MW00939664

HEALING THE WOLF

Paranormal Security and Intelligence Ops Shadow
Agents: Part of the Immortal Ops World (Shadow
Agents / PSI-Ops Book)

MANDY M. ROTH

Raven Happy Hour, LLC

"Mandy M Roth is a true master of her craft! Her breathtaking stories sweep me up, mesmerize and leave me desperate for more. She is my drug of choice!"
- Gena Showalter, *New York Times* bestselling author

"Roth has the kind of characters and books that leave you hungry for more and stay with you long after the last page is read. One word sums up her writing style-addictive!"
- Shannon Mayer, USA TODAY bestselling author

"Roth writes from the heart, and her characters and worlds are guaranteed to suck the reader in and hold them hostage until the very last page!"
NYT Bestselling Author, Yasmine Galenorn

"The perfect mix of sizzling romance and heart-pounding action. If you like your heroes smoking hot…and not quite human, you can't go wrong with a Mandy M. Roth book." – **Laurie**

London, NYT and USA Today bestselling author

Midnight Echoes

Isolated Maneuver

Expecting Darkness

Area of Influence

Act of Passion

Act of Brotherhood

Healing the Wolf

Wrecked Intel

And more…

This list is NOT up to date. Please check MandyRoth.com for the most current release list.

More to come (check www.mandyroth.com for new releases)

Books in each series within the Immortal Ops World.
This list is NOT up to date. To see an updated list of the books within each series under the umbrella of the Immortal Ops World please visit MandyRoth.com. Mandy is always releasing new books within the series world. Sign up for her newsletter at

MandyRoth.com to never miss a new release.

You can read each individual series within the world, in whatever order you want…

PSI-Ops: Paranormal Security and Intelligence

Act of Mercy

Act of Surrender

Act of Submission

Act of Command

Act of Passion

Act of Brotherhood

And more…

(see Mandy's website & sign up for her newsletter for notification of releases)

Immortal Ops:

Immortal Ops

Critical Intelligence

Radar Deception

Strategic Vulnerability

Tactical Magik

Administrative Control

Separation Zone

Area of Influence

And more…

(see Mandy's website & sign up for her newsletter for notification of releases)

Immortal Outcasts:

Broken Communication

Damage Report

Isolated Maneuver

Wrecked Intel

And more…

(see Mandy's website & sign up for her newsletter for notification of releases)

Paranormal Security and Intelligence Ops: Shadow Agents

Wolf's Surrender

The Dragon Shifter's Duty

Healing the Wolf

And more…

(see Mandy's website & sign up for her newsletter for notification of releases)

Paranormal Security and Intelligence Ops: Crimson Ops Series

Midnight Echoes

Expecting Darkness

And more…

(see Mandy's website & sign up for her newsletter for notification of releases)

Paranormal Regulators Series and Clear Sight Division Operatives (Part of the Immortal Ops World) Coming Soon!

Immortal Ops (I-Ops) Team Members

Lukian Vlakhusha: Alpha-Dog-One. Team captain, werewolf, King of the Lycans. Book: Immortal Ops (Immortal Ops)

Geoffroi (Roi) Majors: Alpha-Dog-Two. Second-in-command, werewolf, blood-bound brother to Lukian. Book: Critical Intelligence (Immortal Ops)

Doctor Thaddeus Green: Bravo-Dog-One. Scientist, tech guru, werepanther. Book: Radar Deception (Immortal Ops)

Jonathon (Jon) Reynell: Bravo-Dog-Two. Sniper, weretiger. Book: Separation Zone (Immortal Ops)

Wilson Rousseau: Bravo-Dog-Three. Resident

smart-ass, wererat. Book: Strategic Vulnerability (Immortal Ops)

Eadan Daly: Alpha-Dog-Three. PSI-Op and handler on loan to the I-Ops to round out the team, Fae. Book: Tactical Magik (Immortal Ops)

Lance Toov: Werepanther and vampire hybrid. Book: Area of Influence (Immortal Ops)

Colonel Asher Brooks: Chief of Operations and point person for the Immortal Ops Team. Book: Administrative Control (Immortal Ops)

Paranormal Security and Intelligence (PSI) Operatives

General Jack C. Newman: Director of Operations for PSI North American Division, werelion. Adoptive father of Missy Carter-Majors

Duke Marlow: PSI-Operative, werewolf. Book: Act of Mercy (PSI-Ops)

Doctor James (Jimmy) Hagen: PSI-Operative, werewolf. Took a ten-year hiatus from PSI. Book: Act of Surrender (PSI-Ops)

Striker (Dougal) McCracken: PSI-Operative, werewolf

Carbrey (Car) McCracken: PSI-Operative, werewolf

Macbeth (Mac) McCracken: PSI-Operative, werewolf

Miles (Boomer) Walsh: PSI-Operative, werepanther. Book: Act of Submission (PSI-Ops)

Captain Corbin Jones: Operations coordinator and captain for PSI-Ops Team Five, werelion. Book: Act of Command (PSI-Ops)

Malik (Tut) Nasser: PSI-Operative, werelion. Book: Act of Passion (PSI-Ops)

Colonel Ulric Lovett: Director of Operations, PSI-London Division

Dr. Sambora: PSI-Operative, (PSI-Ops)

Garth Ingersson: PSI-Operative, werewolf. Book: Act of Brotherhood

Rurik Romanov: PSI-Operative, werebear

Johannes "Hans" Bach: PSI-Operative

Jannick Bach: PSI-Operative

Immortal Outcasts

Casey Black: I-Ops test subject, werewolf. Book: Broken Communication

Weston Carol: I-Ops test subject, werebear. Book: Damage Report

Bane Antonov: I-Ops test subject, weregorilla. Book: Isolated Maneuver

Cody Livingston: I-Ops test subject, wereshark

Wheeler Summerbee: I-Ops test subject, vampire hybrid

Ace Hargraves: I-Ops test subject, werehorse

Paranormal Security and Intelligence Ops: Shadow Agents

Bradley Durant: PSI-Ops: Shadow Agent Division, werewolf. Book: Wolf's Surrender

Ezra: PSI-Ops: Shadow Agent Division, dragon-shifter

Caesar: PSI-Ops: Shadow Agent Division, werewolf

Gram Campbell: Shadow Agent Division, werewolf and magik

Armand: Shadow Agent Division, vampire

Seth: Shadow Agent Division, vampire. One of the founders of the Crimson Ops Division.

Paranormal Security and Intelligence Ops: Crimson Ops Division

Bhaltair: Crimson-Ops: Fang Gang, vampire. Book: Midnight Echoes

Labrainn: Crimson-Ops: Fang Gang, vampire

Auberi Bouchard: Crimson-Ops: Fang Gang, vampire

Searc Macleod: Crimson-Ops: Fang Gang, vampire. Book: Expecting Darkness

Daniel Townsend: Crimson-Ops: Fang Gang, vampire

Blaise Regnier: Crimson-Ops: Fang Gang, vampire

Philandros "Landros" Mires: Crimson-Ops: Fang Gang, vampire

Paranormal Regulators

Stamatis Emathia: Paranormal Regulator, vampire

Whitney: Paranormal Regulator, werewolf

Cormag Buchanan: Paranormal Regulator, master vampire

Erik: Paranormal Regulator, shifter

Shane: Paranormal Regulator, shifter

Blurb

Healing the Wolf

Paranormal Security and Intelligence Ops Shadow Agents: Part of the Immortal Ops World

Paranormal Security and Intelligence Operative and Shadow Agent Gram Campbell is not having a great year. So far this alpha-male wolf-shifter has had his heart and his body broken. Now his friends have staged their version of an intervention, sending him off to spend time in a luxury retreat and spa that caters to supernaturals. But this tranquil oasis is more than it appears to be. In it lurks a dark secret. One that threatens to destroy Gram and his destined mate. Is he beyond repair, or will his fated mate bring much needed healing to the man and the wolf within? And can they survive a madman and his vision for the future?

Chapter One

PSI DIVISION B HEADQUARTERS, location classified…

Gram Campbell sat in a chair, looking out of the infirmary-room window at the setting sun. Even being immortal and having seen countless sunsets, the beauty of it wasn't lost on him. Although it was hard to find joy in much of anything as of late.

Not long ago, he'd thought he had it all…a ready-made family, a future. None of that was to be.

He was alone, and doing his best to heal from life-threatening injuries. He'd sustained them a few weeks ago. He'd gotten them by protecting someone he loved, and he'd do it all over again. Though, this time, he'd be sure the assholes from The Corporation couldn't get the jump on him long enough to inject him with whatever they'd given him. It was something engineered for a supernatural with extremely high healing capabilities.

Gram had slightly higher than the average shifter-healing abilities—or he had, until the injection.

It had stopped his ability to heal himself as a supernatural would. And while he was still doing far better than a human would under the same circumstances, he was nowhere near where he should be. He wasn't sure he'd ever be one hundred percent again. That worried him.

He couldn't return to work as a solo operative with the Paranormal Security and Intelligence (PSI) Shadow Ops Division until he was medically cleared for duty. Gram couldn't even get clearance to go home, let alone return to work. It had taken its toll on him mentally. He'd never been one to sit around. Idle hands were the work of the devil, in his opinion. Being forced to do nothing was pure and absolute torture.

Pain radiated through his back and down both

legs. He gritted his teeth and rode out the discomfort. He knew another spasm would follow shortly behind the first. It always did. They were like aftershocks from an earthquake. Everyone knew they were coming, but no one could predict them. He'd been told the pain was caused by damaged nerves. He didn't know or care. He just wanted it to end.

Medication had been offered to help dull the pain, but he didn't want any more. The meds—which were experimental in the sense that no one had ever tried using the concoction before, and no one should really try to use it again—caused him to hallucinate and killed his ability to focus in any fashion. They monkeyed with his ability to use his natural-born magik and made his already pissed-off wolf even more unstable than it had been.

The hallucinations were honestly what bothered him most. They had gotten so bad while on the meds that Gram had thought his mother was in the room with him more than once, and he'd had full conversations with her.

She'd been dead for over a century.

That didn't stop her from weighing in on his love life, or lack thereof. Yes, he understood she wasn't really there. That she was a manifestation of some deeper need to have his mother around him when he was injured—at least that was what the head shrink had claimed; the one PSI had tried to force him to see.

Gram just thought it was caused by the shit they were injecting him with.

If getting lectured by his dead mother about getting up and out into the world to find his perfect someone wasn't bad enough, the damn meds kept making him think a white wolf was in the room with him. It wasn't. At least, he was about ninety-nine percent sure it wasn't.

His wolf, the one who was as broken as he was, would have lost its shit had an actual predator been near. Then again, his wolf had had the shit kicked out of it, too, so it was nowhere near full strength. That being said, it could still sense danger. It didn't seem the least bit worried about the white wolf appearing to him. Even Gram's wolf understood the crap they were giving him was making him loopy and high.

Gram had thought that was the weirdest it would get on the meds. He'd been wrong. Several times in the last week alone, he'd thought a red kickball had rolled into the room, only to find it wasn't actually there. It had been a trick of his mind.

In addition, he'd started seeing a woman in white. She had long dark brown hair and pale skin. The dress she wore hung almost to the floor, leaving her bare feet showing. While the dress was nothing he'd consider fashionable or form-fitting, it was thin, gifting him a glimpse of what she did and did not have on beneath it. His dick didn't really care if the chick was real or not. Each time she appeared to him, he walked around with a hard-on for hours.

He'd yet to see her full face, but each time he hallucinated her being in the room with him, he felt the fierce need to draw her close and protect her. The problem was, the second he tried to make contact with her, she vanished into thin air, having never actually been there to start with.

He understood she wasn't real, that she was simply a by-product of the drugs he was being given, but none of that mattered. He couldn't get her out of his head. She'd only just started appearing to him…and he found that ironic, since visions of her began when he'd started skipping doses of the serum. He'd assumed that would lessen the number of weird things he was seeing.

It hadn't.

A few times, she had been standing next to the red ball, looking to be staring off at something in the distance—not that he'd seen her face or anything. He could sense her anguish, her despair, and her desperation. He could also smell her fear, as if she was real and truly near him. In addition, the hallucination of her was always accompanied by the smell of honeysuckle and vanilla. Both scents he found soothing and alluring.

Kind of like her.

She was tall for a woman but nowhere near Gram's height. And she was thinner than he felt comfortable with. It was as if she was supposed to have more to her but didn't. As irrational as it sounded, he wanted to feed her, care for her, and protect her.

Not to mention fuck her.

It had been three days since he'd taken the injections but he still saw her. His last time seeing her had left him acting like a fool. He'd rushed into the hallway as fast as he could, considering the condition he was in, and he'd nearly knocked over his close friend Garth, who had been coming to check on him.

Garth humored him when Gram told him of

the woman in white. It was painfully clear Garth hadn't seen her, or the white wolf who had appeared just after the woman vanished. It was also clear Garth thought Gram had lost his damn mind.

So did Gram.

His two main doctors, James Hagen and Auberi Bouchard, had threatened to hold him down and give him the meds regardless of his thoughts on the matter. He knew they'd do it at some point if he didn't start healing on his own soon. For all the meds' faults, they had assisted in kickstarting his healing abilities, though not to the point where they needed to be.

Still, something was better than nothing.

That was what they kept telling him.

If roles were reversed, he'd have done and said the same things to them. It was difficult to fault them for wanting the best for him. But Gram didn't want to be under the influence of the medication any longer. He'd either heal on his own or he wouldn't. He couldn't continue to be out of touch with reality.

And he had to stop fixating on a woman who didn't exist, all while also dwelling on the woman he'd cared for and lost to another.

The plus side of no meds was that he no longer had conversations with people who had long passed or saw wolves that weren't there. The down side was that his pain was high, and his healing had crawled to a virtual standstill. He still had burns over large portions of his back and down the back of his left leg. And his right leg, which had been effectively shattered, wasn't healed fully. It had a long way to go. The damn thing had turned into a jokester in the sense he never really knew when it was going to give out on him and stop bearing his weight.

"Trick knee, my arse," he said gruffly. "Try trick leg. Hell, trick body."

He was under the care of the best medical minds in the world. But that meant nothing to him. He wanted out of the infirmary—out of headquarters. He could *not* heal just as well at home as he could *not* heal there. He missed his bed and the smell of his house. The damn infirmary smelled heavily of disinfectants, all of which bothered his sensitive nose. He had a constant low-grade headache as of late, and he blamed it on the smell of bleach and pine-scented cleaners.

No pine tree he'd ever been near smelled like the stuff they used around the infirmary.

He actually longed for another woman-in-white sighting, just so he could smell something good—like her.

"Och, she's nae real," he reminded himself.

As pain spread down his back and into his right leg, numbing his foot, he considered changing his stance on the meds. Maybe even taking just a small dose to take the edge off.

"Even a small amount is nae guid for my mind," he chastised himself for his moment of weakness.

The medication not only made him feel high and see things that weren't there, it didn't do his magik any favors, either. The same magik he'd been born with, that he'd learned to control centuries ago, was now a stranger to him thanks to the injuries and the meds. The combination left Gram's power erratic, and that was dangerous.

Downright deadly even.

No amount of practice seemed to help. Of course, he hadn't exactly been able to open up and go wild with his power, mainly because of his weakened state.

As much as he disliked admitting it, he wasn't the same man he had been before the attack, before his world had turned upside down. His magik and his body should have been back to business as usual. Being stuck in a room, subjected to test after test and pumped full of experimental drugs, shouldn't still be a thing for him.

But it was.

In fact, it was his full reality as of late.

And he hated it.

Gram had lost track of the number of days he'd been in the infirmary. Felt like forever. Far longer than he'd ever needed to be treated for anything before. The days ran into the nights and the hours ticked by painfully slowly. Some moments, he swore time stood still. If his injuries didn't kill him, boredom likely would. Most of his friends and fellow PSI-Operatives had missions to go on that took them away from headquarters. That was great for them but sucked for Gram.

He disliked knowing he wasn't out there helping fight the good fight. The Corporation was enemy number one, and it seemed like new revelations concerning them came daily. They had their hand in everything. They backed countless governments, controlled huge businesses, and were far bigger than anyone ever thought them to be.

They had one end goal, which seemed to be total world domination.

Aim high and all that shit.

It seemed as if they were able to regenerate at an alarming rate. PSI would cut the head off one faction only to have two more pop up elsewhere. It had been all hands on deck with PSI and its affiliates for months now. They could spare no one. He was needed in the field, not sitting on his backside, doing nothing but seeing things that weren't there.

Besides that, he had to admit he missed his friends. The company was appreciated. He'd spent twenty years as a solo operative, but even that had given him contact with some of his friends. His handler, Armand, for one, and a network of contacts he'd acquired over the years and trusted fully. One of which was a wereshark named Cody.

Prior to being a solo operative, Gram had been part of PSI Team Eight. That had given him a close-knit set of men he considered brothers. His friends all stopped in to check on him as time permitted but he could see the pity in their eyes, and it stung.

He'd had that same look on his face more

than once when visiting an injured brother-in-arms. He knew what they were thinking. If he didn't actually heal and soon, his days with PSI were over.

Fuck that.

As if on cue, a visitor arrived.

Chapter Two

JUST OUTSIDE OF DENVER, Colorado...

Amelia Fabius stood at the back of the large outdoor assembly, doing her best to fade away from notice. She smoothed down the front of her white dress, noticing she'd gotten a bit of potting soil on the bottom. No surprise with as much time as she spent in the greenhouses at the compound. They had become her domain. She loved nature and growing things. It gave her a much-needed sense of peace.

That was one thing she'd miss about the compound when she was gone—her gardens and the greenhouses. She loved everything to do with healing and herbal remedies. It was her passion. She'd spent the greater part of the afternoon making a salve for burns. It was simple yet worked wonders. St. John's Wort, comfrey leaves, calendula flowers, lavender, and a few other special touches come together to make a fantastic salve. It hadn't been on her to-do list, but she'd felt compelled to make a large batch. The reserves in the main spa area had been running low anyway, so it wasn't as if she'd wasted her time. Then again, she didn't plan to be around to see the salve get much use.

Besides, it gave her something to do other than work on various things that were supposed to help a VIP guest who had only just left. The guest was one who made her shudder just thinking about him. She'd been tasked with coming up with new salves and remedies to help what ailed him; the problem was, she didn't know how to fix his issues, nor had she been fully versed on what his troubles were.

In a nutshell, she'd been kept in the dark, and that was fine by her. The vibe the man had let off said he wasn't a good guy.

That being said, she'd done her best to offer him some relief, despite her gut telling her to allow the man to suffer. She had been able to offer him something to help him sleep. It had been a special blend of natural remedies she'd been toying with. She'd made a tea with valerian root and passionflower. Getting the taste just right had taken some work, but she'd found honey did nicely.

Amelia picked a bit of dried calendula flower from under her fingernails as she glanced around the gathering, staring at so many faces who should have been friendly to her but weren't. Very few allies were among the massive group. The area, a grove that had a clearing in it, with fallen trees that had been halved and set up as benches, was packed with people. Everyone was dressed in white, as was the standard. It promoted unity and reminded everyone that they were the same—no one better than the other (at least that was the slogan, anyway). They had their arms in the air as they held the hand of the person next to them. They swayed, singing a song in unison that was special, just for them. For their beliefs.

It spoke of having the protection of a powerful god. Of finding a path to everlasting enlightenment and riches of the spirit. Beliefs Amelia had been raised with and wholeheartedly bought into—until the blinders had been ripped from her eyes.

Since then, she saw the world around her in Technicolor—warts and all. It wasn't full of beauty and wonder. It was full of lies, deceit, and evil. And she lived in the thick of it.

Amelia stood partially behind one of the trees, hoping to avoid detection. She didn't want to be singled out yet knew it would happen. It always happened at impromptu gatherings. As of late, it was happening at non-impromptu ones as well.

She was a misfit among the group of follow-ers. They knew her heart wasn't into it, but that didn't seem to matter. She just wanted to fade away from notice.

A tall, well-built man stood at the head of the area on a raised platform, a pulpit he preached at often. He held a book in his hand. Not a Christian bible, but a book of scripture he, himself, had written throughout his incredibly long lifespan.

She wasn't entirely sure of his age, but it was rumored to be around three thousand years. Though the man didn't look to be out of his twenties. There was a certain wisdom in his dark brown eyes. At times, he looked caring, nurturing even. Other times, a monster stared out from his hard gaze. His mood changed on a dime.

While his wrath had never been directly

aimed at her, it had been focused on someone she'd loved dearly. She could still remember hearing the screams of her loved one. Of knowing there was nothing that could be done to help. And knowing the very man who should have given his all to keep the woman safe had been responsible for her death had driven home every warning she'd ever gotten about the man. Every red flag that had ever been raised.

He and his followers, or the Flock, as they liked to be called, had all gone off the sanity deep end long ago.

Probably before Amelia had even been born.

There was a high chance the leader had never actually been sane. Apparently, sanity wasn't a requirement when organizing your own religion and amassing followers. Charisma, a charming smile, good looks, confidence, and power were.

Caladrius "Cal" Fabius had all those things in spades.

He held the Flock's attention as he paced on the raised platform, gripping the Book of Peace.

She nearly choked on the irony of the title. Its teachings were anything but peaceful. His followers were hardly innocent sheep, lured by the lion into the den. They were people who blindly obeyed his every twisted command. Who did his bidding even when it was painfully clear his wishes were dark, his desires equally as perverse.

He saw himself as a god. The Flock helped to permeate that falsehood.

They blew a lot of smoke up the man's backside.

But not Amelia.

She was a constant thorn even when she was doing her best to be a good little soldier.

For good reason.

He'd had it in his head she was going to help lead the cult into the next stage of enlightenment. That she was special, chosen, born to help usher the Flock to bliss. To nirvana. To endless power.

Amelia wanted nothing to do with any of it. Nothing to do with ushering the Flock into anything, unless it was jail cells—where they all belonged. But none of them would ever be held accountable for their actions. They'd been getting away with so much for so long that they were invincible. And their numbers grew each year as more and more wayward supernaturals found their way to the Flock. Some found a new home within the compound walls. Others were simply never found again.

She had no idea how Cal had managed to ensnare so many and get them to not only believe in him and his ideology, but to give up all their worldly possessions and follow him in whatever he did. They worked for him, running various businesses the nonprofit owned, and all the proceeds went into a communal pot (which only a few charmed Flock members had access to). The funds were used to keep the businesses running, feed and clothe the members, and to make Cal one of the richest men in the world.

He made television evangelists look like lightweight amateurs. They may have been blessed with leadership skills and the gift of charming others, but he had honest-to-gods magik. Powers that he'd been born with that helped him heal others, influence others, bend their minds to a degree—much like a vampire could. But Cal was so much better at it all. And his powers had only increased over the centuries. Amelia wasn't even sure of everything he could do. She just knew he might very well be one of the most powerful supernaturals out there.

And why not?

He'd gained the additional power through

means that were ruthless and unspeakable. Very few could stand against him.

She didn't understand the sheep and their obedience. Then again, she'd been born with an independent streak. One her mother had feared would get Amelia punished or harmed by Cal. So far, it had only served to help her, but she suspected her time was limited in that respect. There was only so far she could push Cal before he'd push back. It didn't matter who she was to the man.

She'd seen him direct his rage at Flock members before.

It was horrific.

And even as traumatizing as witnessing his fury had been, Amelia still refused to bend to his every whim, to conform, to be a brainless, mindless twit. She saw through him and his silver tongue. His false promises and prophecies that never came to be.

He'd predicted the end of the world twice that she was aware of. Neither time had it occurred. Amelia had been scared that Cal would do something drastic and either launch an attack against humans and their government or talk all of the Flock into a mass suicide. The only saving grace was that he was too bent on achieving ultimate power and control to check out on life. And he needed the Flock to reach his goals.

At least for now.

When the day came that he didn't need them anymore, they'd all be dead. They were disposable in his mind. She was sure of it. What she wasn't sure of was why none of them seemed to wise up and smell the cult leader. He didn't have them on a path to enlightenment and better days. He had them on a highway to hell.

She'd have thought the fact the world had not ended on any of Cal's predicted end dates would have proven Cal to be a fraud or, at the very least, mentally unstable.

But no.

The Flock didn't question him.

When the supposed end came and went, with no one dead and the world still standing, Cal explained it away. Saying the great gods had been testing the Flock. That it had been a way to prove their loyalty. He drove home the fact his visions were shown to him in a way that he had to interpret, and since he was a man, error was possible.

The sheep, as she liked to call them, bought it hook, line, and sinker.

He could do no wrong.

To them, Cal was the embodiment of perfection and a higher power. To her, he was a nightmare. She didn't need to be told that she was fast running out of time before he'd do what he'd been promising to do since she was born—force her to lure some supposed Bringer of Change into the Flock. Some powerful being who was going to either take the Flock to new heights of enlightenment or destroy them.

She really hoped it was the latter.

It would serve Cal right if his savior actually turned out to be his destroyer.

"Prepare thyself for the upcoming trials. For the battle that is upon us. The time is now," he said, his voice booming out and over the large crowd. He didn't need a microphone, yet there was a sound system there just in case. "A vision has come to me. The gods and goddesses have seen fit to give me the knowledge that the Bringer is nearly upon us. His arrival will test our resolve. Test our dedication and loyalty. We may even be required to take up arms to defend our way of life. Some of our own may even turn their back on the cause."

Whispers and gasps made their way through

the crowd. Accusatory looks flew between the members as each tried to figure out who among them would betray the Flock. Amelia nearly raised her hand. She intended to betray them all.

"Do you have what it takes to stand up to this test?" asked Cal of the group. "Is your faith strong enough? Are you ready to move to our next evolution?"

Amelia had to use all her willpower to avoid rolling her eyes at Cal's statement. He'd been doomsday prepping ever since she could remember. So far, the end hadn't occurred. Didn't mean he stopped getting his followers ready. Though he normally just said that one day the Bringer would arrive. This speech sounded a lot like he was expecting the Bringer guy to show up at the front door of the compound at any minute with bells on—or in the Flock's case, dressed all in white since that was the standard outfit among them.

"We will not back away from this challenge. We will rise up out of the darkness," said Cal, his long dark hair hanging down to his midback. He wore loose-fitting white cotton pants and a tunic-like baggy top. The shirt was cut lower in the front, showing off his muscular chest. He was barefoot, only serving to lend to his peaceful-guru-hippie vibe. To most, he was handsome, intelligent, and the answer to their prayers.

To Amelia, he was a madman.

One she'd been unable to totally break from, despite the effort and sacrifice that had been made to do so.

She lowered her gaze, wanting to avoid crying. She'd spent enough tears on the man. She'd give him no more. Not if she could help it. He was beyond redemption.

"We will walk in the light. We shall no longer be forced to live in secret. We will be the ones who marshal in the times of peace and prosperity," he said, grinning in a way that sent a shiver down her spine.

The Flock hummed together, nodding, hanging on his every word. As usual, they were enthralled.

Sheep.

She caught Cal's word choice—marshal. He most certainly would enforce changes on the world if given the chance. Though she doubted anyone would think they were better off.

She continued to hang back, wondering why the emergency meeting had been called. Could it be his message about the Bringer really meant he believed it to be happening now? Normally, they only met as a group twice a week for sermon and worship. But the sound system had played the calling bells only an hour before, signaling a gathering. Everyone had stopped what they were doing to attend. Well, all but the children and a few select adults who watched over the young ones.

There weren't many children in the Flock, but the few the group had were not included in the meetings. Nor were they permitted access to the main compound building at the resort the group owned, operated, and lived on the grounds of.

The cult, for lack of a better term, had many faults. Keeping the little ones from seeing anything they shouldn't didn't tend to be one of them. Though they had failed in that respect two years back, and once before that as well.

The latter had been a night she would never forget. It was the night she'd first seen her father attack her mother, his intent to kill her. He'd unleashed a fury on her mother the likes of which Amelia had never seen before. He would have killed her then and there had it not been brought to his attention that she was expecting. The child was newly formed but there all the same. That

25

had been the only thing that had stopped Amelia's father from completing what he'd set out to do.

It had saved her mother's life that night and given them the opportunity to flee, but ultimately, it had not been enough to prevent the inevitable.

The death of Amelia's mother at the hands of her father.

Tonight marked the two-year anniversary of her mother's passing. No one had ever paid for the crime. Mostly because within the Flock, the act had not been seen as law-breaking at all, but rather fitting punishment for going against Father.

Amelia nearly gagged at the fact the Flock called Cal Father when he'd not actually fathered any of them. In all his thousands of years, the man had only had two children—Amelia and her sister, Andie.

And he'd then murdered their mother right before their very eyes.

Andie, who was now just over the age of four, was tucked away in her bed, being watched over by adults who specialized in caring for children. For all the caregivers' faults and their stupidity in buying into the cult's rhetoric, they were good to the children. Unless, of course, they all forming a circle around someone they saw as a threat to them and their way of life. Then they were downright terrifying.

"I've called you all here on this night to tell you the time is upon us," said Cal, causing a ripple of gasps to go through the large crowd. "The one we have waited for is nearly here."

They lowered their hands, all of them falling silent as they stared up at their leader.

He offered a smile that was meant to be reassuring. "I have seen it. The one who will usher in change is nearly upon us. He will arrive any day now."

The crowd cheered, having waited so long for this special someone Cal often spoke of. Most of the cult members were hundreds of years old. Being immortal allowed for that. Even with all those years under their belts, they still allowed themselves to be brainwashed.

They bought into hype.

Into madness.

"Is he the bringer of light or darkness?" asked one of the followers in the front row.

Cal stroked his long, well-kept black beard. "Time will tell. I have hope that the Bringer will lead the Flock in my stead."

He'd been talking about who would take over

the Flock from him since Amelia was little. It wasn't as if he was going anywhere. For one, he was immortal and one of the most powerful supernaturals out there. For two, he would never willingly hand over control of the Flock. He liked being seen as a god in their eyes far too much to walk away from it all. He'd already proven he picked the cult above all else.

"One of our very own, as predicted, will be instrumental in bringing him into the fold," said Cal, looking up and over the crowd. His dark gaze landed on her and his smile widened.

She stiffened.

He pointed to her. "Amelia, come. Join me."

She took a small step back, only to find herself being shoved forward by a woman who got on her last nerve.

Susan was a medium-height blonde woman who desperately wanted to be Cal's main love interest. Problem was, he wasn't really a one-woman kind of man. No. He preferred to bed nearly all the women in the cult. It didn't matter if they were already paired off with a male. They were fair game. And the men in the cult saw it as an honor to have their women selected to bed Father.

The men also had no issue sharing their significant others with one another. Some of the rituals of the Flock were nothing more than huge orgies.

"Come, daughter," he said, still holding his arm out. "Join me in your rightful place—by my side."

The Flock cheered as Amelia walked slowly toward the platform. She felt a lot like she was on death row, doing a last walk on the way to the electric chair. In place of death would come the taint of darkness that would never wash off.

Susan stayed directly behind Amelia, forcing her in the direction of the stage. Amelia had half a mind to turn around and claw the woman's eyes out, but she held back. Already her plan for escape had been set into motion. She wouldn't risk it now over someone as pathetic as Susan.

All eyes fell onto Amelia as she made her way to her father.

When she was close enough to the platform, her father's security team, who were called his advisors but were really just muscle, converged on Amelia. Taggert, the scariest one of them all, made sure he was the one who touched Amelia. He grabbed her hips tighter than need be and lifted her with ease, setting her on the platform.

He then ran his hands over her in a manner that was anything but appropriate, but in a way that others couldn't see.

Her father took hold of her hand quickly, steadying her. He drew her closer and kissed her temple. "Sweet daughter, the day is near for you to fulfill your destiny. You will ensure the Bringer of Change comes to be with us. You are the glue that will hold him to us."

Amelia's gaze flickered downward to Taggert, who stood at the base of the platform with his arms crossed over his massive chest and a look of pure hatred on his face. She already knew his thoughts on the entire Bringer of Change. He wanted the man killed. He thought the change the man ushered in would be the end of the Flock.

Amelia could only hope Taggert was right.

That someone would put an end to the madness.

Taggert also had a warped idea in his head that Amelia would accept a forced mating to him, and he'd then inherit the Flock one day. Not likely. Amelia would never mate with him, forced or not. And Cal didn't seem to be in any hurry to increase Taggert's responsibilities, as if he felt Taggert was already working to his capacity.

Cal lifted Amelia's hand in the air and the crowd cheered louder. "It's important we all be prepared for the arrival of the Bringer of Change. You all know what must be done."

A round of yeses came from the people.

Cal motioned for one of his men to bring him his acoustic guitar. They did, and he looked to Amelia, giving her a slight nod. She didn't want to join him in song and worship. She wanted to go back to the cabin she shared with her sister and then head out to meet with a contact. The impromptu gathering was cutting into her time for the evening. Already she'd be late enough as it was.

Chapter Three

EDEE ENTERED Gram's hospital room, her long dark red hair pulled back in a tight ponytail. Her gaze swept over him and she frowned. "Want to tell me why I got a call from the physical therapist telling me you were a no-show *again*? He's pissed. Can't blame him."

Gram shrugged. He didn't really want to get into a discussion of his therapy with her again but knew she wouldn't let it go. "Aye, because I'm nae there."

She scowled, her disapproving looks something for the record books. "Oh really? I came up with that on my own. But thanks for clearing it up for me."

"Then why ask?" He returned to staring out

the window. The sun was now gone from view, replaced by the moon's soft glow. The wolf in him unfurled slightly, a sense of longing for the night coming over it.

When he'd gone through his first shift, when he was an adolescent, he'd thought his wolf to be unstable. After centuries, he'd grown to trust it, and it him. Now the man and the wolf were at odds and too broken to want to bother pursuing anything more. They both wanted to curl into a ball and sleep. That or be sent out on a mission to take their minds from their troubles.

Edee approached and sat on the edge of the bed. She wore a long blue dress with a pair of flats. Gram noticed years ago that the woman tended to gravitate toward dresses. The white lab coat she wore over the dress was something Gram was getting used to seeing her in, and it was nice. It meant she was getting out there and living life again, not hiding away, always on the run, as life had been for her for years.

It also meant that she was always around, since she worked at PSI Division B Headquarters. She wasn't inclined to take any of his bullshit: that was an issue. He could bluster and grumble all he wanted with everyone else on staff. Edee would throw something at him and tell him to get bent all while wheeling him directly to the physical therapist herself.

She had that kind of temperament.

Edee knew him well and had been a close friend for five years. She was like family to him, and she saw him in the same light. Their late-night conversations over the years had revealed as much. She possessed Fae magik, similar to his, though her control over it was nearly nonexistent as trauma had been what had triggered her gifts. Not birth.

His control wasn't winning any prizes lately either, so he didn't really have a lot of room to judge.

Truth be told, Edee probably had more control over her magik at the moment than Gram had over his. That was a scary thought. He'd once seen her blow up a microwave by accident all because, in a fit of anger, she'd let her magik loose near the appliance. Edee had effectively microwaved the microwave.

Edee and Gram had gone through a lot together. She was best friends with Gram's ex-fiancé—Brooke. She was the last person who would allow him to wither away in a hospital room, swimming in self-pity.

"I know you miss Brooke and Bethany," said Edee softly, compassion in her voice.

"They were in to see me again this morning," he returned, doing his best to school his expression. Talking about Brooke and Bethany hurt. He'd thought he had a future with Brooke. That he'd adopt Bethany, her daughter, as his own and they'd be as happy as they could considering they weren't true mates. That hadn't been meant to be. She'd reconnected with her true mate…and he just happened to be a man who got on Gram's last damn nerve.

Malik Nasser.

An ancient Egyptian lion-shifter who fancied himself the gods' gift to women. Or he had before mating. His bed hopping had been legendary until Brooke. Now Brooke had him by the shorties. The woman had effectively neutered the bastard.

Good.

Gram got a bit of satisfaction from that knowledge.

Edee stared at him. "Brooke is worried about you. So am I."

"I'm fine," he said, his words clipped. He

wanted off the subject. "Getting better every day."

"Bullshit," she snipped. "Can the crap and try that on someone else. Someone who doesn't know you like I do. You're about as far from fine as you can get."

"You know your bedside manner is somewhat lacking," said Gram with a slight grin.

"That has been mentioned before." Edee smiled wide, the action lighting up her face. She was a very attractive woman. One who was slowly finding her way back to being self-assured and strong-willed.

He glanced at the door. "Did you come in here to check on me or hide from Striker?"

Dougal "Striker" McCracken never seemed too far behind Edee. He'd become an oversized giant shadow who hovered in the vicinity wherever Edee went. Gram wasn't sure she noticed even though Striker was hard to miss.

She grumbled. "That man gets on my last nerve."

Gram snorted. "He does not. I know yer tells, woman. You like him. You just do nae want him to catch on to as much."

"Can you imagine if he found out I consider

him a friend?" She put the back of her hand to her forehead in a dramatic fashion and did a partial fake swoon. "I'd have to go into witness protection or something to get away from him and his *help*."

Gram had heard all about Striker's version of helping Edee the day before. "I do nae think he meant to knock you down the stairs at Malik's house. Sounds to me like he was trying to make sure you dinnae fall down them in yer heels."

"Oh yeah. I know. Thank God he has fast reflexes. He at least caught me before I tumbled *all* the way down them," she said with a half laugh. "You should have seen his face."

"I heard all about it."

"Brooke told you?" she asked.

Gram shook his head. "Bethany. She told me all about her uncle Striker *helping* her aunt Edee. She was quite animated when she told me. I especially enjoyed seeing her flail her arms about, with wide eyes, shouting half-done sentences in a fit of anger. She really does mimic you well."

Edee snickered. "I bet. Did she mimic Striker's brogue when she got to his portion? She's got it down pat, between you and him."

It was impossible to hold in his pride over that

fact. He'd worked with Bethany from an early age to teach her Gaelic. She knew a fair amount and could sound like she was Scottish when she wanted. It was adorable.

So was she.

All of it drove home how much he missed the idea of a family. Of something more in life.

"I thought I'd found happiness," he confessed.

She sighed and then stood, putting an arm around him and squeezing him gently. Neither said a word as they looked out the window together. They stayed that way for several minutes before she patted his chest lightly. "There is someone special out there for you, Gram. I know it."

"That is a pretty notion, but it's nae the reality of it," he said. It was true. Mates were rare. Not all supernaturals were gifted with one. He'd been alive for centuries and not a single whisper of his mate had found its way to him. Granted, a number of men who were even older than him were only just now finding their mates, but still. The odds were stacked against him.

Holding out hope for such a thing was too much. Especially when Gram felt as if everything in his life had turned on its head as of late.

He glanced at Edee. "Has seeing Brooke mated to Malik made you think about one day mating yerself?"

Edee paled. "God no. I don't want to be tied to one man all my life. You're all so moody and needy."

His lips curved upward. "Thanks."

"Hey. I call it like I see it."

"That you do, lass," he said.

"Have you showered today?" she asked, never one to beat around the bush. She wrinkled her nose.

"Aye," he said before thinking harder on it. "Maybe. I do nae recall, nor do I care."

"Yeah, well I care. You smell horrible. Either you shower or I'm going to bring a hose in here and have at you," she threatened.

She'd do it, and she'd smile the entire time.

"I do nae smell that bad, do I?" he asked, sniffing himself. He had to admit he didn't smell the best. "I think I showered yesterday."

"Nope. Try the day before that."

"Yer keeping track of when I bathe?" he asked, giving her a sideways stare.

She shrugged. "Someone has to. You're clearly not worried about it. Which is really weird because you normally shower twice a day when given the chance. You make the rest of us smell bad. This new you is less anal but also less hygienic. I'd rather have anal you back."

"Thanks. I think."

She nudged him lightly. "I overheard some of the guys talking. They think you need to get laid. They think getting you in bed with a woman is what will do the trick to help you heal your mind and body."

Gram did his best to avoid flinching at the idea of touching or being touched by any woman. That was the last thing he wanted.

"But I don't think you're ready to jump back into dating," said Edee, watching him closely. "Are you?"

"No." He wasn't. He needed time to lick his proverbial wounds. Time for his heart to heal.

"Brooke is happy with Malik. And while I know that has to kill you inside, I think you're also happy for her, which has to be really frigging confusing." She took a seat on the end of the bed once more. "She has a lot of guilt over it all. She never intended to hurt you, and the fact you were injured saving Bethany weighs on her heavy too. I tried to explain you'd have it no other way, that you'd do it all over again. She doesn't listen well."

Gram let out a long breath as he looked down at the floor. "She has nothing to feel guilty about. She found out her mate was alive, and they made a life together. They put their family back together. And yer right. I would do it all again in a heartbeat, even knowing what the final result would be."

Even talking about it made his chest tight and his eyes moisten. Edee was right: he was happy for Brooke and for her mate—even though he personally thought Malik was an asshole. But none of that took from the fact he hurt. Everything he'd thought he'd built for himself had been ripped away. On top of it all, he still wasn't healed fully, and he itched to get back out into the field and go on missions again. Being cooped up in the infirmary sucked.

Killing bad guys was just what he needed to take his mind off things. He just needed to get back on the horse and off his ass.

He tried to stand, but his right leg was so stiff that he nearly fell. Glancing nervously in Edee's direction, he waited for her to make a smart remark. It was sort of her thing.

"You're doing a hell of a lot better than you have any right to be, considering what you went through," she offered, calming his fears a bit.

Reaching out, he put his hand to the wall, to the right of the window, to help steady himself. "I should have healed all of this by now."

"Correction," she said sternly. "You should have died in that explosion. Let's be honest here. That isn't something any supernatural should have lived through. I've read the medical reports. I've talked to James and Auberi, not to mention any other medical personnel I could get my hands on. You're a damn miracle. Start acting like one."

"Dragon-shifters would have been fine," he returned.

She groaned. "Well, since we're just overrun with them, I stand corrected."

He grinned. "I get yer point."

"Do you, Gram? Because it seems to me you're wallowing in self-pity. This isn't like you. Where is the fire in your eyes? Where is the stubborn Scottish iron will that I wanted to throttle you over for years? I can't believe I'm going to say this, but I miss that side of you."

"Lent all my stubborn Scottish-ness to Striker," said Gram, knowing the mere mention of the other Scot in the building at the moment would get Edee going again.

From the word go, Striker and Edee had a strange tension between them. Gram had to wonder if it was sexual. Knowing Striker, it was. The man lived and breathed sex.

Not that too many red-blooded males didn't.

Edee, from what Gram had learned of her before life had brought them together, used to be very free with her sexuality. Incredibly open with it all. He understood why that side of her was hidden from others now. She'd lived through horrors he didn't even want to think upon. She'd bounced back and seemed to grow stronger emotionally every day.

And here he was doing exactly what she accused him of—wallowing in self-pity.

"Shite," he whispered.

"You finally seeing the light or am I going to need to track down that stubborn Scot you mentioned?" she asked, leaning forward on the edge of the bed. "You should know, I heard him on the phone yesterday, right after he tried to kill me on the stairs at Malik's. He's up to something."

Gram stared at Edee. "Do I even want to know what?"

"Probably not since I'm positive it involves you." She stood and stretched her arms above her head. "He mentioned a couple of names. I've never heard of them before. He also said something about family and Colorado."

Gram tensed, already having a fairly good idea who Striker would reach out to in regard to Gram. "Were the names he mentioned Mac and Car?"

Her eyes widened. "Yes."

"Double shite." Gram stepped back from the window, mindful of his stiff leg. "I should shower. If the twins show, they really will hose me down."

"Twins?" asked Edee, eyeing him closely.

"Two of Striker's cousins."

Edee gasped. "Oh dear gods above, tell me they have more manners than that beast."

"Edee, they make Striker look tame. Like a teddy bear even," answered Gram, meaning every word of it. He'd known the McCracken clan for centuries. They were a rowdy bunch. They drank too much. Fucked too much. Got in too many fights. Everything with them was done to excess.

"I didn't think anyone could out-Striker Striker," she replied.

"Och, I heard that." The Scot in question appeared in the doorway. He had on his tartan, a pair of biker boots, and a T-shirt that read "Vamps Suck."

The Crimson Ops Division of vampires at PSI had to just love the shirt. Which was more than likely why Striker was wearing it—to get a rise out of them.

Edee put her hands to her cheeks and pulled lightly, annoyance showing brightly. "Were your ears ringing?"

"No, but my dick was hard. Figured you were talking about me," said Striker with a wink.

Edee glanced at Gram. "Feeling up to killing him? Could get you back in the game."

Striker ran a hand over his wild, deep red beard. It matched his hair, which was also long now but currently pulled back from his face at the nape of his neck. "Och, lass, Campbell willnae kill me. We go way back."

"Then he totally will kill you. I've known you less than a month and I want to strangle you most of the time," said Edee, easing closer to Striker despite her words.

Striker grinned. "I've that effect on the ladies."

Gram laughed. "Aye. It's true. He does."

"Great. You're a character witness for him now?" asked Edee, sounding anything but annoyed. She looked to be fighting a smile.

"Character witnesses for him are few and far between. Seems the least I could do," said Gram, heading in the direction of the bathroom that was attached to his hospital room. "I'm going to shower. Unless you two want a show, I'd suggest you step out."

"Och, Campbell, I've seen you naked more times than I can count. You've nothing I have nae seen before," said Striker, earning him a sideways glance and a snicker from Edee. Striker's face reddened. "I dinnae mean it the way yer taking it, lass."

"Uh-huh, sure."

Edee glided past the man, leaving Striker's head turning as he watched her leave the room.

"Bonnie lass."

"So you've mentioned," said Gram. "Do you really want to bed her or are you just in it for the chase?"

Striker looked at Gram. "I do nae know what I want with her."

Gram was quiet a moment. "Striker, how many women have you had that you'd label a friend? Someone you talk with, confide in, care about, but who yer nae bedding. Women who aren't mated to yer friends."

He opened his mouth and then closed it, a pensive look coming over his face. He started to say something and stopped, frustration evident. He lifted a hand but lowered it.

Gram snorted. "I'm going out on a limb here, but is Edee yer first?"

The big man nodded. "Aye. She confuses me."

"And you think Mac and Car will help clear it up?"

Striker grinned. "The lass ratted me out, did she?"

"She did. Though she did nae believe me when I told her that yer cousins make you look like a tame teddy bear."

Tossing his head back, Striker laughed loud and long. "She's in for a surprise then."

"That or you're in for a run for your money because I know the twins. They'll think Edee is hot and be trying to get in her pants about two seconds after they meet her," said Gram in all seriousness. "She'll castrate them...or maybe she'll think they're good-looking and decide she wants to have a threesome."

Striker's face reddened more but Gram knew it was from anger this time, not embarrassment. "She'll nae be having any way with them let alone a three-way!"

"Dougal!" yelled Edee from down the hall.

Striker cringed. "Aye?"

Gram snorted. "I thought no one was allowed to call you that."

"I told her I dinnae like it," said Striker before he looked tired. "Only made her call me it more."

"She sounds pissed." Gram didn't bother to hide his laugh. "What did you do this time?"

"Is this your half-eaten sub sandwich on my research samples?" Edee asked, coming around the corner, holding a partially eaten sub. It was dripping with mustard and mayo.

"Nae if it ruined any samples," said Striker. "If it ruined anything it was Boomer's lunch. Nae mine. Kill the cat-shifter, nae me."

Edee narrowed her gaze on the tall man. "I wonder how long it will take James to dislodge this sub from your ass?"

49

Striker eyed the sub. "An hour, give or take a few minutes."

Gram lost it, laughing so hard he needed to bend. "How the hell do you know that?"

"Well, there was this one time I thought it would be funny to try...och...never mind," said Striker, snapping his mouth shut quickly.

Gram wasn't sure the man's face could get any redder. He looked like a tomato.

Edee raked her gaze over Striker. "I'm going to check the Asshole of the Week wall to see what it is you got stuck up your butt."

She hurried off.

Striker ran after her. "Fine. It's nae Boomer's sub! Let's nae talk about my arse anymore."

Chapter Four

AMELIA SLINKED along the side of a large building, walking down a darkened alley, hoping no
one saw her. She kept the hood of her black
sweatshirt pulled up and over her long hair. With
her head down, she walked with purpose. The
gathering had gone into the night, taking precious
time she didn't have. She'd been left no other
choice but to reach out to her contact and ask him
to reschedule for tonight.

It had taken some doing and she'd been left
waiting on pins and needles until she heard back
from him, but she'd been able to reschedule the
rendezvous. Unfortunately, she'd gone through
all the trouble only to find Susan shadowing her
the entire next day. Briefly leaving her alone

when Amelia escaped to the greenhouse. Susan wasn't fond of the greenhouses or of Amelia's herbal medicine mixing area within it. She thought the entire area was boring because it was tucked away from any kind of heavy foot traffic.

Amelia thought the location was perfect and often got lost working on perfecting various remedies. Since the goal for the day had been creating a new masking agent—one that would keep the supernaturals from smelling another—she'd opted for the percolation extraction method. The process was more time consuming than other means but, in her opinion, the end results were more potent and worth the effort and energy.

If all went according to plan, Amelia would have what she needed in time to make her escape. She'd already come up with an oil, a mixture of cinnamon, cloves, and allspice, that did a very good job of confusing the senses of a supernatural —especially shifters. But the Flock was accustomed to it, as well as the oversaturation of lavender scents around the resort and compound. She needed something new, something better. Something that could fool even Cal, even if just for a short period of time.

Long enough for Amelia to flee with Andie and never look back.

Sadly, the toll of prepping to go on the run, and extra hours in the greenhouse, had caught up to her. Earlier in the day, she'd dozed off without meaning to. The strangest dream had come to her. In it, she was running, holding a man's hand. His back had been to her and he'd been shirtless, wearing jeans and black boots. He had long dark hair and a body to die for. He also had what looked to be burn scars on his back. They didn't take away from his appeal or the fact he was trying to keep her safe—that much she was sure of.

She was sure of something else, too.

Without any question, Amelia simply knew she'd been intimate with the stranger. That she'd given herself over to him and felt something for him. If she had to label it, she'd have said love.

That was ridiculous. She wasn't in love. She didn't know a man who fit the bill as the hunky hero from her dream. And she'd never been with any man. Period.

When Amelia had woken to find Susan standing over her, sneering, it was on the tip of her tongue to call out for the dream man. The problems with that were, she didn't know his name and he wasn't real. Still, Amelia had fought the urge to let her magik loose to roam the ether for the mystery man, to send out a flare to him that she needed his help.

She didn't.

But she'd very much wanted to.

Instead, Amelia had artfully gotten Susan away from the greenhouse and the mixture to mask scents. It needed another twenty-four hours to continue to drip before it would be ready. Susan's insistence that everything Amelia found interesting was boring had helped. But it had done nothing to shake the bitch for the remainder of the day. When Amelia learned Susan had been dispatched on Cal's orders to spend time with her, she wondered if he'd discovered her escape plan.

The fact she was still among the living said he hadn't.

Tina, one of Amelia's only allies in the Flock, had managed to create a diversion at the resort that called for Susan's full attention. Since Susan prided herself on everything running smoothly— she, herself, answered to a group of powerful males—the plan had been a success. That had afforded Amelia the opportunity to sneak over to the nearest neighbor of the compound for a ride into Denver.

Jeanie Tippons was in her early sixties and had a long-standing distrust of the Flock. She was a trained emergency-room nurse who had seen a number of cases come through the local hospital that she was sure could be traced back to the Flock. She wasn't wrong. She'd been vocal about it as well, which was for the best. It was harder for the Flock to get rid of her if the public was watching. If anything happened to her now, most eyes would turn to the Flock.

Cal couldn't have that.

And he couldn't bend Jeanie's mind as he could that of so many other humans. Amelia was pretty sure it was from the woman's iron will, but there could have been something more to it. She'd led a hard life and didn't take crap from anyone, and that was just part of what Amelia liked so much about the woman. Jeanie often came to Amelia's cabin to help with Andie. The woman didn't care that Cal forbid her from being on the property. It was as if Jeanie was daring Cal to do something about it all.

So far, he hadn't.

Andie responded well to Jeanie, trusting the woman fully.

Amelia trusted her, too.

The fact Jeanie had dropped everything to give Amelia a ride into Denver, which was about an hour from the compound, said a lot about the woman's character. She'd understood the change of plans at the last minute and the need for secrecy. She was a rare gem. Amelia would miss her when she was gone.

Jeanie and Amelia's mother, Abigail, had been close. The women had developed a strong bond of friendship over the years. The local towns-people were told Amelia's mother ran off with a young lover. Most people bought the story because they wanted to or because Cal gave them no choice.

But not Jeanie.

She knew Cal had been behind Abigail's disappearance from the start.

He was behind a lot.

When Abigail had tried to run with Amelia five years prior, pregnant with Andie, they'd real-ized just how ill-prepared they'd been for life outside of the Flock. Everything had been new and overwhelming. Blending in wasn't easy for them at first. They stuck out like the hippie-chicks they seemed to be compared to by everyone around them.

They'd had no money, no identification, no means to support themselves. While they'd managed to survive on their own, and on the run, for nearly three years and learned many tips and tricks for living under the radar and off the grid, ultimately, Cal and his followers had found them.

Emotions swelled in Amelia as she thought of her mother and how desperate the woman had been to keep her daughters far from their father and the Flock. Abigail had known what fate was in store for a woman in the cult.

Nothing good.

Women were either passed around between the men, used for manual labor, or used to seduce perspective Flock members. Sometimes they were required to do all of it. Abusing them wasn't against Flock rules. A man was well within his right to backhand *his* woman if he felt it was warranted.

Amelia and Andie had been spared so far, but that would change before long. Already Cal had promised Amelia to Taggert, once she completed the task required of her—securing the Bringer of

Change. Cal fully intended to force his own daughter to be party to assuring the male joined the Flock. It didn't matter that Amelia wanted no part in his plan. And it didn't matter that she knew without a shadow of a doubt she would be expected to use sex and her body to lure the man. While her father had never said as much outright, his people had.

Susan, in particular, liked to point out just what would be expected of Amelia when the time came. It had been Susan and the women in her close circle who had worked with Amelia, teaching her how to give erotic massages, how to be alluring to the opposite sex, and what to do to please a man.

The lessons had been humiliating.

That was part of the way the cult broke people down. It was textbook brainwashing techniques. Everything from isolating the person from their friends and family to breaking their spirit to the point the person felt worthless without the Flock. Amelia even knew of instances where Cal had renamed members upon joining. Giving them a new sense of identity and reality.

They thought it was out of love.

It wasn't.

Amelia lost track of the number of embarrassments she'd suffered in front of the Flock, at the authority of her father or his inner circle of trusted males. The most recent was being forced to watch other female Flock members as they performed spa-like treatments, and also sexual acts on the men. It had started off innocently enough, instructing Amelia on the ways in which to give a massage, how to handle healing stones, and so forth, things she already knew, but had escalated quickly. Amelia had found herself frozen in stunned disgust as she'd been made to remain in the room when the normal spa services turned into sexual acts.

Not just any acts, either.

Each time Amelia had tried to avert her gaze, Susan had intervened, drawing attention to Amelia and holding her face, making her watch. Everyone involved had found it all hysterically funny. Everyone but her. She'd been mortified and sickened by the level of depravity some of the members displayed.

Some were sexual sadists.

She was positive of it.

In her brief time in the real world, living away from the Flock, Amelia had crammed in as much knowledge as she could, learning all there was to learn on cults. Knowledge was power, and she knew deep down that she needed to be as prepared as she could be.

That she would not be a sheep.

One of the people who had jumped at the chance to help instruct Amelia in the ways of sexually pleasing a man was Taggert. He was most certainly a sexual sadist. He got off on pain, receiving and inflicting it. He got off on mental and physical torture. And he'd gotten off on Amelia's humiliation.

A quiver ran through her as she thought back to the look of sheer satisfaction Taggert had worn as one of Susan's women went to her knees before the man. The woman had started off drawing Taggert's erection into her mouth and then licking the head and shaft of it. She sucked on his balls, all the while watching Amelia, looking amused. But Taggert had taken the already embarrassing moment to a whole new level when he'd grabbed the woman by the sides of her head, burying his fists in her hair. He'd then controlled how much of his cock she took in her mouth and for how long. He'd rammed in so deep and held so long that she'd gotten sick all over the place.

That hadn't stopped Taggert.

He'd kept going, kept forcing her to accept him orally in a brutal manner. He'd done so until she'd passed out and then he'd jerked himself off, his gaze locked on Amelia as he'd jetted seed all over the woman.

He'd then forced another woman to clean up the mess from it all and drag away the one who had given him oral sex.

If that hadn't been bad enough, other males had been brought in, displaying other acts of sex and violence. Taggert had remained through all the training sessions, staying close to Amelia, smirking, trying to steal caresses from her all while she flinched and her stomach churned. Once he'd even cupped her chin, demanding she look upon the acts occurring and not look away as she'd been trying to do.

When blood play had come into the mix, Taggert had watched her, desire in his dark gaze and a sinister smile upon his face. He'd licked her cheek and whispered how he couldn't wait until the day he was able to do that to her.

She wanted to be ill just thinking about it all again.

There was no way she could be part of luring

anyone into the fold. And no way in hell she'd permit her little sister to grow up in the Flock. Andie's age kept her protected for now, but she'd grow and that would change. She'd be handed off to someone Cal felt could benefit the Flock. Rumor had it the man chosen for Andie was Brian, who was as bad, if not worse than Taggert. He'd also been in on the entire training ordeal. That didn't matter. If it gained Cal power, Cal would sacrifice his daughters.

No one was safe.

Already Amelia danced on the edge of his patience. If he found out she'd snuck away from the compound and was planning to escape, for good, there was no telling what he'd do.

Odds were, she'd end up like her mother.

Murdered in front of the Flock. Used as a life lesson to those who would dare to stand against him or the path to enlightenment. A cautionary tale to be told to others for years to come.

She knew of dozens of murders that could be linked back to them, and those had just happened in the last few years. There were probably hundreds more that she wasn't aware of. She wasn't certain. She did know the cult was deadly, despite the face they put out to the world. The peace, love, and happiness lie they spun to make everyone in the outside world think they were great.

It helped them get recruits.

They were media darlings.

All of it was smoke and mirrors.

A public relations campaign that cost them millions but paid off in the long haul. They saw themselves as untouchable.

In many ways, they were. They operated above the law. It was easy for them. They used their power to influence the minds of most humans and bought off the ones they couldn't. Anyone who stood in their way went missing, never to be seen or heard from again.

She'd tried to get outside help before. It had resulted in the death of the person attempting to assist. Now, at the end of her rope, Amelia was desperate. Everything that had happened in her life led her to this point. To sneaking around in the dark for clandestine meetings with shady people. Had she been permitted to select another path, she would have gladly done so. But this was her life and it was a dangerous one.

Amelia pushed onward in the darkened alley, acutely aware of every noise and movement in her area. She was hypervigilant and with good reason. The Flock had eyes and ears everywhere. Not to mention, the contact she was meeting was far from human. And from what she'd been able to gather, he was anything but harmless.

Still, the risk was worth it if it got Andie to safety. If it spared her sister the same fate Amelia was staring in the face, she'd make any sacrifice, and risk it all. Just as her mother had tried to do for her.

Failure wasn't an option.

She checked her watch, mindful of how much time she'd already lost in an effort to sneak away from the compound undetected. Even with the little bit of help she'd gotten, it had taken a lot of effort to be able to leave without notice.

As Amelia came around the back of the building, she found herself in a tucked-away alcove that had recyclables piled high on one side. An eight-foot chain-link fence blocked anyone from getting through with any sort of ease.

She turned in a slow circle, looking for any sign of her contact.

There was none.

"No," she whispered, fearing her contact had grown tired of waiting for her and left.

He'd been her last hope.

The name she'd been given was Ace. That was all she knew about the man. That, and he was said to be one of the best. And she needed the best right now.

Hot tears welled in her eyes and she held tight to them, her jaw clenching. Running without forged papers would make it even harder than simply going. If it was just her, she'd be fine, but she had someone else to consider—her little sister.

Bending her head, she wiped her eyes and collected herself enough to head back to the compound.

As she turned to go, she found herself staring at a tall, well-built man. She'd never heard him approach or sensed him there. That was saying something.

He wore sunglasses despite the fact it was the middle of the night. That never meant good things in her world. Supernaturals often had to hide their eyes from others.

The man had to be over six and a half feet tall. He had a head of long dark brown hair that hung down and over his shoulders. It wasn't exactly T-shirt weather, yet that was all he had on with his jeans and black boots. The shirt was dark gray and snug-fitting to the point she wondered if the arms would burst at the seams trying to accommodate his biceps.

If he wanted to harm her, she wasn't sure she could defend herself well.

She didn't know a lot about him. A friend of a friend had put her in contact with him. They said he had access to the best forged paperwork out there. The price tag had been steep. More than she could easily handle, but she'd spent five years squirreling away everything she could for this day.

"You Amelia?" he asked, his voice deep.

"Yes," she said softly, nerves getting the better of her. "Are you Ace?"

"I am." The edge of his mouth turned upward. "I'm not going to eat you or anything. You can relax. You're staring at me like I'm the big bad wolf or something. I'm not. Hell, I'm not even a wolf."

He tapped his upper right arm, showing off a tribal tattoo of a horse.

She swallowed hard.

He shrugged. "All I can do is tell you I'm not going to hurt you. Not much I can do to settle your nerves any. Though I can't blame you. With the number of women turning up dead around here in the last few months, you've every right to be concerned. You should know, I had nothing to do with the deaths."

She knew he hadn't.

The Flock had.

She calmed slightly. "I'm sorry I'm late. I swear I tried to get here on time."

"You from that hippie commune?"

She tensed. Never had she let him know where she was from. For him to guess accurately on his first try was cause for alarm.

Ace motioned to her sweatshirt pocket. The emblem for the compound where she lived and worked was on it. Clothing was sold in the gift shop section of the resort. It was where Amelia had gotten her street clothes. Running around the streets of Denver in the all-white wardrobe the Flock preferred would have drawn a lot of attention.

"Again, relax. I guessed as much because of the patch. I didn't read your mind or follow you. You really should stop thinking the worst of me."

"Oh." She exhaled slowly and wiped her palms on her jean-covered thighs. "Sorry. I'm not sure how all of this works."

He lifted a dark brow. "This your first time needing forged paperwork?"

She debated on lying to the guy but decided against it. "Yes. I wasn't who handled this before when it was needed."

His lips tightened. "You okay? If you and your kid are in a bad situation, I know people. We can get you out of there."

The tears she'd only just managed to get to stop returned at his offer. "Thank you but it's complicated, and she's not my kid."

He held a manila envelope up slightly. "Tell me I'm not handing you documentation, so you can steal someone else's kid. I'm a lot of things, but okay with kidnapping isn't one of them. And you look like a kid yourself. Hell, you even legal?"

She couldn't help but laugh slightly as she shook her head. "I'm legal. And she isn't my child. She's my little sister."

"And your mother?"

Amelia closed her eyes tight, fighting away her emotions. "Dead."

"Your father?" he asked, seemingly uncon- cerned with his invasive line of questioning.

She'd never met a crook with a moral compass before and any man who dealt in obtaining illegal paperwork for wasn't exactly winning any saint awards. Neither was she since she was purchasing the goods.

It was somewhat refreshing. Ace either really cared or he was trying to find out if anyone would notice if she went missing.

He lifted his other hand. "You look and smell freaked. Sorry I'm prying. I see a lot of shit in my line of work."

She bet he did. "My father is part of why I need the papers."

"And you're in a situation that you feel you need to run from? That it's so extreme you need fake papers for you and your sister?"

"Yes," she said, reaching into her back pocket to get the cash she'd brought for the exchange.

"Listen, kid, if you need help, tell me," he said before handing her the envelope. When he didn't take the wad of cash, she stared up at him, confused, and tried to push it at him. He shook his head. "Hang on to it."

"But I still owe you the other half of the payment. The agreement was I'd pay you half up front and the rest on delivery," she protested.

He grinned somewhat, and she had to admit he was handsome. She'd have noticed sooner if her nerves hadn't gotten the best of her. "I do just fine, and you look like you could use it far more than me. I'm guessing that wasn't easy for you to come by."

"No. It wasn't." She continued to hold the money out to him. "Please take it. I owe it to you. I don't want charity."

He put his hand over hers and closed her fist around the money. "Listen, it's pretty fucking clear to me that you're in a bad spot. Most people I deal with are. I don't know what is going on or who it is you're trying to run from, but I can see it in your eyes. You're scared shitless. I don't have it in me to let a woman and a kid suffer. I'm real close to demanding you tell me what's going on and then handling the matter myself."

She gasped and shook her head. "No. Stay far from the compound. It's not safe for you. They seek out alpha males. Shifters are especially alluring for them."

"Really? Isn't it supposed to be a safe haven for supernaturals?" he asked, his tone saying he knew different. "And how is it you know I'm a shifter? I'm sure that information wasn't shared with you prior to our meeting."

She glanced away. If people started to poke

around, it could alert the others and tip them off. She couldn't have that. "I'll be fine. Just please stay away. Trust me when I say the resort is not what it appears to be."

"Few things are, kid," he supplied. "How old are you? Because from where I'm standing, you look like you're maybe eighteen. I have to admit, when I saw the pictures you provided for the passports, I had to wonder if you had a kid when you were barely into your teens."

She shook her head. "I'm twenty-three."

"Still nothing but a baby really," he returned, pushing her hand back toward her body. "Keep the money. Keep the papers. Keep that number you called. The one that put you in contact with me. If you need anything, and I do mean *anything*, you call that number. They'll find me no matter where I am. All the men I work with are good men, Amelia. We can help you. We understand what it's like to be scared and think you have no way out. Part of our life's mission is to help others who can't help themselves. The way we see it, there is a bit of Outcast in all of us."

"Outcast?"

He winked. "It's not important. It just means we get it. And none of us will be okay knowing you and your little sister are in a dangerous situation."

She lost her battle with her tears and they began to flow freely. "T-thank you."

He stiffened a moment before he reached out and gave her something that resembled a hug. She was sure it was meant to be comforting but it was evident the man wasn't much of a hugger. The act was awkward at best. "Amelia, I mean it. Call and I'll come."

She nodded, hugging the man in return, still crying.

He patted her back. "Tell you what, you call that number regardless. If I don't hear from you in the next two days, telling me you're okay and fine, I'll step in. Am I clear?"

"Yes," she managed as she hiccupped. "It's hard for me to make calls without someone noticing."

"Hard or dangerous?" he asked, still hugging her.

"Both."

"Do your best. If I don't hear from you, I'll reach out in some fashion. Either I'll come, or I'll send someone I trust. Okay?" he asked.

She stared up at him. "Why are you helping me?"

"Because I can and it's the right thing to do," he answered. "It's not often I find myself on the right side of the fence. Figure I should act on it to help even out all the hell I raise."

She smiled against his chest and composed herself as best she could. "Thank you again for everything."

"How are you getting back tonight, Amelia?" he asked.

"I have a ride. They're waiting on me. I need to hurry so no one notices I'm missing."

He nodded. "Take care of yourself, kid. And remember, if I don't hear from you within forty-eight hours, I'm coming in, like it or not. I really do not want to get a phone call telling me your body was found next. Got it?"

"Yes," she whispered. "I should go. They'll notice I'm gone soon."

"Forty-eight hours," he reminded.

She nodded.

Chapter Five

JUST OUTSIDE OF DENVER, Colorado. Twenty-four hours later...

Gram shot another annoyed look in the direction of his captors. He'd not been kidnapped by bad guys.

No. It was far worse.

His own friends had done it. They claimed it was an intervention. He'd give them an intervention the second he got his hands on them all.

When he'd learned Striker was planning something involving Colorado and his cousins, Gram had assumed the pair would arrive at PSI and do something crazy, like show up with thirty women they'd hired to strip for him.

It wouldn't have been their first time doing

something such as that. They'd once hired two busloads of strippers for a week and holed up in a rented beach house. There had been endless booze, women, and partying. That had been years ago, but Gram grew tired thinking about it all. He wasn't that same man anymore. He didn't see women as he once did—something to get him off and find release with.

He'd grown up.

Matured.

And he wanted more from life than a quick fuck with a nameless woman who meant nothing to him.

Gram had every reason to be leery of the plans the McCrackens had cooked up to help him get on the mend. Nothing had happened at first, and Gram had thought he'd dodged a McCracken bullet. That the men had been tied up and unable to break away to stage their version of an intervention.

Nope.

He'd not been so lucky.

Striker hatched his plan bright and early in the morning. Catching Gram off guard. When Gram had gotten out of the shower (which meant he'd been clean a whole two days in a row—

record-breaking for his last few weeks), he'd found a fresh set of clothing laid out on the bed and breakfast on a tray for him. He'd thought nothing of eating the food. Why would he? He'd been eating meals in the infirmary for weeks. He had no reason to worry about the food or what was in it.

The next thing he remembered was waking up on one of PSI's jets, with his Shadow Agent handler and good friend, Armand, near him, reading over reports, and their good friend Cody, who was reading a book on poetry. The two acted as if it were no big deal that Striker had clearly slipped him something and they'd abducted him. Probably a horse tranquilizer, knowing the Scot.

Worse yet, upon landing in Denver at a private airstrip, the men were greeted by two PSI agents from the Denver office.

Not just any two operatives.

No.

These two just happened to be first cousins of Striker. The very same twins Gram had feared would show for him. They thought it was hysterical that Striker had one-upped Gram and managed to get him all the way to Colorado.

It wasn't even noon yet and Gram was losing

track of the number of felonies his friends were committing. Drugging him, kidnapping him, transporting him across state lines, unlawful imprisonment—the list went on and on. Though none of it would compare to the murders he was about to commit if they didn't stop trying to help him.

He was fine.

He didn't need help.

"Carbrey, if you do nae pull this SUV over, I'll nae be held responsible for my actions," he warned, his attention on the driver of the SUV. "I can promise you that there will be two less McCrackens to worry about. There are so many of you I do nae know if anyone will notice if two go missing."

The six-and-a-half-foot-tall hulk of a man had a head of jet-black hair and a close-cut matching beard. Carbrey McCracken's hair hung just past his shoulders and had several small random braids in it, typical for men who hailed from the same time period as Gram—like the McCrackens did.

The troops had been called in to help him heal his body and mind, and right now, they were driving him crazy.

"Did you hear that, brother?" asked Macbeth

"Mac" McCracken, Car's twin, as he gave the driver's seat a slight shove from behind. "He's going to inflict bodily harm on us."

Carbrey and Mac were identical twins. They even kept their hair and beards the same length, making it hard to tell them apart unless you knew them well and memorized which tattoos went with which man. Their scents were very close, but Gram had learned centuries ago to pick up on the subtle differences. He'd also learned that trouble tended to follow the twins wherever they went. More than once Gram had found himself sitting in a cell, next to the twins, after a rather long night of hell-raising. Those days were long behind him.

If anyone counted twenty years ago as long behind.

He had a sneaking suspicion he'd end up behind bars again if they were around.

The pair seemed to be in a race to see who could tattoo more of their bodies. They also had a fair number of silver piercings, which confused him, seeing as how silver actually burned shifters. Both men could shift into wolves, so silver was not their friend.

Wouldn't know it to look at them.

You also wouldn't know they worked in law enforcement for PSI. They looked more like criminals. Hell, they probably broke more laws than criminals even.

Carbrey snorted and glanced in the rearview mirror. "I'm up here shaking in my boots. Really. I do nae think I can keep driving. I'm *that* terrified of you, Campbell. You planning to glare at me? That'll teach me. Hey, I have an idea. How about you shift shapes and come at me. Oh, wait, yer refusing to try to shape-shift. Pussy."

"Yer an asshole," snapped Gram, folding his arms over his chest and pouting. He didn't care how juvenile it was. All he wanted to do was go home, shut himself in and lick his wounds—both physical and mental. "And I'm nae refusing to try, my wolf is giving me the finger."

"Yer wolf is a dick, like you," added Carbrey before grinning wide. "How about you shift and make me regret calling you out?"

"Goading me willnae get the results yer after," said Gram evenly. "Unless death is the end game for you."

The twins laughed more.

Mac's cell phone rang, and the sound of bagpipes filled the SUV. Gram had a fairly good idea that meant Striker was calling. Mac answered and then laughed. "Oh, he's awake now. Woke on the plane. We considered restraining him. Aye, he's good and pissed with us. He's been pouting for at least an hour or so now. I do nae think he's much enjoying yer surprise getaway for him. No. I dinnae tell him it's supposed to be loaded with hot chicks. Aye. He's an ungrateful fuck. Maybe his cock is broken too. I dinnae think to ask. I know his wolf is. Hold on, I'll tell him." Mac lowered the phone and grinned at Gram. "Striker says get well soon and get laid."

Gram flipped off Mac.

Mac snorted. "I cannae be sure but I think he just propositioned you, cousin. For the record, I'm better-looking than you. Why would he want you when he could have me? What do you mean, yer milkshake brings 'em all to the yard? I do nae have any clue what yer talking about, cousin. Are you high? Dipping in the same shite you slipped Campbell?"

Gram rubbed the bridge of his nose. He was in for a very long retreat.

Mac moved the phone from his ear and eyed Gram. "He's now singing something about his lady lumps or humps. I'm Scottish and even I'm having trouble understanding him."

"Do nae look at me. He's yer kin," said Gram.

"Do nae remind me." Mac groaned and put the phone back to his ear. "What? No way is Carbrey better-looking than me. He's an ugly fuck."

Carbrey grunted from his spot up front behind the wheel. "I look like you."

"No," said Mac, holding the phone from his ear once more. "I'm drop-dead sexy. Yer nae."

Armand, a vampire, and the only non-shifter male in the SUV, sighed from his spot in the front passenger seat. The SUV's windows were treated with extra-strength UV protectant so that vampires could ride safely within during the daylight hours. Armand would have been extra crispy without the treated glass. "Children, am I going to have to break up another argument? It has been at least twenty minutes since the last one."

"He started it," the twins said at the same time.

"Enough, boys." Armand reached back, much like a parent would while trying to deal with a toddler when driving, and took the phone from

Mac. "Striker, the last thing we need right now is another Scotsman weighing in on this. The three with me now are more than enough. I really do not understand how your country survived all these years, not with the way you all behave. I'm frankly shocked Scotland was left standing after the McCrackens and the Campbells. How did it survive your clans at all?"

Carbrey waggled his brows. "The French are dicks."

Armand ignored him and continued to speak to Striker. "We are en route to drop Cody off with his contacts here. I'll join him to see what help I can offer. The twins will see Gram to the doorstep of the retreat. Yes. They will assure he remains there."

"We're babysittin'," said Mac.

Car laughed. "Wolf-sitting."

Gram gave them both stern looks, only serving to make them laugh more.

It wasn't long before Armand appeared annoyed with the direction of his phone conversation with Striker. No real surprise. Striker brought out the best in most. He hung up and handed the phone back to Mac. He then turned in the seat and eyed Gram. "It's a sad day when I realize you are *by far* the calmest and sanest of the Scots I know. These two make Striker look well-behaved. Not to mention Searc. He may be mated now but he is still a pain in my ass."

Gram laughed.

Armand glanced at Car before continuing to speak to Gram. "Striker said something on the phone. Apparently, Garth told him that you've been seeing a woman in white and a ball on the meds you were being given. You never mentioned either to me."

Being Gram's handler meant that Armand was not only his point of contact in the event of an emergency, he was often Gram's backup, and the one whom Gram got his mission briefings from. They'd forged a tight friendship over the past two decades. That being said, Gram had been a member of Garth's PSI Team Eight for centuries before that. Old habits apparently died hard.

"Yer seeing a woman with balls wearing white?" asked Mac, an expression of sheer horror on his face.

Armand rubbed his temple, murmuring something about Robert the Bruce and William Wallace.

All the Scots in the SUV narrowed their gazes on the French vampire, waiting for him to dare to say more.

"William was a great lycan," said Mac, lowering his head, putting a hand to his chest. "A moment of silence for him, please."

Car went to lower his head too, but Armand shoved him.

"You are driving. Watch the road," warned Armand.

"Yer already dead. Lighten up," replied Car.

Gram shot the man a hard look. "Stop taking jabs at him being a vampire. That never ends well for you, or do I need to remind you about what happened when you pushed Auberi the last time he was out here?"

Auberi was another good friend of Gram's. He was not only a trained physician but also a member of PSI's Crimson Ops Division, which was full of vampires. The last time he'd been around the twins, Auberi had ended up tying the men together and leaving them bound before heading out to a club to party. No one could blame the guy. The twins no doubt pushed him into it all.

Car glanced at the rearview mirror. "Rumor mill has Auberi with a kid now. That true?"

Gram snorted. "Nicolette is hardly a kid. She's a young woman who is mated to Garth."

Mac gasped. "The Viking mated? Wait, Garth and Auberi do nae get along. At all. They're now related?"

Armand grinned. "They are. Auberi has not only found himself an instant father of a grown woman, he's found he's now Garth's father-in-law."

The twins lost it, laughing so hard Gram worried Car would wreck the SUV.

"You're all loud as fuck," said Cody Livingston from the third row of the SUV. The large wereshark had managed to lie down with his feet propped on the back of the second row of seats. It didn't look comfortable to Gram but to each his own. Cody leaned up, his blond hair piled into a messy knot on top of his head. The man always looked as if he'd just rolled out of bed and was on his way to surf.

Everything about him always seemed so laid-back, so carefree, but Gram knew better. He knew a fraction of the horrors Cody had been subjected to in his life. Frankly, he was stunned the man wasn't in a corner crying or a homicidal maniac. It wasn't like life hadn't been doing its best to drive him in that direction.

Mac looked back at Cody. "Look. The shark lives."

Cody lifted a hand and flipped off Mac.

"You wish," said Mac. He then rubbed his jaw. "Livingston, want to tell me why it is yer even here? You Outcasts do nae generally mix in with us."

Gram growled, disliking the term Outcast, even though Cody and the others like him who had been created by the government referred to themselves as such.

Mac put his hands up. "I'm nae saying anything against the Outcasts. I do nae like the way they were treated either, but I'm nae wrong. Cody has never come out here to work with us on a matter before. Why now?"

"When I heard Gram was being sedated, I didn't want to miss it." Cody remained reclined with his eyes closed as he answered. "Seriously, though. I got a call from a friend of mine out here. He's an Outcast, too, named Ace. Asked me to put some feelers out, and it just happened that what he's having me look into overlaps with Gram's vacation, so here I am."

"I'm nae on vacation," corrected Gram. "I've been kidnapped."

"We should stuff a gag in his mouth," said Car. "I hear it's all the rage with kidnappers nowadays."

Armand eyed the man. "And I hear you enjoyed being bound. At least that is what Auberi said. Or was it not you who Auberi tied to a bed with full body paint that resembled the Union Jack? We all know how much you love England. How does one end up so drunk that they have no memory of getting naked with a vampire and then being covered in body paint and tied to a bed?"

Car's eyes shifted to amber quickly. "I will eat you, vampire."

"I am sure you like to think so," returned Armand, clearly unafraid of the shifter male. No shock, since Armand was one hell of a powerful vampire.

Gram stared up front. "I'm curious how it is you ended up naked with Auberi, too. He never did say."

Car cleared his throat. "We're nae gonna talk about that."

Mac cracked up.

"Brother, I will pull this car over and deal with you," warned Car.

Cody groaned. "Seriously? This? Again? I'd rather go back to talking about my dick."

Gram laughed. The twins had spent the first hour after meeting Cody grilling him with question after question on being a wereshark. It was evident they'd never met one before. They had gotten stuck on the topic of a shark's dick, and what it may or may not look like in shifted form. Cody refused to show them.

Thankfully.

Mac glanced over his shoulder at Cody. "I swear I hear a bit of an Aussie accent when you talk sometimes."

"You do," was all Cody offered on the matter before lying back down and closing his eyes.

"He's a real conversationalist," said Car with a grunt. "The dead guy is more fun to talk with."

"Thanks," said Armand, glancing out the window at the Rocky Mountains in the distance. "It's peaceful here."

"You ever been to Denver before?" asked Mac.

Armand shook his head. "It is somewhere I have wanted to see but time has not permitted. How long have the two of you been out here?"

"Maybe twenty years or so. We were in New York for a while before that. And then prior to that we were pretty much everywhere," said Mac. "Really thought we left behind the days of finding mutilated bodies on a nearly daily basis. That was way more New York style than here."

Gram perked. Dead bodies? He hadn't heard anything about dead people. "Wait. What's going on?"

Car glanced back at him quickly. "That's right. Yer nae up to date on what's happening. We've got a serial killer on our hands out here. Targets women, ages twenty to thirty-five. Supernaturals. Brunettes so far. Signs of sexual assault and more."

Armand tensed. "It's partly why I am here, Gram."

"They think it's vampire-related?" asked Gram. "I've never heard of a vamp going on a killing spree out here. The local ones normally keep a close watch on their own."

Car nodded. "Aye, but they do nae know who is doing this. And they want him caught as much as we do. It's reflecting badly on them. And they do nae want our attention on them any longer than need be."

"No. I'd guess they'd nae want that," said Gram, worrying his jaw with one hand. "That settles it. I'm nae going to a retreat. Take me to the PSI offices here. I'll help."

Car glanced back at his brother. "It's as if he thinks that will work."

"He's nae getting out of going to get better," said Mac.

Armand nodded.

Gram groaned.

Cody laughed.

Chapter Six

GRAM ENTERED the spa's lobby and was instantly hit with the overpowering smell of lavender. They apparently soaked everything in it from the strength of the scent. Undertones of cinnamon, allspice, and cloves made their way to him, all confusing his senses.

His wolf did its version of an internal sneeze, unhappy with the strong odor as well. Soft music filled the room. It was a mix of classical music and the sound of the ocean. The sound of it all together agitated Gram, making him feel antsy, like he wanted to get away from it. He strongly suspected it was supposed to be soothing. He'd heard of binary beats before. They never worked for him like they did some.

Basically, they annoyed him and made him fidget. The opposite of their intent.

The entire right wall of the lobby was made to look like a giant waterfall, complete with running water and everything. The walls were cream-colored, as was all of the furniture. Everything had modern, clean lines to it, and was what Gram heard termed minimalist. While he was sure it was in vogue, it felt sterile to him. For a place that prided itself on its open-arms, welcoming attitude, as noted by the billboards on the side of the highway leading into the remote, isolated facility, it was failing miserably in his opinion.

Though Gram did find himself oddly drawn to a large vase of flowers that sat off to the right of the counter. Never before could he recall a time when he'd stopped to take note of flowers, let alone admire them.

Weird.

Car pointed to a large floor display that had photos of relaxing spa amenities. One was of a woman leaning back with green goop on her face and cucumbers on her eyes. Another was of a man soaking in what looked like mud. "Know that I'm gonna pay them extra to take yer photo when yer covered in mud with vegetables over yer eyes. Then I'm gonna frame all the photos and send them to yer headquarters. I think there might be an Asshole of the Week mention in there for you. If for no other reason than it will amuse me greatly."

Gram rolled his eyes. No one really wanted to win the award. While it wasn't official or anything, it had become a thing that PSI guys did on a regular basis, nominating one another whenever an operative did something particularly stupid. With the abundance of alpha males in PSI, it was amazing they didn't rename it the Asshole of the Day, rather than week.

"Smells like they dunked the place in a field of lavender and then hosed it down with more for guid measure," remarked Mac, rubbing his nose, his wolf displeased as well. "It's so much that it's giving me a headache."

"Aye," said Gram.

For a place that supposedly catered to their kind, it wasn't doing so great in the scent department and its music was shit.

Carbrey took one side of Gram, and Mac flanked him on the other. They knew he was a serious flight risk. The second the opportunity presented itself, Gram was out of there. No way in hell was he going to sit around in a mud bath with cucumber slices on his eyes. And he certainly wasn't going to talk about his feelings.

Not happening.

No way.

No how.

"I can see it in yer eyes, Campbell," warned Mac, placing one hand on Gram's shoulder, giving it a squeeze. "I'll break your leg if you try."

"You do realize yer forcing me to be here to heal and yer threatening bodily harm if I do nae stay," he said, quirking a brow at the man's logic.

"Aye. I know full well what I said. And I mean it. To get you right as rain, I'm willing to break yer leg. Car will help," he said, nodding his head in his brother's direction.

Car grinned. "I will."

"Sure. The two of you *finally* decide to get along just in time to team up on me." Gram let out an annoyed breath. "You both suck."

"Nah, but we enjoy getting sucked," said Car with a throaty laugh. "I need to get laid. My balls are turning blue. Why couldn't we stop off at a house of ill repute? Instead, we're at a place that will want to feed us bean sprouts and hummus.

Where are the hot chicks Striker swore would be here?"

"What do we have here?" asked Mac as a group of women walked out and behind the front counter area.

Car grinned. "Ask and ye shall receive."

A blonde offered a flirtatious smile, focusing on Car. "Welcome to Caladrius Wellness and Healing Center Spa & Resort. How can we service you today?"

"Service us?" asked Car, his voice trailing off as a dreamy look came over his face.

"That's it, I'm taking yer place, Campbell," said Mac, stepping forward. "No one told me they'd be flat-out offering to *service* you."

Gram shook his head. "Not like *that*."

The women all stared at him like he was the crazy one for suggesting they weren't offering to perform sex acts on him.

He blinked several times, wondering just what kind of retreat Striker had hooked him up with. As the thought hit him, he stiffened. Knowing Striker, it was really a bordello that was designed to look like a spa.

Shite.

Car sighed, still looking as if he'd found his

version of heaven. "Mac, break my arm. I want to have a legit reason to stay."

"Aye. Only if you break mine in return, brother," responded Mac, swept up with the women before them as well.

The blonde woman grinned. "You don't need to be injured to be a guest here. This is the spa and wellness portion of the resort. You'll find the resort itself offers many activates and amenities. Golf, tennis, swimming, fencing, gyms, two bars and three restaurants that are open to the public as well as a private dining area for staff. I think you'll find Caladrius has something for everyone."

Car waggled his brows. "Aye, but if we're injured, there is a guid chance we'll have pity taken on us and get our boo-boos kissed."

Mac snorted.

"As I said, we offer something for everyone. Injuries are not required to have body parts kissed. That is a bonus that is free of charge," said the blonde, her tone suggestive.

Mac and Car high-fived in front of his face, as if he wasn't even there.

Gram groaned. The twins were making dealing with Striker look like a breeze. They would end up in bed with three chicks very soon.

One too many times Gram had seen the twins work their seductive charms on the opposite sex. He couldn't think of any time their advances had been rejected. Then again, he'd only had one rejection in his long life as well.

Brooke.

He didn't want to continue to feel as if someone was sitting on his chest whenever he thought of her. He wanted to just be happy for her and for Bethany. Maybe Striker had the right idea. Maybe time away from the situation to rest and relax was called for. As he looked over the women, he had to admit they were very attractive. But he had no interest in sex. At least not with them.

Car took a step toward the women. "Campbell. He's a reservation."

"I do?" questioned Gram. "Since when? I assumed that, like everything Striker does, this had very little thought put behind it."

"Striker made it for you yesterday before he called us," supplied the feisty Scot. "So there is a higher-than-average chance you'll be getting a *special* massage if you know what I mean."

Yes. He knew exactly what he meant. And he planned to kill Striker the first chance he got.

Gram was about to say as much when he found himself oddly fixated on the fresh-cut flowers once more. The strangest urge to keep his mouth shut and remain came over him. That in itself was odd.

The women giggled in a way that said they were receptive to the twins' antics. In fact, two of the women came out from behind the counter, one going to each twin. The women touched the twins' arms, petting them in a teasing manner. The last thing Car and Mac needed was encouragement.

The women gave it in spades.

Oh yeah. The twins would be doing the horizontal bop with the women soon enough. It really was impossible to take them anywhere and have them behave. They were basically overgrown teenage boys. They had women, booze, and food on their minds at all times. That was about it.

"Mr. Campbell," said the blonde. "Welcome. We've been looking forward to your arrival."

"Can't you stay with us, too?" asked the redhead, slinking her body against Car's. "Everyone can use some downtime to relax, unwind, and unload."

"Unload?" asked Car with a large swallow.

She licked her lips and nodded, her gaze sliding down him, settling on the man's groin. "Most certainly unload."

Car whimpered.

Mac laughed until the woman near him began to pet him once more. Then he looked as if he was caught between running away and dry humping her then and there. Knowing the man, the latter would win out.

The woman nearest Car made eye contact with Gram briefly. The way her eyes caught the light made Gram wonder if she had a bit of cat-shifter in her. He couldn't smell any on her, not that he could smell much beyond the overpowering scents the spa had, but his senses did alert him to the fact she was more than human. All the women present were. Made sense if the place catered to supernaturals.

There was something else there. A scent he couldn't quite place with all the lavender in the air. Whatever it was, it reminded him of the scent of a succubus.

The woman slid her hand down the front of Car and came to rest on his groin, cupping him through his jeans. "Is that a yes to staying and unloading?"

Car jerked and cleared his throat. "Dear gods above, I wish I was staying to be serviced too."

Mac eyed his brother. "Maybe we could be late for the other thing."

"Not an option," said Car with a long sigh. "But we'll be back. We've something to take care of first. In the meantime, yer welcome to keep our friend here company. If anyone could use servicing, it's Campbell."

Gram lifted a hand to stop Car before he went any further. "I'm guid. I do nae need servicing. Can someone show me to my room?"

Mac grunted. "Och, Campbell, you more than anyone need servicing. If these women are nae to yer liking, just say so. Striker told us you like yer women tall, dark-haired, green-eyed, and smokin' hot. Maybe they take orders here."

Gram was going to kill Striker slowly.

Mac looked to the blonde behind the counter. "I do nae suppose you have one of those women handy, do you?"

She grinned. "As a matter of fact, we do."

Mac waggled his brows. "Guid. He'll take two."

"Arsehole," whispered Gram, knowing Mac could hear him with ease.

"Stop yelling at me. I know you don't like Brussels sprouts, okay?" A small man with wiry hair, a knit cap, and a towel wrapped around his waist came walking out from a back area. His pudgy, hair-covered torso stuck out as the towel rode dangerously low. He had on a pair of pink flip-flops and appeared to be a man on a mission. He spun and pointed to another man.

A tall, lanky male followed close behind, this one wearing a white robe and a pair of blue flip-flops. Under the tall man's arm was a football helmet, and in the helmet was a head.

Gram did a double-take.

The head was fake and looked to be from a mannequin, but it was a head nonetheless.

The smaller man turned to face the other fully. "Gus, I heard you the first ten times. I'm sorry I got Brussels sprouts juiced for you. It sounded good, and I wanted to see one get juiced. Didn't know it could be done. The carrot was one thing. Big deal. Everyone does that. But a sprout, that was great. What? No. They don't juice peanut butter and jelly sandwiches here. Wait. Maybe they do. Wonder if that comes in a smoothie. You know, smoothies are all the rage

MANDY M. ROTH

with the young folks. I stay hip. I know these things."

Gram glanced at Car and Mac to find them both staring at the scene before them, looking as lost as Gram felt.

"Uh, is the little guy talking to himself?" asked Car, not bothering to lower his voice any.

"Aye," said Mac. "And is that a head in a helmet under the silent one's arm?"

"I think yer right, brother." Car nodded. "We should nae be shocked. Striker picked the spa. Stands to reason there would be people walking around talking to themselves and carrying heads."

"Bill," said the blonde woman, her lips pressing into a thin line as she rushed from behind the counter in the direction of the little man. "I thought you were all set up for facials this afternoon. Shouldn't you and Gus be there now and not here, in the lobby, where other guests can see you?"

Bill thumbed in the tall guy's direction. "Gus won't stop going on and on about my juice screwup. He's a big baby when it comes to a good cleanse. Hey, speaking of that, can you guys juice peanut butter and jelly sandwiches? Nothing does a body good better than peanut butter and jelly. Yum."

"Um, no," she said, keeping her calm.

It was amazing.

Even the twins were captivated with the spectacle before them, and they had the attention spans of gnats on crack.

"Grilled cheese juices?" asked Bill, sounding hopeful. "Maybe put them in a smoothie or something. I'm known as something of a problem solver. Also, if anyone needs some good shit, you know what I'm talking about, I got a good hookup." He glanced at his silent friend. "I know it's legal here but mine is better. Grown with love."

"I'll see what we can do," replied the woman, clearly wanting the crazy little man out of her lobby area.

The taller male looked in Gram's direction but didn't make eye contact. He seemed to look everywhere but directly at Gram. It was unnerving to say the least.

The slightest of buzzing began around Gram, and he could have sworn he felt Fae magik. As quickly as it came, it left.

She's here.

He froze, glancing around, trying to figure out who had just communicated with him on a mental path reserved for the men he worked with. It wasn't Car's or Mac's voice he'd heard. In fact, he'd never heard the voice before in his life.

He nudged Mac. "Did you hear that?"

"What?" asked Mac, never looking away from Gus, who was now petting the helmet in a loving manner. "It's like a train wreck."

"The voice," said Gram. "In yer head."

Mac glanced at him. "Yer hearing voices now? Looks like we're nae a moment too soon with getting you help."

"Dick," said Gram, partially under his breath.

Mac motioned to Bill. "You'll fit right in here, Campbell. Maybe we can find you a head to carry, too."

Protect her.

Gram turned partially, trying to figure out who the source of the clearly male voice in his head was and what the hell they were talking about. Who was here? What woman did he need to protect?

If you go, she will die.

He rubbed his ear, as if that could possibly make the voice stop.

Mac eyed him. "You still hearing voices in yer head?"

"Aye."

"Freak."

"Arsehole," returned Gram. "I'm telling you, someone is in my head."

"Uh-huh," said Mac, nodding and making over-the-top slow gestures to drive home the fact that Gram was talking crazy.

"I haven't lost it. Someone is telling me to protect a woman. Tell me that isn't one of the offered services because I'm having a hard-enough time separating fact from fiction as of late. I do nae need help or anyone trying to drive my personal crazy train."

The three women stopped what they were doing and glanced at one another.

Was it one of them who needed help? Had they found a way to make a male-sounding voice project into Gram's head? He didn't know of too many species of supernaturals who could pull off something like that.

"Protect who?" asked Mac, sounding as if he didn't believe Gram.

"I don't know."

"Yer head-voice isnae verra helpful," added

Mac. "Tell it to fuck off. There are hot chicks and crazy-time theater going on here. It'll have to take a number. Yer busy right now."

Gram glanced around again, unable to shake the feeling that the voice wasn't a prank or the result of the women. It was serious, and if he ignored it, really bad shit would happen.

Protect who? he asked, pushing his thoughts out on what he hoped was the mental pathway to the mystery person.

Your mate.

Air swooshed out of Gram's lungs at the reply. His mate? Was this someone's idea of a sick joke? Kick him while he was down? Pour salt in his wounds?

Bill rolled his eyes dramatically. "You're meddling again, Gus. I thought you said we weren't allowed to do that."

Gus seemed aloof, his attention elsewhere while he clutched the head.

"Oh, sure. It's okay if *you* do it. Got it. Just not when I do," snapped Bill. "For that, I'm not gonna let you have any of my grilled cheese smoothie that Susan is gonna make me."

The blonde woman cringed. "Bill, I'll look into

it. I can't promise the smoothie will happen. But if I can't get the kitchen staff to make you one, I'll put a grilled cheese in a blender for you. Okay?"

Bill winked at her. "You're all right, Susan."

"Thank you, Bill. Now, how about we get you two over for your facials?"

Gus appeared agitated at the suggestion.

Gram found it difficult to fault the guy. He wouldn't want a facial either.

Car leaned in Gram's direction but continued to stare at Bill. "Have you ever seen anyone so hairy? I have nae, and we all know what we do at least once a month."

Bill stared at them in a way that said he was sizing them up. From the man's expression, he wasn't intimidated by the sight of three large alpha males. If anything, he looked ready to challenge them.

Yep. The little man was crazy.

"What are you looking at?" demanded Bill, puffing his chest, making his towel come loose. One second it was up, the next the terrycloth towel was pooled on the floor next to the man's pink flip-flops. Bill stood there in all his naked, hairy glory, giving them all the stink-eye.

Car jerked backward. "Good gods, he's as hairy as a werewolf."

"Och, he's more so," added Mac. "None of us are that bad."

Bill narrowed his gaze on the men. "I know some werewolves. You got problems with them? Huh? You start talking smack about them and you'll have me to deal with. Wild Bill. You'll rue the day you crossed paths with me."

The blonde woman tried to get Bill to cover himself with the towel, to no avail. The other two women moved in at once to lend a hand.

Gus turned in a circle, staring at the ceiling, still clutching the head under his arm.

"Och, you do nae suppose he's the same Wild Bill we've heard tales about riding a mechanical elephant in Vietnam, do you?" asked Mac.

Bill shot Mac a hard stare. "One and the same, bucko. So fear me. I'm a badass."

Mac snorted. "I assumed he'd be taller."

Car nodded. "And less hairy."

"Oh, and nae human," added Mac. "Though I was right to assume he was crazy."

"Stop yelling at me," said Bill, looking at his friend, who hadn't said one word. "What do you mean they're friendlies? Striker sent them? I'm not sharing my grilled cheese smoothie with anybody but you, friends or not. There are some things in life a man holds sacred. Grilled cheese is one of them."

"You know our cousin?" asked Car. "Striker?"

"You're kin to him?" asked Bill, eyeing them warily.

"Aye," said the twins.

Bill grinned, showing off his crooked teeth. "Why didn't you start with that? Yeah, we know Striker. He's a good buddy of ours. We once held him at gunpoint. It was great."

Gram wondered if Striker had actually booked him a private suite in a funny farm, not a resort with a spa. He wouldn't put it past the guy. He'd get great amusement out of it all and no doubt think he was helping in some way.

"Tina," said Susan. "Can you see to our VIP?"

"Mr. Campbell, if you'd follow me," said the redhead as Susan resorted to holding the towel in front of Bill's groin herself. "I'll show you to your room and get you all set up for your first booking of the day."

"My what?" asked Gram.

Tina walked back to the computer at the desk

and then looked at him. "We have you down for massage in about an hour."

Mac laughed. "Be sure the woman rubbing him down fits the bill for his tastes."

Tina grinned. "Actually, he's booked with me."

"For now," added Susan. "Who knows. That could always change."

Mac threw his hand up. "I'll go in his place!"

Gram groaned.

Susan smiled. "I'm sure we can find space for the two of you if you'd like to stay with us as well."

Gram shook his head. "No. They do nae want to remain, and I do nae need a woman rubbing me down. I'll take a man."

They all stared at him.

He grunted. "Nae that way. Never mind."

Car and Mac nodded to him with dual expressions that said they were up to no good. He wasn't so sure leaving the twins alone with two clearly unstable men was wise. It wasn't as if the twins were dealing with a full deck themselves. They didn't need any help in the crazy-behavior area. They did just fine on their own.

Car eyed Susan with hunger in his eyes. "We'll

be just fine, Campbell. Go get a facial or something, or rubbed down by a man, since that was
yer pick and all."

"Dick," said Gram as he followed the
redhead.

Tina led him through a maze of hallways, all
looking the same to him and smelling heavily of
lavender. She came to a stop in front of a large
room. "Here is the physical therapy room. You've
been set up on a daily schedule. You're also set to
get daily massages."

"I am?" he asked and groaned. "My doctors
had a hand in this too, didn't they?"

She glanced over her shoulder at him, giving
him a look that said she didn't know the answer
and was only doing her job. Feeling bad for acting
a bit like an ass, he nodded to her.

"Thank you. My room?"

"You're actually in one of the cabins, not the
main resort. The person booking stressed your
need for privacy." She motioned for him to follow,
and he noticed for the first time that she was
walking slowly, as if already knowing he wasn't
able to walk fast. He wondered if James or Auberi
had spoken to the facility on his behalf. He shuddered to think Striker had taken it on himself to

relay medical information about him. He'd end up neutered or something.

Tina kept going until she was at an exterior door. She opened it for him and motioned him through. She led him down a path that had land-scaping done in a way to make it feel secluded and serene. It opened to an area with small round cabins.

"Right this way," she said, taking him to the one on the far end. "The cabins are fully func-tional. In fact, they are very similar to ones we all live in here on the property."

Gram gave her a questioning look.

She smiled. "Mr. Campbell, have you heard of us before?"

"No."

Her lips twitched. "That is rare around here."

"I'm nae from the area."

She nodded. "So I hear. Well, Caladrius is run by a large group of people. We see each other as a family of sorts. We all live on the grounds. Since there are nearly two thousand acres to the facility, there is plenty of space. The staff living compound is set a ways back. If you enjoy golfing, you might catch sight of it since it's in that direction."

He'd not golfed in years. He was almost ashamed to admit as much, seeing as how it was basically a national sport of his countrymen.

"Keys are on the counter in the kitchen area, but you shouldn't need to lock up. Caladrius is very safe and secure. The local town, about fifteen miles down the road, has had a rash of incidents recently, but it's not spread to here. It's more than likely people coming up from Denver causing problems," said Tina, something off in her voice.

Gram wasn't too worried. Even in his current state, he was hardly defenseless. A bunch of humans on a crime bender didn't really stand a chance against him. Hell, Wild Bill could probably handle them.

"Dinner is at seven tonight in the main dining room. You'll find that located in the building we just left. Your daily itinerary will be slipped under your door each morning. If you want, yoga starts at six in the morning."

Yoga?

No.

He pushed a fake smile to his face. "Thanks."

"You'll find your bags inside."

"My bags?" he echoed.

"Yes. They arrived a few hours before you did."

Of course they did. Striker was going to get an earful from Gram when he next spoke to the man.

"I'll send someone to retrieve you for your afternoon massage," she said with a smile.

"Thanks," he said and watched her walk off.

If he grabbed his stuff and called for a car service, he could be out of there in an hour, maybe two tops. Perfect. No yoga. No facials. No neutering.

Chapter Seven

AMELIA MADE her way down one of the many walking paths that ran from the main resort to the Flock's compound and living quarters. It was all kept very separate for good reason. It wouldn't do any good for guests to see what went on with private rituals, and the reverse was also true. There were certain areas of the retreat that were not for everyday average guests. No. They were for the sexually deviant or the ones with needs that could not be met by normal—safe—means.

For those supernaturals who got off on blood-letting in the extreme or even killing.

The retreat supplied *everything* they'd need. It was easy for Cal and his followers to find fodder to be lambs to the slaughter. They preyed upon vulnerable humans and supernaturals. Those on the streets were their favorite. Runaways were pure gold in their eyes. No one would miss them if they vanished from the streets, never to be seen again. They were easy targets for the cult. The Flock had recruiters whose entire job was to seek out these "strays."

The Flock brought them into the fold, making them think they were joining a family of sorts, a higher calling, a group with like-minded individuals who shared ideological ideas. But they weren't. They were signing up to be food or worse.

Most of the fodder recruits were humans with a few weaker supernaturals sprinkled in. The humans didn't know supernaturals were real or how dangerous the cult was. Hell, they didn't even know they were joining a cult. It wasn't like anyone woke up and said, "Today sounds like a great day to follow a madman." No. They were finessed. Persuaded to be part of something more. Something beautiful. Something wonderful.

Lies.

Many of the teen runaways thought they were going to live in a place with warm beds and hot food. And what they thought was safety.

It was anything but.

For most, it was hell and their final resting place.

Amelia wasn't supposed to know the full extent of what went on in some of the VIP areas of the retreat. Her duties with the greenhouse and herbal remedies kept her busy and, for the most part, isolated. Very rarely did she even find herself off compound grounds and in the resort area. She'd only just been there because she was dropping off fresh-cut flowers for the lobby area. The request for them had come in bright and early.

Normally, she avoided the resort for good reason. The path to it also led to another gathering area. This one was more secluded, but it wasn't for Flock members. It was for guests to do unsavory things without notice. What had happened there was still burned into her brain, forever etched into her memory—haunting her nightmares.

She'd been looking for her mother one night, to ask her opinion on some cuttings that weren't thriving. Amelia had happened upon one of the cult's acts of violence by accident on the eve of her eighteenth birthday. She'd stumbled upon two shifter males who had been VIP guests at the resort, eating what was left of their victim—a young woman Amelia had befriended in passing two weeks prior. The girl had been a teen runaway who had been picked up from recruiters in Salt Lake City. She'd thought Cal and the others were the answer to her prayers.

All they'd done was serve her up to monsters.

Amelia didn't want to think about everything her friend had endured prior to being granted the freedom of death. There were nights she'd close her eyes and still see it all in her head again. See the shifters biting and tearing into flesh. Hear their snarls. Smell the evil pouring off them.

The sounds of an engine roaring pulled Amelia from remembered horrors.

It wasn't shocking to hear a vehicle approaching on the path. It was one of the paths that were made to accommodate small all-terrain vehicles, golf carts, and snowmobiles when the area was blanketed in snow.

Most of the women born into the cult didn't know how to drive anything, let alone a golf cart. It wasn't something the men thought the women needed to know. There was a lot they felt that way about.

They'd single-handedly done their best to set

back the women's rights movement some hundred-plus years to the glory days, in their opinion.

Thankfully, Jeanie Tippons didn't share their viewpoints. Jeanie had been instrumental in teaching Amelia's mother there was more to the world than what the Flock and Cal had presented. Jeanie taught Abigail and Amelia how to use a computer, how to operate a cell phone, and how to drive. Without her, they'd have been even more ill-prepared to flee than they had been.

Amelia stepped off the path just in time for Brian, one of the men from her father's security detail, to come flying down the path on an all-terrain utility cart. Unlike many men in the Flock, Brian kept his dark hair cut close to his head. He didn't wear all white, either. Though he did wear a white T-shirt with an emblem for the resort on it.

Brian slowed when he saw her, and a sick-looking grin spread over his face. "Susan find you yet?"

Amelia stiffened. If Susan was hunting for her, it wasn't for anything good. "No. Why?"

Brian wasn't just one of her father's right-hand men and part of his security detail; he was tight with Susan, making him extra dangerous and anything but a friend. More than once Amelia had happened upon Brian and Susan engaging in various sex acts. And she knew for a fact Brian had had a hand in the disappearance of several female Flock members over the last few months. He wasn't someone anyone would want to be alone with on a back path with for any length of time.

"Susan says you're getting the VIP guest arriving today. That you're set up to handle all his needs."

"Me?" asked Amelia, her eyes widening. She'd never before been tasked with handling any guests. Each of her training lessons had been conducted with Flock members only. Her father made sure to keep her far from outsiders. "Are you positive?"

"Oh yeah," he said. "I heard Cal give her the order myself. So did Taggert."

Amelia flinched at the mention of Taggert. She didn't need to be told Taggert took the news of Amelia handling any guest poorly.

The man snorted. "Father seems to think this guy arriving is someone special. The Bringer was mentioned. Might be him. Would make sense.

That is who Father has been saving you for, isn't it?"

It couldn't be. The Bringer of Change? Was that who her father thought was coming today? Was that why he was having her service the male?

She'd spent her life being told she was destined for some Bringer. Some man she didn't know. The Bringer had become a cross between a boogeyman and a god in Amelia's mind. Someone she was sure would never actually come. That he, like a number of Cal's prophecies, would never pan out.

If Brian was right, and the male Cal was sure was the Bringer was arriving, or worse yet, had already arrived, Amelia's time had run out.

The urge to flee was great but she couldn't. Not yet. She'd planned to make her move under the cover of darkness tomorrow night. Right before she sent word to Ace that she and Andie were safe. Nothing was ready for her just yet. Tonight was one of the mandatory normal gatherings. Her absence would be noticed. But tomorrow was the night Cal and his men went off to his large cabin and held private meetings.

She knew what went on at the meetings.

Sex. Mind-altering drugs. Blood play. Murder.

Everything that would keep the men occupied while she took her sister and vanished into the night.

"You look a little pale there, Amelia," said Brian, a teasing note to his voice. "Everything all right?"

It was on the tip of her tongue to tell him exactly what she thought of him, but she knew better. He could make the next twenty-four hours extremely difficult for her. It was best she continue to remain silent on the matter and focus on her escape plan. "Everything is fine. I'm just, erm, excited to be allowed to finally do my part and contribute to the Flock. I know how you all see my work in the greenhouses as anything but a real contribution."

It took all she had to avoid choking on the words.

Something she couldn't read passed over the man's face. "You should head back in the direction of the resort. Taggert wants to speak with you."

"I will. Thank you." Amelia waited as Brian drove off toward the resort. She then hurried on her way, which was in the opposite direction of Taggert. Dealing with him when he wasn't riled was bad enough. If he was in a mood because of talk of the Bringer, he would be impossible to handle.

If that wasn't a big enough issue, she had to think of a way to get out of servicing any guest—Bringer or not. If she couldn't, she'd need to do what had to be done. Like it or not. Her future depended on it. So did Andie's.

Panicked on how to handle servicing a guest, Amelia wasn't paying attention and missed the small path that forked off to her cabin. When she stepped out into a clearing near the river, she sighed.

When she turned and ran directly into Taggert's large form, fear raced over her.

She also knew then that Brian had realized she'd want to stay away from Taggert, so he'd lied about the man's location.

Taggert licked his lips, staring down at her. "Hello there, Amelia. I've been looking for you. You weren't in any of the greenhouses and you weren't at your cabin."

She backed up somewhat, trying to put distance between herself and the madman. "I need to go check on Andie and then—"

He caught her upper arm in his steely grasp.

"And then what? Handle the new VIP? See to the needs of the fucking Bringer?"

She stared blankly up at him, at a loss for what to say to talk her way out of the situation. Some of the males could scent a lie. She was sure Taggert was one of them.

Just then, Andie came rushing out of the tall brush, the red ball she was never without under one arm. She was dressed in all white with her dark hair pulled back into white ribbons. There was a pure innocence about her that always melted Amelia's heart.

Andie was gentle natured yet had seen great horrors in her short four years on earth. Her gaze landed on Amelia, and she froze.

Taggert cursed under his breath at the arrival of the little girl.

Amelia darted away from Taggert's grasp and bent in front of her little sister protectively. "Hey, sweetie. I was just coming to check on you. Did you have lunch yet?"

Andie nodded. She'd not spoken a word since their mother's death. Witnessing it had trauma-tized her. No help had been provided for her despite Amelia's desperate pleas for assistance. Andie needed to see a professional. She needed more help than Amelia, alone, could provide. Their father didn't seem to think the fact the little girl hadn't uttered a word in two years was a problem.

He wouldn't.

His thoughts were that she'd speak when she had something worth saying. Not until.

Amelia put her hand over Andie's stomach and kissed her sister's forehead. "Come on, sweetie, let's get you up to the cabin for a nap. I can read you a book, too. Sound good?"

"She's old enough to see herself back to your cabin," said Taggert, coming up behind Amelia. "She doesn't need you with her nonstop."

"She's only four," protested Amelia.

"And that's old enough." He took Andie's red ball and threw it long and hard, up and over the trees. "Go fetch, little girl."

Amelia spun around fast, her gaze narrowing on the man. It wasn't like her to stand up to the bully, but she wouldn't let him harm or scare Andie in any way. For her sister, she'd do anything, even if it meant facing down the devil himself—or his right-hand man in this case.

He grinned. "Careful, Amelia. You look like you might be considering issuing a challenge.

Father isn't here to step in and protect you. And I'm not feeling very forgiving right now. Especially not with knowing what he'll have you doing in hours. You are to be *mine*. Not some Bringer's."

Amelia tensed and touched her sister's head lightly. "Sweetie, go back to our cabin. Go inside. I'll come for you in a little bit, okay?"

Andie nodded but Amelia didn't miss the cold glare her little sister directed at Taggert. It actually sent a shiver through Amelia. In that moment, Andie's expression looked a lot like their father's when he was angry. That was chilling. She didn't want her sister to let hate into her heart. It would be all too easy to turn out like their dad if she did.

"No," whispered Amelia, worried Andie might reveal she was gifted with magiks in an attempt to protect her. "Go."

Andie ran off in the direction Taggert had thrown her ball.

The second Andie was gone, Taggert began advancing on Amelia.

Chapter Eight

GRAM WAS ABOUT to head into his cabin when a red kickball rolled to him from the left. It came to a stop at his feet.

Closing his eyes, he did his best to shake off the hallucination. It shouldn't have happened. He'd been off the meds long enough. Yet the damn red ball was back, and it was apparently following him.

He opened his eyes, expecting it to be gone. It wasn't. There it was, next to his foot. It took him a second to realize it was actually touching his foot.

Bending, he grimaced and then poked the ball. It didn't disappear. It was solid, something it had never been before. It rolled slightly with his touch.

Gasping, Gram grabbed the ball, lifting it, wondering where it had come from and if others could see it as well or if his mind had finally snapped fully.

Just then, a little girl who looked to be around the age of three or four came from a small opening in the trees and plants. She had on an all-white dress with white ribbons in her dark brown hair. She looked up at him with huge hazel eyes.

Instantly, he thought of Bethany. She was around the same age. Was he now hallucinating children? Had his mind invented a child to compensate for the one he felt as if he'd lost?

Gram bent again, despite the pain in his leg and back. He held the ball out to the little girl, wondering if she was real or a figment of his imagination. "Here you go, lass. Is this yer ball?"

She nodded. With a tentative step, she eased toward him, watching him closely before smiling wide. "Hello. I'm Andie."

"Andie is a verra pretty name. I'm Gram."

"I know." She touched his arm, and Gram knew then she was real, not a hallucination.

"You do?" he asked.

She nodded again and then tipped her head. "Your voice is different."

"Aye, my voice is different," he returned, unable to hide his smile. "Have you heard of Scotland?"

She shook her head.

"'Tis far from here."

"Are you from there? From far from here?" she asked, dancing on one foot.

Gram had seen such a dance before. It was the potty dance. There was no way in hell he was taking a child he didn't know to a bathroom. Nothing screamed stranger danger and life behind bars more than taking someone's kid to a bathroom, alone.

"Li'l one, where is yer mother?" he asked.

She frowned. "In the ground."

Her mother had passed?

"I'm sorry, lass. Have you an adult you answer to?"

"I have a sister. Is that what you mean? She's bigger than me."

It wasn't but he nodded all the same. "Aye. Yer sister. Is she close? I'm guessing she's worried about you."

She tugged at her lower lip and then glanced in the direction of the path she'd come from. "He made me go away. And he threw my ball."

"Who did?" asked Gram, still holding the red ball while he remained bent. His leg and back screamed in protest but he ignored the pain, his concern for the child outweighing it. He'd seen the very ball she had been playing with in his visions. That was no coincidence.

He had been alive far too long and had seen too many strange things to ignore the signs. He was supposed to help the child. He knew it deep in his bones. While the facility was secure, it was also full of supernaturals. He didn't want to think any of them would ever harm a child, but he'd seen far too much in his long life to put it past them.

"Taggert. He's with Amelia now, by the river." She eased forward more and touched the ball, meeting his gaze full on. "Can you help her?"

"Who? Yer sister?"

She nodded and leaned more, putting a hand up to her mouth as she lowered her voice to whisper to him. "Taggert is mean. He scares Amelia, but I'm not supposed to know that. She told me no when I wanted to help. Can you help her?"

"Aye," he said, handing her the ball. "Is she that way?"

She pointed to the path. "Yes. She's that way. Mr. Gram, don't tell no one I told you, okay?"

"Aye." He stood slowly and touched Andie's head. "Lass, is there somewhere safe you can go while I check on yer sister?"

"Yes."

"Go there now."

She went to the door of his cabin.

He tensed. "Lass, I do nae think yer sister would want you going into a place where you do nae know the man staying there. You should go to the main building."

"I'm not ever allowed to go into the main building." She smiled at him but opened the door all the same. "Here is safe. Here is good. I knew you'd come."

He stiffened. "What?"

"We all knew you'd come," she returned.

"Lass?"

"But he's wrong about you."

"Who?" asked Gram.

"My father. Help Amelia." She smiled up at him.

If she was worried for her sister, he'd check on the other little one. It was probably nothing, but he'd look into it to be sure. And then he'd get to the bottom of the red ball and her cryptic words. Was the child gifted in the art of magik? If so, had she somehow tapped into his mind, seeing his hallucinations and manifesting one? It wasn't an easy task but there were some supernaturals who could do such a thing.

Another thought occurred.

What if he'd been shown the red ball before arriving so, when he did meet Andie, he'd know for sure he was supposed to assist her?

No matter the reason, she'd asked for his help and he'd give it.

"Lass, yer welcome to use the toilet when yer in there," he said.

She smiled even wider. "Good. I gotta go."

He hid his laugh as he went to the path and followed it. Since the path wasn't paved like the other, it took him more time than he'd have liked in his current condition. As it opened to a large grassy area, near a river, he instantly felt as if he'd been hit with a bat.

He stumbled but managed to remain upright despite the wall of magik he'd just passed through. Whoever had created it was powerful. It was meant to keep others out. To repel them. Had he been a lesser supernatural, it might very well have done that. As it stood, it wasn't pleasant, but he'd survived worse.

He came out of the brush fully—and his breath caught.

There, near the river's edge, was the very same woman he'd been having visions of.

The woman in white.

Her long, dark brown hair hung to her slender waist. For the first time, he got a really good look at her face, and for a second, he forgot to draw in air.

Never had he seen a woman as beautiful as her.

In that second, every bit of sorrow and pity he'd been feeling for himself over having loved and lost faded away. The constant pain that had racked his body dissipated. All that remained was the sight of the woman before him.

The beauty all in white.

His wolf came to life, stirring in him, wanting out. It wanted a better look at her, too. He sniffed the air, and the scent of honeysuckle came to him with light undertones of vanilla. His gaze locked on the woman. She was the source of the smell. He knew it with every fiber of his being.

She's real.

He finally took a moment to study the man with her. Said man was crowding her space, backing her in the direction of the river. Fear pulsed from her, finding Gram, making him want to kill something.

Anything.

He narrowed his gaze on the male. He'd do nicely.

Chapter Nine

AMELIA CONTINUED TO BACK UP, praying Taggert would lose interest in her and go away. She doubted that would happen. The best she could hope for was that Andie was far enough away to avoid being harmed by the man or seeing anything she shouldn't.

Taggert grinned. "Amelia, we both know who will need to sweep up the mess this supposed Bringer leaves behind when he goes. You're beautiful, but let's be honest, you're weak. For being the daughter of a great man, you have no gifts. Neither does your sister. Do you think this man Cal is so stuck on is going to want a woman who is basically human?"

Her gaze flickered. She hoped the guy *didn't*

want her. That he took one look at her and did a hard pass. Let them all think she was defenseless. That she was nothing more than human. Underestimating her was the best thing. If her father or the others learned the true extent of her gifts, they'd find a way to exploit them. To twist them and use them for evil. And there was no way Amelia was permitting Andie's gifts to be exploited.

"I see the way you watch me," he said. "You couldn't take your eyes off me the other day when Susan was showing you how to give a massage—and other things."

The only thing she ever watched him with was disdain. She hated him and everything about him. His cruelty knew no limits and she'd long since given up hope the man had any redeeming qualities.

He didn't.

Taggert eyed the river and then her. "Planning to try to swim away from me? You should know, that won't work. You can't outrun me. You know it; so do I. In fact, your days of running from me are nearly over. Cal's protection will end the second he realizes you can't give him what he wants—the Bringer. I saw the look in your eyes during your training sessions. You don't have it in you to lure a man into the fold."

She stepped into the water, trying to back away from him more.

He followed, his hand coming to her cheek.

She recoiled at the feel of his fingertips on her skin. Straightaway, she was hit with what felt like snakes slithering along her skin. She hated snakes. They were often used in Cal's ritual ceremonies and they had always scared her. Taggert's touch always made her feel as if creepy-crawlies were on her.

She glared at him.

His gaze narrowed. In the next breath, he snatched hold of her hair with his other hand, wrenching her closer. He inhaled deeply, his eyes filling with flecks of amber. That meant the wolf he carried in him was nearing the surface.

Taggert was deadly enough all on his own. Adding in the fact he was a shifter who could also wield magik made him the ultimate threat. One that, if she dared attempt to stand against it, could cause everything she'd worked so hard for to unravel.

But letting him do what he intended wasn't an option, either.

Amelia pushed on his chest, knowing if she dared to use her gifts on him, her plan wouldn't work.

"Let go of me," she breathed out, wanting to strike back but resisting.

Taggert grinned and licked her cheek. "Make me."

She shoved at him, to no avail.

All she managed to do was amuse him.

He yanked harder on her hair, forcing her head back more. He then shoved his face into the crook of her neck, licking the vulnerable area. If he so chose, he could bite her throat out with ease. Her only saving grace was that she knew he wanted her in a carnal way. If she was dead, that couldn't happen. And if he dared to kill her, Cal would unleash hell upon him.

She pushed at his face, trying to get his mouth away from her neck, before raking her nails down his cheek.

Hissing, he released her hair so fast that she fell to the ground. Taggert stepped over her, eclipsing the sun behind him, fury lighting his eyes as they swirled with amber. He ran his fingers over his cheek, coming away with blood. In the blink of an eye, the wounds on his face healed over. Proof of how powerful he was.

"Cal is not here to save you from me this time, Amelia," he said, his voice so cold that it actually made her shiver. It didn't matter that the day was warmer than normal for the time of year.

She held up an arm in an attempt to protect herself.

He batted it away and pain shot through it.

Recoiling, Amelia held her arm to her chest, blinking back tears. She didn't want to give the sick bastard the satisfaction of knowing just how much he'd hurt her. He got off on pain. It would only turn him on more.

"What's the matter, Amelia? Run out of places to hide from me? Missing a hero to save you?" he asked, reaching down for her.

Growls that didn't come from Taggert filled the area.

Suddenly, someone grabbed Taggert's wrist and jerked him back from her.

At first, she assumed that someone was Cal or one of the other men who worked on the staff. When she saw it was a stranger, anxiety for the newcomer ran over her.

Even more than that, she was instantly reminded of the strange dream she'd had. The one where she'd been running with a man who was holding her hand. A man she'd been positive she'd been intimate with and felt something for. This man, from behind, looked just like the one in her dream—that was, if he had scars on his back without his shirt on.

It took Amelia a moment to remember she'd put up a wall of power around the area, to keep her sister out and protected. Something Taggert wouldn't have been able to sense on his own, but something the newcomer would have had to pass through to get to her.

That didn't mean he could hold his own against the likes of Taggert.

While she didn't know the man, she felt the strongest urge to keep him safe. More than her inborn need to keep all innocents from harm. This ran deeper. Much, much deeper.

It was primal.

Raw.

And real.

The man pushed Taggert back from Amelia and then stood tall in front of her, forming a wall of muscle. An imposing sight indeed. His presence blocked Taggert from being able to get to her with any sort of ease, but it also left the new arrival vulnerable. Taggert wasn't the type of man to back down from a perceived challenge. It was in his alpha-male nature to take on anything and anyone he saw as threatening him. The only other male she'd ever seen him back down from was her father. Taggert was wise to fear Cal. He could kill with the blink of an eye if he truly wanted to.

The good Samaritan was going to get himself killed trying to be chivalrous. As much as Amelia didn't want to be alone with Taggert, she didn't want anyone hurt on her account.

"Move," snarled Taggert to the man.

"I do nae think I will," said the man before Amelia, his Scottish brogue evident and thick.

The sound of his deep voice eased over Amelia, seeming to caress her in places no other had touched before.

The glaring sun made it difficult for Amelia to make out much about the man beyond the fact he was tall and lean, but not too skinny—perfectly proportioned, actually. He was well-muscled, but not too bulky, either.

Just right.

And he smelled amazing. Like mint and rosemary. Both things she very much liked.

"This is none of your business," said Taggert. "And you really don't want to piss me off, buddy."

The man before her snorted. "I'm nae yer buddy, and I'm fine with pissin' you off."

Amelia's lips pulled upward, wanting to form a full-on smile at the man's gumption. He was either very brave or incredibly stupid. She wasn't sure which and didn't want to find out. Already the situation had escalated. She didn't want it to go further.

Growling, Taggert stepped back, but not to retreat. From what Amelia could see, it was to do something that shocked her—partially shift forms in front of a non-Flock member.

Revealing yourself to anyone outside of the Flock was one of Cal's cardinal rules. You simply did not do it. Not if you wanted to live to tell the tale to others.

Taggert in regular human form was an imposing sight, with his height and build. But the man before her rivaled him in more ways than one. He held his ground, crouching slightly and growling as well, though his was deeper and more threatening than Taggert's had been.

There was no mistaking the sound. He too was a shifter. That did level the playing field somewhat, but not enough for Amelia to feel right letting the stranger help.

No one else would be caught in the crossfire if she could help it.

Amelia came just shy of touching the man's back. The urge to make contact with him was nearly all-consuming. That in itself was alarming.

Never before had she felt such longing.

Such a demanding desire.

Somehow, she managed to avoid touching him. Instead, her gaze moved down to his backside, and she swallowed hard. His butt was amazing, and the jeans he was in cupped it just right. She spent her life around hot men. Supernaturals didn't really come in any other form, but this one shamed the rest of them, making them seem like ugly ducklings, and she'd not even seen his face yet. From behind he seemed to have broken the mold.

It was hard to focus on the fact there was a serious threat at hand.

Threat.

Yes.

Concentrate.

She stared harder at the man's backside.

Not on that!

Taggert growled once more, and Amelia pulled herself together. She rushed around in front of the Scottish do-gooder and put her hands out, blocking Taggert from getting to the man.

"No," she said, her shoulders going back, her stance rigid. "Don't."

With nostrils flaring, Taggert glared past her. His gaze was nothing short of murderous. He had the juice to back his unspoken threat. That scared her. She didn't want anyone hurt on her account.

"Move, Amelia," said Taggert.

She shook her head. "No. I won't."

"Who are you and what are you doing out here?" demanded Taggert of the man.

"I'd worry less about me and more about you," said the other man, as if he didn't have a care in the world and wasn't facing down a dangerous alpha-male shifter. "If I ever see you raising yer hand to the lass again, I'll rip it off and feed it to you. Am I clear?"

Amelia reached behind her with the intent of pushing the man farther back from Taggert's reach. Her hand found the man's steely thigh, and she nearly moaned as heat flared up her arm. The heat centered in her chest to start before sliding lower, making her acutely aware of her female anatomy.

If the man's voice didn't make her melt into a puddle of want, touching him would.

The man put his hand over hers, his fingers caressing hers ever so gently, keeping her hand to his leg. The heat continued to build, and she wondered what was causing it because it wasn't natural.

Still, she wanted more.

Much, much more.

She found herself stepping back, pressing her entire body to the man's. She wanted to rub herself all over him.

Sliding his arms around her waist, he moved her behind him in one quick, swift movement, ignoring her gasp of protest and shock.

He put his arms out then, his hands at his sides, claws showing from his fingertips. "Leave here now. Last warning," he ground out in Taggert's direction.

Taggert took a deep breath, additional flecks of amber filling his gaze. "Mating energy?"

Amelia watched in stunned horror as Taggert drew upon his powers. She'd seen him do so enough times in the past to recognize the signs.

The change in temperature around him, the oppressive feeling of static in the air, and the way he moved his fingers in a sweeping gesture, despite his hands being partially shifted. It was as if he was playing an invisible piano, the keys the elements, the song deadly.

The air around them thickened and the sky above them darkened. Lightning crackled and thunder rolled. It went from being broad daylight to night in seconds.

"She is mine," growled out Taggert.

"Taggert, no!" she pleaded, trying but failing to get around the Scottish guy. Not only was he making her body react in ways it never had before, he was apparently made of concrete, because she couldn't budge him.

He kept his arms out wide and laughed as he glanced upward. "I'll turn that dark magik back on you so fast, you won't know what hit you. Yer nae the only shifter here who can do such things. Want to see which of us is stronger? I know I do. And I do nae believe the lass is yers. She does nae seem to care much for you. I cannae blame her. I've known you five minutes and I do nae like you one bit."

Taggert stiffened and locked gazes with

Amelia before standing down—something she wasn't accustomed to seeing him do. The sky cleared, and the pending storm vanished without a trace. Once again, the sun shone bright and birds even began to chirp.

Crisis averted.

For now.

Deep down she knew it was far from over.

Taggert never backed down from a fight.

Ever.

Exhaling, Amelia touched Hot Guy's back and rubbed it absently, thankful he hadn't been hurt in any way in the altercation.

The man's claws receded, and he eased her away from Taggert's reach. Once he had her a decent distance from the other male, he turned to her, boldly putting his back to Taggert. It was a major slap in the face to the other shifter. It said Hot Guy wasn't afraid of him.

While she wasn't a shifter herself, she was a combination of many things, but nothing anyone could exactly label. She did know enough about shifter politics to know Hot Guy's move was a massive insult to Taggert. And she knew Taggert well enough to know he'd retaliate at some point.

He wouldn't let the challenge go unanswered. It was against his alpha nature.

"Lass, are you all right?" asked Hot Guy, searching her for signs of injury.

She stood perfectly still, unable to answer him as she soaked in the sight of him up close and personal. She'd thought the man was hot before. Up close, he was downright spectacular.

The man's long black hair hung past his broad shoulders. His white shirt was undone partially in front, showing off a light dusting of black chest hair that she instantly wanted to run her hands through. His strong jawline was covered in dark stubble. The kind that looked like it was always there. And it was amazing on him. It gave him a sexy yet rugged vibe.

A man's man.

A moan wanted to come from her. She fought hard to internalize it.

Dear goddess, the man is amazing.

It took Amelia a second to realize she was staring at him rather awkwardly. She cleared her throat and gathered her wits about her before nodding. "I'm fine. Thank you."

He stared at her for what felt like forever before putting his hand close to her face. He came just shy of touching her. Deep down she knew he wanted to make contact with her, but was refraining out of respect for her and her personal space.

To hell with personal space. She wanted to get very personal in his space as soon as possible. She took his hand and held it in hers, causing the heat to return.

He curled his fingers around hers and the heat intensified. For a moment, she thought for sure she'd go up in flames.

"If he hurt you in any way, I will kill him," the man warned.

She'd all but forgotten about Taggert, who was still near them. Hot Guy didn't seem to care and kept his back to the threat.

She eased closer to the hot guy, wanting to be held by him notwithstanding the fact he was a stranger.

He felt safe.

He felt right.

"Amelia," said Taggert, causing her to look at him.

He was still by the edge of the river. His gaze slid to the newcomer, and she knew Taggert's tells well enough to know the good Samaritan would end up hurt if she wasn't careful and didn't tread lightly.

She weighed her options. If she sided with the new guy, there was a high chance Taggert would go in search of his buddies and seek out the man to kill him at a later date. It's what he and his friends did.

If she went to Taggert and gave him what he wanted—herself—she could possibly distract him and keep his attention from the man. But could she really do that? Could she let the sick bastard touch her?

She wasn't sure. What she did know was that if she kept hanging on Hot Guy, matters would only go from bad to worse.

She jerked back from Hot Guy and pushed her hair behind her ears, glancing away. "Thank you for your help, but you should go now. Everything here is good."

"Guid?" he asked with a huff. "Hardly. That douchebag was manhandling you. He's lucky I do nae rip his fucking hands off and cram them down his throat. To harm a woman is the sign of a coward. Nae a man."

She gulped as testosterone rode the air around them.

He moved closer once more and his scent washed over her. "Do nae fear me, lass. I'd never harm you."

"I know," she said without thought. And she did know without a shadow of a doubt that he'd never harm her. She didn't understand why or how she knew as much, but it didn't take from the fact she did.

Taggert's nostrils flared, and he opened his mouth to speak but didn't. Instead, he glanced off to the right, in the direction of one of the many paths that led to the river. The path he was focused on just happened to lead past the greenhouses as well. It didn't take a genius to know he heard someone approaching—and there was only one person Amelia knew of who would cause Taggert to mind his words.

Her father.

Chapter Ten

"AH, TAGGERT, THERE YOU ARE," said Cal as he came through an area flanked by large bushes. He was dressed head to toe in his signature all-white ensemble. His long dark hair was pulled up in something of a topknot, as was often the case when he wore it off his neck. When he saw Amelia, he paused in his step, his dark gaze whipping to Taggert. "Is there a problem?"

"No," said Taggert. There was no mistaking how nervous he suddenly sounded. "Amelia was just about to show one of the guests back to his cabin. He got turned around. I was just checking on her. As is my duty."

Hot Guy's brow quirked at the lies that rolled off Taggert's tongue.

"I see," said Cal, his face unreadable. When his attention came to her, Amelia squared her shoulders.

"Amelia?" he asked, and she knew if she dared to tell him that Taggert had cornered her again, he'd see to Taggert's punishment himself. That would have been fine by her...if it didn't mean Taggert would seek retribution and exact it tenfold. It was his way. Plus, if Cal knew how drawn she was to Hot Guy, he'd more than likely unleash Taggert and the others on the man.

She eased even closer to the newcomer, feeling safe near him. She didn't know him but that didn't change the pull she seemed to have to him. Not to mention the immense heat by proximity. She had to wonder if the guy was some sort of fire-starting supernatural who could turn into an animal. She'd seen a few fire starters pass through over the years. One had been a dragon-shifter, if she wasn't mistaken. She'd been young when he'd come through. What she remembered most about him was how kind he'd been.

How safe he'd made her feel.

A lot like the man before her now.

Maybe the man turned into a dragon, too.

"Amelia, are you all right?" asked Cal,

concern in his voice. She was surprised, as he'd never sounded genuinely worried for her before. "Are you not feeling well?"

Pressing a smile to her face, she met her father's gaze. "I'm fine. Sorry. I skipped breakfast this morning and got lost in my work today. I'm a little out of it."

"I can have Susan come and get you," he said.

She fought the urge to cringe at the suggestion of Susan being anywhere around her. Susan was as bad as Taggert, if not worse. She shook her head. "I'm fine. I promise. I'll get the guest back to where he needs to be."

"Thank you." Cal came closer, his hands folded before him. "You must be Gram Campbell. Our newest guest. I was told you were coming and have been eager to meet you."

"Aye," said Gram, remaining near Amelia. In fact, he stepped forward, his body nearly touching hers. "I am. And you are?"

"Caladrius, or Cal, as most call me." Cal approached and put out a hand to Gram.

Gram shook Cal's hand. "You'd be who this place is named after?"

Cal's smile widened. "I am. I'm the founder."

Gram eyed him as he released the man's

hand. "Is Caladrius nae a bird from Roman mythology thought to take sickness from others?"

"Why, Mr. Campbell, you surprise me. Yes, it is. Most don't know that," said Cal as he continued to watch Gram.

Amelia held her breath, fearful Cal would try to hurt Gram. He was unpredictable like that. As she watched the glee in Cal's eyes, she knew then he didn't want to harm Gram; he wanted to recruit him. Bring the man into the Flock. Gram was exactly the type of man Cal preyed upon. The type he liked to indoctrinate into his ideological beliefs.

No.

She wouldn't allow that to happen.

"I've dedicated my life to the healing arts," said Cal, laying on the charm. "My dream is that one day there is no more sickness in the world."

Amelia nearly choked on the man's lies.

"But this is nae for humans," said Gram. "So yer dream does nae include them?"

No one normally questioned Cal. It was refreshing to hear someone do so now. Even though it scared her.

Cal continued to smile. "This is one of *many* facilities I own either fully or partially. Most are dedicated to servicing humans. This and a few others are intended for fellow supernaturals. Your concern for humans warms my heart. Maybe, before your stay here is complete, you'll share in my vision and want to be a part of it all."

"I've been doing my part for centuries," said Gram. "And I'm nae looking to take up any causes. I've enough of my own to worry about."

"I was told you suffered a traumatic injury recently. An explosion? Is that what I was told?" asked Cal. "Something about you not healing properly."

A slight nod was the only response Gram gave.

Taggert eased up to them, his gaze locked on Gram. It didn't take a genius to see he intended to give Gram a hard time, and he no doubt sensed an opening, hearing Gram wasn't at one hundred percent.

Amelia rounded on Taggert, putting herself before Gram. She narrowed her gaze. "I put up with a lot from you. On this, I'll stand against you."

Taggert's brows lifted in surprise at her boldness.

"Ah, Amelia," said Cal, something close to pride in his voice. "Having a lovers' quarrel?"

"Lovers?" asked Gram.

Amelia met his gaze. "No."

Cal laughed. "Taggert has been given first rights to Amelia after a few matters are attended to. They will be wed, for lack of a better word."

Amelia cringed.

"Does the bride nae have to be willing?" asked Gram, surprising her more with his courage. "Because she does nae seem verra willing to me."

"Things here are different. Matches are decided upon by me." Cal eyed her. "Amelia finds most of our customs out-of-date and archaic. Her words, not mine. She's young. Unsure what is best for herself."

"But you do know what is best for her?" questioned Gram.

"I believe so, yes," replied Cal.

"And why is that?"

Cal smiled. "Because she is my daughter."

Amelia had to fight to keep from cringing at Cal's public acknowledgment of who he was to her. It was rare that he ever said anything to anyone outside of the Flock about being her father. The Flock members knew that Amelia and

Andie were Cal's only children. They were supposed to be treated with kid gloves and shown the same respect the others showed Cal.

That wasn't the case.

Jealousy was an ugly beast.

"Lass, he's yer father?" asked Gram.

Cal tipped his head, clearly wondering if she'd claim relation to him as well.

She never had before. She didn't use her position as his daughter to win any favors in the Flock. In fact, she avoided talking about being blood to Cal at all. And it was never discussed in front of non-Flock members.

Ever.

"Yes," she admitted, hating that it was the truth. The man's blood ran through her veins. It was a truth she greatly disliked.

Cal paid close attention to the way Gram slid even closer to her. "Mr. Campbell, you find my daughter pleasing to the eye?"

"No," said Amelia quickly, answering for him, wanting him safe from her father and Taggert.

Gram chuckled. "Aye. I do find her verra pleasing to the eye. Is there an issue with that?"

"Not at all," said Cal, a slow smile touching his lips. He was up to something. Amelia knew as much from his body language. "Amelia, why don't you spend the rest of the day with Mr. Campbell? You can show him around the resort and make sure he gets to his scheduled appointments. He has a massage coming up, if I'm not mistaken."

He wanted her to be the man's tour guide? He normally forbade her from interacting with the male guests in any way. This new change was disconcerting to say the least.

"Cal," protested Taggert, earning him a hard stare from Cal. He shut up. He was smarter than he looked.

Amelia cleared her throat. "Cal, I'm guessing one of the other women would be better suited to show Mr. Campbell around the resort. I was going to work with Andie this afternoon."

With a long sigh, Cal came to a stop in front of Amelia. He took her hands in his. "I remember when you used to call me Daddy. Are those days forever gone?"

Amelia wanted to shout yes but she didn't want to set him off. While he'd never before turned his rage on her, or permitted another to harm her, he more than had it in him to hurt another. She'd seen it all firsthand. She teared up and looked away.

He touched her chin lightly. "My sweet, big-hearted Amelia. I know your trust in me is shaken. I would like to make things right between us. I greatly dislike the lengths you go to in order to avoid me. And how much you want to leave here—leave us."

Did he know about her secret meeting with Ace? Did he know she was planning to run?

She did her best to remain calm. Panicking would only tip him off if he hadn't already figured it all out.

"You give her everything a girl could want," said Taggert, edging closer. "You spoil her and Andie."

"Of course I do," said Cal, still touching Amelia's chin. "I'm nearly three thousand years old. They are my only two children. The apples of my eye. I want the best for them."

"Then don't make me marry Taggert," Amelia blurted, before thinking better of it.

Taggert growled. "Amelia, this is tiresome. You already know your father made his choice years ago. Once *things* are in place, I'm the next step. He doesn't change his mind. Ever. And he knows I'm right for you. I'll protect you. Keep you safe."

"Och, I do nae think you and I have the same definition of the word 'protect,'" said Gram, pushing his way into the conversation once more. "I've known her a verra short period of time, and I can tell you I'd kill anyone who dared to harm her or raise their hand to her. Can you say the same, Taggert?"

Cal looked between the men. "Something I should know?"

"Aye. You picked a douchebag for yer daughter," said Gram, lacking any fear of Taggert.

Amelia's eyes widened. She waited for her father to reprimand Gram for daring to challenge a decision he'd made. She'd seen him do far worse to Flock members who questioned him. That was why very few did.

Instead, Cal's eyes lit and crinkled with mirth. "And if you were in my position, Mr. Campbell, who would you have selected for her? Perhaps a man such as yourself?"

She shook her head, preparing to tell her father that she didn't know Gram and he'd only happened upon her.

"Aye. 'Tis exactly what I'd have done. Though I'd make sure she wanted me, too. I'd nae just make demands of the lass. I'd want to be sure she came to me willing, nae because her father, a man who should want her to be safe and happy, deemed it so."

Positive she'd heard the man wrong, she twisted to face him fully. "You'd pick me for you?"

"Aye." He grinned, and it was so sexy that she felt her cheeks heating once more.

Cal beamed. "This is an interesting twist of events. More than I could have ever hoped for. I have to admit that I did some digging when I learned you were coming. I like what I found, Mr. Campbell. I'm hoping you more than enjoy your stay with us here at the resort. To that end, Amelia, would you kindly show him around?"

She nodded, still shocked by Gram's words.

Jealousy poured off Taggert to the level Amelia thought she'd drown in it.

Cal apparently sensed it too, because he inserted himself between Taggert and Gram before facing his head of security. "Taggert, I got a call from the sheriff. He was hoping we could check our surveillance footage to see if we noticed any suspicious cars or characters about two days back."

"Is all well?" asked Gram.

"I'm sure you've seen the papers or news by

this point. Someone is harming and killing young women in the area. Another body was found a few hours ago. An eyewitness swears they saw a vehicle coming from our direction," said Cal. "I assured him my head of security would look into the matter and report in anything we may happen upon. We want this killer brought to justice as soon as possible."

Amelia held her tongue.

She knew better.

She knew the truth.

The very man her father was sending to speak with law enforcement was more than likely the reason the woman was dead to start with.

"Yes, Father," said Taggert, giving Gram a once-over before he backed away.

Gram touched Amelia's hand. "I'm confused. Why is he calling you Father? You said you only have two daughters and he's nae married to Amelia."

Cal laughed softly. "Those who reside here permanently, who are part of *the Flock*, call me Father. It was not by my choosing."

"The Flock?" asked Gram.

"Those who follow my teachings and hope for

a better future." Cal lifted his arms out and glanced around. "Peace for all."

Amelia nearly gagged.

"So yer a cult?" asked Gram, his question making Amelia laugh.

She tried to hide it behind a cough, but it didn't work.

Cal shrugged. "I dislike the negative connotations the word evokes, but if you mean I have a large mass of people who are devoted to my teachings, the answer is yes."

"If it's all the same, I'll nae be drinking any purple fruit-flavored drinks while I'm here," said Gram.

Cal laughed long and hard.

Chapter Eleven

CODY LIVINGSTON SAT at the table in the Outcast safe house hidden in the thick of Denver's downtown area. Armand sat across from him. There were other, smaller safe houses set up around Colorado, but this was by far the biggest. It wasn't that far from PSI or the Para-Reg offices that serviced the area, as well.

It was hardly Cody's first Outcast safe house. He'd been in hundreds over the years. Hell, he'd even helped to set up many of them. That being said, the Denver one was impressive for sure. Everything in it was state of the art. Whoever was in charge of the IT department there needed to be commended. There were monitors on one wall, going from floor to ceiling, each displaying different feeds.

Some had lines of code running endlessly on them. Others were scrolling lists of names. He knew algorithms had been set up to help search a variety of areas to find and flag any possible issues related to the supernatural, and the Outcasts specifically. He'd been instrumental in getting the network set up decades ago.

One of the monitors with names running on it pinged something, marking it in red. Since the location popped up as Utah, Cody knew the Outcasts closer to the area would look more into it.

Some of the other monitors had static images flashing. And some appeared to be live feeds. Three looked to be displaying satellite imagery footage. He could only guess which satellites they were tapped into. A lot of what they did piggy-backed on existing systems. They did so in a way that didn't tip anyone off that they were even there.

They were that good.

Nothing was out of the realm or reach of the Outcast organization. They may have been forced to go to ground decades ago when their own government turned against them, but they hadn't taken defeat lying down. While most of them had scattered with the winds after the shit hit the fan with the Immortal Ops program, nearly all of them kept in contact in some form or fashion. The network was elaborate and its reach deep.

Cody was very involved with the Outcast network, doing his part to assist others who couldn't help themselves.

Armand was not, nor had he ever been, an Outcast but that didn't stop the vampire from wanting to help where he could. From the moment Armand had come into Cody's life (at the exact moment Gram had, as well), he'd trusted the man fully.

Having him close whenever he got devastating news helped Cody somewhat. Staring down at the surveillance photos on the table before him, Cody was happy to have Armand there for moral support. He'd seen firsthand what Cody had lived through. What he'd been put through all in the name of science and for the sake of madmen wanting more power.

And because one sick fuck, in particular, was desperate for a cure to an ailment that had plagued his family line for generations.

Having his not-too-distant past thrown in his face once more was nearly more than Cody could handle.

There were photos, receipts, and more, all proving what he was being told. That didn't make it any easier to wrap his mind around. His gaze traveled from Armand, with whom he'd formed an unbreakable bond nearly five years ago, to a man he'd once served with—Ace Hargraves.

Ace had been born with trace amounts of supernatural blood in him, just like Cody had. It made them prime candidates for Immortal Ops testing. The experiments had been an attempt by the U.S. government to genetically engineer super soldiers. Men who were more than human and could be controlled—or so they'd thought.

Cody, Ace, and the other men like them had been told they were signing up for testing to serve their country—to be all they could be and more. In the end, that's exactly what they ended up.

More.

Much more.

In some cases, too fucking much.

Then, after all the horrors they'd gone through, their government turned their backs on them, going so far as to order their extermination.

After all, loose ends weren't something black site operations were big fans of. Hiding the evidence of the atrocities committed had been the choice made by the men in charge.

They'd made a lot of decisions that made no sense to Cody and the others. Then again, Cody never saw a human being as a number, like a lab rat. These people did. Many of them had played a part in Nazi eugenics, even pioneering some of the testing used at the time.

All of it was sickening and horrendous, yet history never spoke of the Outcasts or what they'd lived through. Why would it? It wasn't as if humans knew about supernaturals, so keeping all the failed experiments a secret was much easier than one would think. And distancing themselves from the Nazi doctors and scientists somehow made those in charge feel better, as if they'd taken a higher road. They hadn't. They just got better at hiding what they were doing.

It had been decades since Cody had undergone what had ultimately made him the man he was today, but that didn't lessen the sting any. It was done but not forgotten. Not to mention Outcasts had been, for the most part, hunted for decades. If it wasn't their own government trying to find and eliminate them to hide what they'd done, it was someone wanting to exploit them or study them. It was always something.

They'd been given the name Immortal Outcasts, and it stuck. Some of them looked down their noses at the term, but not Cody. It was accurate and summarized how he felt.

Like an outsider.

Unlike many supernaturals he knew, he hadn't been born with the ability to shift forms. Sure, he had always been healthier than others around him, had always been taller, buffer, stronger, faster, but not so much that it was obvious to everyone. The testing he'd signed up for changed every-thing. It flipped his entire world on its head. He'd had to leave his old life behind and go on the run as the monster the scientists had made him into.

Cody had been born and raised in Australia. When he was in his teens, his family made a move to America. By the time he was eighteen, the first World War had broken out. He'd felt it was his duty to help defend the nation he'd taken to calling home. He'd enlisted and was quickly shipped off to France. While there, he'd been shot. When receiving treatment for his injuries, Cody suddenly found himself being approached by the brass and outsiders. They'd offered him a chance to help change the course of history. To help ensure mankind was safe from evil.

He'd jumped at the opportunity, never reading the fine print.

Ace had been in the same testing facility as him. The men had been in the same unit prior to the testing. The two had watched a number of their brothers die during the experiments. They'd assumed they would, too.

Cody's first time shifting had not only been terrifying, it had been extremely painful. He still didn't know what the scientists were expecting, but from their expressions, having a wereshark wasn't on the list.

It hadn't been on Cody's, either.

The smallest amount of great white shark DNA had been used in his cocktail. From Cody's understanding, that was common practice back then. It was thought to help get the desired outcome. They didn't expect any of the men to actually take to the DNA fully.

Cody had.

Later, he'd learned that far, far back in his ancestry were men who could shift into sharks and other marine animals. That had left his system far more accepting of the shark DNA than anything else.

It could have been worse. He knew one guy who'd suffered the ill effects of a lab mishap and could shift forms into a giant rat. He knew men who could turn into just about anything, really. A snake. A spider. A gorilla. A bear. The list went on and on. A close friend of his had gargoyle and vampire DNA introduced to his system, leaving him some strange mix of both, yet not fully either. Wheeler was a good guy, dealt a raw deal. Like all the Outcasts.

But Ace was no different. Though he didn't turn into a shark, rat, or vampire. No. Ace shifted into a huge horse. When fully shifted, he made Clydesdales look like miniature ponies.

Ace wasn't big on shifting. Cody couldn't blame him. He didn't exactly look forward to doing so, either. Thankfully, he wasn't a slave to the moon like some shifters. He did suffer from a strong pull to the ocean. Every so often he shifted fully and swam, letting the shark side of himself out to play. During those times, he tended to spend a week or more in the ocean, far from people, far from land, from worries and drama.

Ace took a deep breath from his position near

the door as he held a cup of coffee in one hand. "It's all true, Cody. I wish it wasn't. That bastard is alive and kicking."

The bastard in question was someone who was well-known to the Ops community. Walter Helmuth had made a name for himself by being a ruthless paranormal underground ruler in Seattle. He made his money off the trafficking of supernaturals and paranormal death matches—a fight club comprised of nothing but supernaturals. The man was insane on the best of days.

Cody would know. He'd been a prized pet of the man's for long enough.

Helmuth was part gargoyle and lacked control over that side of himself. In an effort to stave off shifts, Helmuth had taken to injecting himself with serum derived from Cody's DNA. When that stopped working, he'd apparently set his sights on a succubus he thought might be able to help.

The succubus was now mated to a fellow Outcast who happened to be able to turn into a gorilla, and they had a little one on the way. The last anyone had seen of Helmuth had been weeks ago, when he'd gone head to head with an Outcast and a former Immortal Op.

The grapevine had given Cody the information quickly when it came to light. Rumor had it that Helmuth was seriously injured and thought to possibly be dead. From the photos in front of Cody, that theory was wrong. The sick bastard was not only alive, but he looked healthy and happy. All smiles in the photos as he sat near the edge of a pool sipping some fancy drink from a glass with an umbrella in it. The people around him were all dressed in white.

He tapped a photo. "And this was taken at some hippie commune, you said? And you're not sure he's still there?"

Ace sipped his coffee and nodded. "The Caladrius Center. Yeah. We've had our eye on the place for a few years now. It tickled our computer program's algorithm, drawing our attention, and from there, we noticed a lot of things weren't adding up. We had a man on the inside there. We lost contact with him unexpectedly. Either he's been unable to reach out to us or he's dead."

Armand leafed through files in front of him. "And this Caladrius who runs the resort is what?"

Ace shrugged. "We don't know for sure. We do know he's not human. Far from it. Neither are any of his immediate circle. Not a surprise since the resort section of the center all caters to our kind."

"How did Helmuth end up there?" asked Cody, unable to look away from the photo of the man who had tortured him for months.

"From what we can piece together, Helmuth went there to heal after getting his wing ripped off in that fight with Bane and Lance. Caladrius is rumored to have healing powers, and it's no big secret that the center gives supernaturals what they need. And I do mean anything they need," said Ace. "It was smart for Helmuth to go there to get better. No one thought to look for him there. And the guy who runs everything is clearly in bed with some shady people.

"I met with a young woman from out there, and she's terrified. I didn't want to let her go back in but her little sister is there. Seemed wrong to keep them apart. I considered going in for them myself, but when I reached out to you and found out Gram was set up to stay there, it seemed wise to let this play out, at least for now."

Cody looked to Armand. "Gram isn't one hundred percent. Did we sign off on sending him to a place that will kill him?"

Armand was quiet a moment as he continued

to read through the files. He then looked up. "I would not have let him go in alone had I known this."

Ace cleared his throat. "Had I known that was the vacation getaway Striker planned for the guy, I'd have said something over the phone. Pulling him out right this second might be unwise. Plus, I feel better knowing he's there. While less than perfect, he's someone that girl I met with can trust."

"But he can't help anyone if he's their next victim," said Cody, wanting his friend safe. "We need to go in and extract him at once."

Ace shook his head. "No can do. Not unless we want the supernatural version of Ruby Ridge or Waco on our hands."

Armand sighed. "They are heavily armed?"

Nodding, Ace stepped closer. "And then some. From what we can tell, the leader runs weekly drills with his security staff. In the event they're converged on by law enforcement, they'll take a stand. If they think they're going to be overtaken in any way, they will kill everyone in there."

"Who cares if a bunch of crazy cult members off themselves?" asked Cody, meaning it. He didn't care if it lacked compassion. Gram was one of his best friends. He wouldn't sacrifice him for some greater good. The guy had saved his life once. Cody owed him as much in return.

Ace lifted his hands. "Hey, I'm not going to argue with you about it, but I *am* going to show you this."

The werehorse moved some of the photos and pulled a few from the bottom. He pushed them before Cody.

When Cody looked down to see a small group of children, all dressed in white, playing on a playground with the resort off in the distance behind them, he gasped. "They have little ones out there?"

"Yeah. And they may have some women held against their will. Honestly, we think they're behind the rash of deaths lately. The ones PSI is looking into. But we don't have anything firm to hand PSI to convince them to go in and investigate it further."

Cody cursed under his breath. There was no way he'd permit children or innocents to be harmed. "Fuck."

"Yes, indeed," said Armand, casually pulling his cell from his pocket. He pressed speakerphone and Mac's voicemail picked up. Armand disconnected the call and tried another number. This time a man picked up who Cody didn't know.

"What? I did answer it, Gus," said the man. "No. This newfangled technology escapes me. You see any two-year-olds? Bet they can do this? What? Oh you're right. I should talk to the person on the other end."

Armand disconnected the call and then dialed the number again, evidently thinking he had the wrong one. When the same man answered, Armand arched a brow. "Is Carbrey there?"

"Who?" asked the man. "Did you ask if I had the chocolate company here?"

Armand appeared confused.

Cody snorted. "No. He said Car-Brey. Or just Car. Not Cad-Bury. Is he there?"

"You called this phone to talk to a car?" asked the man, sounding befuddled. "Oh, I saw a doco on that once. A series of them. The car was named KITT. Real chick magnet. Gus, what do you mean that wasn't a doco?"

Armand tipped his head. "What is a doco?"

"Documentary," said Cody, somewhat amused with the absurdity of the conversation.

"Slang for it?" asked Armand.

Cody nodded.

Armand rubbed his chin. "Why? Wouldn't it be doc-*u*? Not doc-*o*? There is a 'u' after the doc part of the word. Not an 'o.'"

"Dude, I didn't invent the slang for it, and is that really the important matter here?" asked Cody.

Ace snorted.

"Gus, it was too a doco. Remember, I was gonna look for that guy who drove that car named KITT and see if he's interested in retiring. What was the doco called again? Day Rider? No, Dark Rider? Shucks. I can't remember. But I'd be perfect to take Michael's place with KITT." The man made a series of odd noises before returning to arguing with someone Cody couldn't hear. "I could too. Ladies love me. And I have mad driving skills. Hey, you cannot blame Lola on me. That car clearly was neglected by its owner—the big meanie. Yes. I can call Duke a meanie. He is one."

Cody glanced at Ace. "Is he talking about Duke Marlow from PSI? Doesn't he have a sports car he named Lola?"

Armand shook his head. "Not anymore. Someone wrecked it. My guess is the crazy man talking on the phone now."

"Don't you start on me too, vamp-boy," said the man on the phone.

"Who is this and how is it you know what I am?" asked Armand.

"And why in the hell are you answering Car's phone?" interjected Cody.

"I'm Wild Bill. My buddy here is Gus. We didn't answer any car's phone. We answered one of the Irish guys' phones. What do you mean he's not Irish, Gus? Scottish? Huh. That explains why I can't understand a damn word he and his clone are saying. Oh no! Mona's head just rolled off the table. Grab her. She's getting facial stuff all over the floor."

Ace took a deep breath. "Someone's head fell off?"

"It would appear so," said Armand, staring at the phone on the table. "Mentally touched man, would you be so kind as to take the phone to one of the men you can't understand? We have a matter that is of the utmost importance to discuss with them."

The man spoke but it was muffled, as if he had his hand over the phone. Suddenly, it cleared. "Gus says to tell you that the twins are where they should be and that Gram has to stay here right now."

"Who the hell is Gus?" demanded Cody.

Ace scratched his upper chest and then glanced at one of the monitors. He then went to it, tapped a button just under it, and waited as a keyboard slid out from the wall. He keyed in a few things and stepped back as two photos appeared on the monitor. One was a wiry-haired older gentleman who didn't look to be very tall. The other was of a tall, lanky male.

Ace tapped the monitor. "May I present Bill and Gus. I knew those names were familiar. I heard Weston threatening to eat them once when I called out to check on him and Paisley. Then Bane mentioned them annoying him. I think they actually started out with Casey but are slowly making the Outcast rounds."

"We saved a princess," said Bill. "And some other girls. We protected Laney, too. You know, all the shit you guys can't seem to do on your own. Super soldiers my ass. We're like superheroes but better. We don't have a weakness. Well, Gus's weakness would be Brussels sprouts. He's not a fan."

"Did Casey find them after they escaped a mental institution?" asked Cody of Ace.

"I'll have you know that I keep checking in to crazy farms, but they keep checking me out. I swear. What's a guy gotta do in today's day and age to get put away for good and access to endless good drugs?" asked Bill. "This was a lot easier in Vietnam. They locked me away then and kept the good shit coming."

The men all shared a look, each no doubt guessing what Bill meant. He'd been tested on by the government, just like they had been.

"Lass, you wouldnae be willing to kiss all that ails me, would you?" asked one of the twins in the background.

"Put that one on the line, please," said Armand, close to losing his patience, which was saying something, considering he always seemed to be a fountain of calm.

"You wanna talk to the one who is trying to get a blow job?" asked Bill.

Ace stifled a laugh. "Yes. That would be one of the twins for sure."

"Gus says no," said Bill. "He says we've got everything under control and don't go butting in or people will die. Oh, and Gram has to save his mate. He can't do that if he ain't here to do that. Gotta go now. We got a colonics appointment soon. After our facials are done."

With that, the man hung up.

Cody leaned back in his chair. "I'm not sure if I'm thankful they're the backup or not."

"I'll call Casey," said Ace, leaving the room in a hurry.

Armand stared at the phone on the table. "It's been some time since I wanted to drain the life from a human."

"Glad to see you got your vamp mojo back on, but how about we not drain the little guy?" said Cody. Then his gaze went to the picture of Helmuth. "We can't let him hurt anyone else."

"I know. First, let us see to it that Gram and the twins are safe, if from nothing more than the *doco*-loving little man."

Chapter Twelve

AMELIA EASED CLOSER TO GRAM; the compulsion to simply be near him was all-consuming. Her father watched with nothing short of pure satisfaction in his eyes. There was a hint of madness showing through the glee. She couldn't recall a time she'd seen him this enthused about anything, let alone the arrival of a VIP guest. She half expected him to roll out a red carpet for Gram and have flowers tossed at the man.

The idea would have been considered far-fetched if Cal didn't have the same welcome himself whenever he went away and returned. The Flock treated him like he was a god. But not Amelia. She knew better.

"Father," said Taggert, going wide around Gram on his way to Amelia's father. "Can I have a word with you?"

Cal lifted an arm in Taggert's direction. "Mr. Campbell, I'm not sure if you've been properly introduced to the head of my security team, Taggert. You have a great deal in common. You're just alike. Taggert is also a wolf-shifter who possesses the gift of magik, and both of you have a keen interest in Amelia. Though it would seem she is only receptive to one of you. Perhaps a backup selection won't be necessary after all."

"What?" demanded Taggert.

Amelia stepped back from Gram. He was just like Taggert? Did her father mean Gram was as deadly as Taggert?

Gram reached out quickly, his hand coming just shy of touching hers. He righted himself and appeared strained. Deep down she could sense how much he wanted...no, *needed* to make contact with her.

Unable to deny the man, she lifted her hand, placing it in his.

Gram didn't seem to care that they had an audience as he pulled her closer to him in a protective manner, keeping her far from Taggert's reach.

Cal fixated on their joined hands and it was impossible to miss the delight in his gaze. If the act made her father that happy, something was off.

A sinking feeling came over her. Was Gram the man her father had been waiting for? Was he the Bringer?

Amelia worked her hand free from Gram's but didn't step away. It took all she had to keep what little distance she had from Gram. What she really wanted to do was wrap her arms around him and beg the man to run away with her and her sister.

She doubted her father would find that amusing or exciting in the least. He'd have Gram's head on a pike if he knew exactly how Amelia felt about the man she'd only just met.

Gram eyed her. "Lass, I see the wheels spinning in yer head. I'm nae like that asshat."

Taggert growled.

Gram flipped him off. "Let's nae pretend to like one another. And yer an arsehole."

Taggert made a move to go at Gram.

"Do it. I verra much want to kill you," warned Gram, stopping Taggert cold.

Cal smiled wider. "Interesting. I was not expecting this."

Unable to stop herself, Amelia questioned her father. "You can't think he's who you've been waiting for, right? I'm not going to let you…"

Suddenly, Taggert was next to Amelia, to her right, Gram to her left. Taggert eased himself partially between Amelia and her father. He too knew exactly what Cal was capable of.

"Father, Amelia has been out in the sun for a long time today and she skipped breakfast. We should get her inside. You know how easily she burns," said Taggert, who seemed to have abandoned his quest to growl threats at Gram endlessly. He now seemed concerned for Amelia. It never boded well when the criminally insane and sadistic started worrying about what someone else would do. If Taggert was concerned, just what in the heck was he worried about happening?

Normally, Amelia would have done her best to fade away from notice, to keep her head down and go with the flow. Especially with having an escape plan that she was close to launching. But she couldn't stomach the idea of standing idly by and allowing her father to get his taint all over Gram.

Cal stared between the three of them and then winked at Amelia, making her jump in her spot.

Gram snaked an arm around her waist and yanked her against him.

Much to Amelia's surprise, Taggert then put himself in front of her in a protective manner. The challenge wasn't spoken outright, but it was there. Taggert was daring her father to attempt to go through him to get to her, showing he'd side with Gram if need be to keep Amelia safe.

It was official. Hell had frozen over.

"I do nae know what is happening here and I do nae care," said Gram, still holding her to him. "I find myself wanting to keep the lass close to me. Make of that what you may."

Her father clapped. "Wonderful news. Taggert, you can stand down. All is well. Better than expected even. Far better."

Taggert relaxed somewhat but didn't go too far from Amelia's side.

Gram watched her father. "What are you? I cannae get a guid read on you. Are you magik?"

"I am many, many things, Mr. Campbell,"

supplied her father. "And I have waited so long for you to come and join us."

Amelia's stomach dropped.

Gram was the Bringer.

She tried to step away from him, but he refused to release her.

"For me?" asked Gram, paying attention to Cal. "Why? I do nae know you. I would have remembered meeting you. I do nae forget a face."

"Mr. Campbell, as I mentioned, I am a great many things. One of them is a seer of what is to come." He lifted his hands in the air. "The great gods and goddesses speak through me."

Gram's brows drew up more. "Said every cult leader who fancied himself the next messiah."

Amelia assumed her father would lash out at the comment.

He didn't.

He grinned more. "Cult is such an ugly word."

"One man's messiah is another man's cult leader," supplied Gram, seemingly unconcerned with what her father thought of him.

That in itself was refreshing to a degree, but it didn't change the fact that Gram was the Bringer.

"Did these gods and goddesses tell you I was

coming?" asked Gram. "Because I heard it was my arsehole of a friend who made this reservation for me, nae some secret god and goddess society. Unless Striker started one of those. I'd nae put it past him. If anyone was ever born to want his own cult, it would be that one."

Cal's expression was even. "The higher powers did tell me of you, and they gave me visions of your arrival."

"Visions?" asked Gram, seeming very interested all of a sudden. "Are they of a white wolf or dead mothers? What about a woman in white?" His gaze snapped to her.

Cal's brow furrowed. "No. They are not. Why? Have *you* had such visions?"

Amelia found herself holding her breath, waiting for Gram's answer, though she wasn't sure why she cared so much.

Gram caressed her hip as he kept his arm around her waist. "Aye, 'tis part of why I'm here I suppose. I'm guessing my doctors mentioned as much. I thank you for trying to help me save face by pretending you dinnae know I've been hallucinating. I will admit that I cannae explain why it is I had visions of Amelia before I came here, though. Or the red ball."

He'd seen her before his arrival?

Red ball?

Could he mean Andie's? She was very rarely without it.

"Mr. Campbell, *you* had visions of Amelia?" asked Cal, stealing the question from her lips.

Taggert's entire body tensed.

Gram nodded. "Aye. I couldnae see her face but it was her. I've no doubt of that. The visions even had her scent—honeysuckle and vanilla. Strange. I know. So, I'll ask you again, what are you, and are you the reason I saw her before coming?"

Amelia twisted into Gram and put her hand to his chiseled abs. She didn't want him pushing her father too far. "Don't."

He gulped as he stared down at her hand. "Lass, if you touch any lower, I cannae be held responsible for my actions. There is only so much a man can take."

It took her a moment to follow along with his meaning. When she did, her eyes widened, and she jerked her hand free from him. "Oh, I…that wasn't what, erm…never mind."

He grinned sheepishly.

She found herself starting to smile as well.

"Tell me, Mr. Campbell," said Cal. "Do you find Amelia to your liking?"

"Aye, verra much so," replied Gram.

Amelia blushed.

"Though I am wondering what she is," said Gram. "And how it was she appeared to me before I came. So what of you, lass? What are you?"

Cal and Taggert laughed softly at the question.

Flinching, Amelia averted her gaze. Her mother had always kept what Amelia could do a secret, letting everyone assume she had no gifts. That she was nothing more than human-like. When she was growing up, lying about what she could and couldn't do had confused her, but she'd trusted her mother and abided by her wishes. That didn't mean the subject wasn't a sore one.

Cal came to her and drew her into a hug before kissing her forehead. If a strong wind came it would blow her over from the shock of her father's affection and concern.

He met her gaze. "Amelia, I'm sorry. My laugh wasn't meant to be cruel. I found it amusing that Mr. Campbell has taken such an interest in you so suddenly. It is more than I could have ever hoped for. I know you will make sure his stay here is *enjoyable*."

She cringed at the implication.

Taggert muttered something about whoring out Amelia.

Cal gave him a scolding look and he shut up. Cal then patted her cheek lovingly. "You are a true gift. As is Andie. You are as much a part of the Flock as any other. I think you know just how *special* you are. It matters not to me that you are more human than not. You and Andie are to be protected at all times. You have a very bright future here. I was clear on this, right, Taggert?"

Taggert grunted. "Yes."

Cal winked. "Amelia, can you show Mr. Campbell to his quarters? Something tells me he'd much rather prefer you be the one to do it than me."

"Father," said Taggert.

Cal eyed him. "Is there an issue?"

"Amelia isn't normally around the guests," replied Taggert. "She's kept away from others for a reason. Right?"

Cal shrugged. "No time like the present to have her assist. Mr. Campbell is a VIP. If he wishes to have Amelia escort him, then so be it. I know Amelia will see to his needs." He looked at Amelia, as if daring her to disobey.

She nodded.

Cal focused on Gram. "Would you care to join me for dinner this evening?"

Gram's gaze eased over her, and Amelia felt her cheeks heat.

"Amelia will be there," added Cal, surprising her by how quick he was to thrust her toward Gram. He must really want Gram in the Flock, because Taggert was right. Cal had never before permitted her to be around any male guests.

"Aye, I'll join you." Gram put his arm out to Amelia. "If the lass wouldnae mind showing me back to my quarters."

She hid her smile for fear it would set off Taggert even more. Amelia looked to Cal for guidance. She didn't want him changing his mind and issuing a kill order on Gram.

He nodded, and she touched Gram. Even more heat flared through her, making her breath catch. "We should head back. I need to find Andie and check on her."

"The wee one is fine," said Gram, drawing her closer. "I passed her on my way here."

Relief ran over Amelia as she teared up once more. "We should go now."

They walked off, leaving Cal and Taggert. She didn't need to be around to know Cal wasn't going to reprimand Taggert. She just hoped Cal kept the man busy enough for the rest of the day to keep him far from her.

Chapter Thirteen

TAGGERT SEETHED WITH ANGER, wanting to lash out at the man he'd once seen as a god, as a father figure of sorts.

Cal had taken him in when Taggert was barely in his teens, starving, hungry, cold, and having to sell his body for coins. It wasn't a time in his life Taggert liked to discuss. And very few knew the truth of it all. That was how he liked it. He didn't like showing weaknesses.

When Cal had shown up in the alley, just outside of a well-known and well-used brothel, Taggert had assumed the man was there for sex. Either from Taggert or one of the whores Taggert palled around with. The ones who were the closest thing to a mother he'd ever had.

That hadn't been what Cal wanted at all. Cal had offered Taggert a warm bed for the night, food, and clean clothing. Of course, Taggert had been suspicious of the treatment. He'd seen a lot of sick shit in his short life back then and wondered if perhaps the man was simply buttering him up for devastation later.

He hadn't been.

Cal had sensed the wolf-shifter and Fae in Taggert and he'd nurtured it, guiding Taggert on using his gifts and controlling his beast. When it became clear that Taggert's Fae side required sexual energy, Cal saw to it women were provided. And when Taggert's appetites in the bedroom grew darker, Cal never questioned him—or the number of dead bodies that had to be cleaned up and removed after the fact. Body counts that to this very day continued to accumulate.

No.

Cal told him it wasn't a sickness. That his cravings were natural. That supernaturals were created to kill and the ones with animals in them had been fighting their nature for far too long. That they should be permitted to hunt, fuck, kill, eat, and repeat the steps. Cal stressed that Taggert's powers were divine and could be used to help in Cal's vision of a brighter future for supernaturals. A vision that would one day leave supernaturals controlling the world, not humans. A time when there would be no shame for doing as they were born to do.

Rule over humans and weaker supernaturals.

Over the centuries, their bond had only strengthened. That was, until Abigail, Amelia's mother, came on the scene. Cal had taken an unnatural interest in the woman when she was hardly old enough to be considered of legal consenting age. That hadn't stopped the man. He'd ordered the girl's parents to give her over to him, to be one of his harem women who were often called wives.

Taggert, who was no choirboy, remembered what it had been like to be young and used by adults sexually. He'd found himself encouraging Cal to wait until the girl was slightly older. The morning of Abigail's eighteenth birthday, her parents had led her to Cal's cabin, dressed in a sheer gown, a crown of flowers on her head, her long dark hair flowing all around her. Her green eyes had been wide, and she'd radiated fear. That had excited Taggert's wolf side.

Hell, thinking back on it now still made

him hard.

She'd been a vision of beauty. In fact, Amelia looked a great deal like her mother. But in Taggert's opinion, Amelia was even more beautiful than Abigail had been.

Abigail's parents had joined the rest of the Flock at the celebration held in honor of Cal selecting her. Afterward, Taggert had been instructed to remain behind and assure no one bothered Cal as he bedded his new bride (although no wedding ceremony ever actually took place).

To this day, Taggert could still hear the woman's pleas for Cal to stop, to be gentle, to let her go.

He hadn't.

No.

He'd kept her locked in that cabin with him for days, breaking her spirit. When he was done taking what he wanted from her, he'd set her up in her own cabin and forced Taggert to watch over her. To keep other Flock members far from what was his. And then the kill order came on her parents. In Cal's eyes, the two were a liability. He wanted them eliminated. He'd charged Taggert with doing so.

Taggert had done as commanded. He'd killed Abigail's parents and then watched over her. It hadn't taken long for the woman's scent to change and for Taggert to realize she was expecting. The news had shocked him, as he knew she wasn't Cal's mate.

The rest of the Flock took it as a sign of Cal's divinity. Of his power. His strength. Taggert knew better. He knew the man had spent centuries absorbing the power of the alpha males he'd killed, and that Cal had tapped into that power to ensure he'd have an heir. He'd drawn upon that stolen power to be sure his seed took root.

And it couldn't have happened with just anyone. Abigail had been special—divine in her own right—making her the perfect choice to bear Cal's offspring.

The entire time Abigail had been pregnant, she was kept under close supervision to be sure she didn't attempt to end the pregnancy in some fashion. Like Amelia, Abigail had a natural-born talent with plants, flowers, and natural remedies. It would have been easy for her to take something that would have caused the babe in her to be no more. The pregnancy was monitored closely, and Cal seemed to have real concern for the child. When Taggert learned why—that Cal had fore-seen his daughter would be instrumental in assuring some Bringer came into the fold—he'd been jealous.

He'd always been Cal's favorite prior to Amelia.

Once Amelia had been born, nannies both supernatural and human were brought in to assist in her upbringing and make sure her mother did nothing to harm her. Abigail's dislike of Cal was well-known. While the woman hated Cal, she loved Amelia, so much so that the baby became the perfect way to control her.

Threaten Amelia and her mother obeyed. Doing whatever was asked of her. That included pleasing Taggert and the other men on the secu-rity team sexually whenever they wanted.

Cal hadn't cared. His only demands had been that the woman not be killed or seriously injured during their sexual escapades. And that Amelia never be present for any of it. The men who were given turns with her obeyed.

Taggert had fucked the woman so many times he'd lost count. In truth, he'd started to develop something close to feelings for her. She didn't reciprocate them. She had always seen him through the same tainted lens she saw Cal. More than once, Abigail had called Taggert a monster.

Sick.

Twisted.

And when she'd noticed the way Taggert watched Amelia when she was in her late teens, Abigail had tried to stand against him.

He'd beaten her into submission.

Cal had been fine with that, too. In fact, he'd encouraged it, disliking the disobedient streak the woman had begun to develop.

Then one day, shortly before Amelia was to turn eighteen, Cal had approached Taggert and informed him that he was no longer allowed to lie with Amelia's mother in a carnal way. Nor could hands be lain upon her in anger. That she was to be placed in Cal's cabin, where she would stay until she became pregnant with another of Cal's children—hopefully a boy.

And it was then that Cal had told Taggert that one day, after Amelia did what was required of her—guaranteed the Bringer joined the Flock—Taggert could have her. He could wed her, and Cal would even lend his power to make sure Taggert could have children with Amelia. The same power Cal had used to have his seed take root in Abigail.

Taggert had longed for that—for a family and a woman of his own. Unlike Cal, he had no intentions of sharing his woman with any others—that included the fucking Bringer. Amelia would be his and his alone. While she may not like him or trust him, she would learn to obey and serve him, as a woman should. With time, she might even begin to care for him, as he cared for her.

She was different from other women.

Special.

He didn't want to squeeze the life from her while he fucked her and made her bleed. He wanted her to join him in inflicting pain on others, all while they found sexual release in one another. And he would not stray from her bed as Cal had done to Abigail. No. Taggert would be loyal to his wife. Together they'd one day take over the Flock.

Taggert had thought he'd end up happy and with a family years ago.

Then Amelia's cunt of a mother had learned of Cal's plans for his daughter and had run with Amelia. She'd run, pregnant with Andie, with no help, no friends, no money. And she'd managed to stay gone for two years. She'd even managed to give birth to Andie while on the run without sending up a giant flare into the ether, alerting Cal to the birth of his next child. That was impressive.

To a point.

He grinned, thinking of what had happened to the bitch when she and her daughters had been brought back to the compound. It had been against Abigail's will. She'd put up one hell of a fight. He'd give her that. But the second Taggert dared to threaten Andie, the woman had caved. She folded and came willingly, begging and pleading the entire time for her daughters to be allowed to go free.

Not a chance.

Amelia would be his come hell or high water.

The bitch learned what happens when you cross Cal, when you go against the greater good of the Flock. She'd learned, and her daughters had been there to see what happens as well. It was a life lesson he knew Amelia and Andie would never forget.

A smile touched his lips as he thought of the punishment Cal had served Abigail.

A close business associate of Cal's named Walter Helmuth had been acquiring failed experiments from another of their friends, Gisbert Krauss. These failures were termed original hybrids, and Helmuth had found a way to crank up their lethal tendencies even more. They had been given the label berserkers. They were magnificent creatures. Singular visions. They followed a command to the letter.

When Cal had issued orders to the hybrids, he'd told them to rip the bitch to shreds. To feast upon Abigail's flesh.

And they had.

It had been a sight to see.

Beautiful.

He still jerked off to the memory of it to this day. The terror in Abigail's eyes, not for herself but for her daughters, had been amazing. Her scent had changed, coated in fear, making her smell so fucking good. Hell, it had sent many of the males of the Flock into a frenzy. Some had even gotten so worked up they'd turned on the women near them and killed them to slake their inner beasts.

No matter.

Nearly all the women were replaceable.

All except Amelia.

Taggert had ensured Amelia and Andie weren't touched or harmed. He'd kept the other men away from them. Brian assisted, having been promised Andie's hand when she was of age.

The expressions on the girls' faces as their mother was consumed by the berserkers amused Taggert. It was important the girls understand their place in the grander scheme of events.

If Amelia ever dared try to run as her mother had, Taggert would hunt her down and punish her himself. Cal wouldn't need to bother. Though Taggert would not allow her to be killed or eaten by anything or anyone. No. He wanted to keep her forever. Instead, he'd hurt her little sister. That would teach her.

Cal's sudden change in plans regarding gifting Amelia to him set Taggert's teeth on edge. He wasn't one to question the man, but this was pushing too far.

Cal stared at the river, lost in thought.

When he finally turned to face Taggert, his expression was hard. "You are unhappy with my change of heart about Amelia."

"You told me I could have her when she was done getting the Bringer to join us," reminded Taggert. "You said she'd be my wife. That you'd lend me power to have a family of my own with her."

Cal shrugged. "Things change. I had not foreseen just how taken the Bringer would be with her. Did you smell the mating energy? You know, they could be actual true mates. That would mean he will do anything to keep her safe, to protect her, to make her happy."

At the mention of mates, Taggert stiffened. "She's not his fucking mate."

Cal arched a brow at Taggert's tone.

Clearing his throat, Taggert averted his gaze. "Father, I've waited years for her. I've done all that has ever been asked of me. I've served you well. Give me her. I beg you. Have another handle the Bringer. Give me Amelia. I will honor the union with all I have."

Cal touched Taggert's arm lightly. Energy radiated from the man. "Taggert, if they are mates, there is no way I can make that promise. The Bringer will not let her be given over to you, and he's far too important to the grander scheme to upset. If having her makes him happy, then he shall have her for keeps."

Taggert's jaw set in a hard line. "Father, I heard you order Susan to make sure Amelia is the one who services the man today. She's never been with a man before. Send one of the others. Tina, even. Tina's a succubus. She can make the Bringer happy. She can get him to join us."

Cal snorted. "Tina and every other Flock female could run naked in front of Campbell and I don't think he'd notice them. His focus is singular and on Amelia and her alone. It must be Amelia who sees to his needs. She will get him to stay. She will be the key to having him align with me."

"What is so special about him?" asked Taggert. He didn't understand. The Bringer guy was clearly broken. He was injured, and he wasn't running at full capacity. What could Cal, who was godlike, possibly want with the man?

"What I see is never clear-cut. It's impressions. Ones I'm left to interpret. You know as much," said Cal, folding his hands before him again, looking serene. "I see great power coming from his presence here."

"It always comes down to power with you,

doesn't it?" questioned Taggert before thinking better of it.

"Caution, Taggert. You are like a son to me, but that will not save you from my wrath. Amelia is of my blood, but if she does not do what's required of her, I will see her dead as well."

Taggert stiffened. He didn't want Amelia dead. He was pissed with her for endlessly rejecting him, but he didn't want her dead. He didn't even want her seriously injured. Sure, he'd scared her some and handled her with a firm grasp, but that wasn't anything out of the norm for the males of the Flock to do to the females—those who were beneath them. But that didn't mean he wanted her dead, and he wouldn't have really harmed her. Scared her, yes, caused her permanent injury, no.

"Father, if I can ensure this Bringer joins us, will you give me Amelia then?"

Cal laughed. "Campbell's dislike of you is very clear and quite sudden. It makes me wonder what happened prior to my arrival."

Taggert sighed. "I was attempting to take what I wanted from Amelia."

"Despite my explicit orders that she was to

remain untouched?" questioned Cal, standing eerily still.

Taggert nodded. "Yes. I know it was wrong, but the darkness in me is growing, Father. I need her. She'll keep it away. She's the key to my happiness."

"She will be with the Bringer. End of discussion."

"She will not obey," said Taggert. "You know her will is strong. Like her mother. Like you."

Shrugging, Cal continued to look at the river. "Then she shall meet the same fate her mother did."

Fear for Amelia crashed through Taggert. "No! I will not allow her to be harmed!"

Cal rounded on him, slashing out with talons that emerged from his fingertips in the blink of an eye. Huge white wings burst free from the back of the man, ripping through his shirt. Cal's eyes turned bright red and fangs flashed as he struck Taggert, knocking him off his feet.

Taggert's wolf struggled for freedom, wanting to go head to head with Cal. That was suicidal and Taggert knew it. He'd seen what Cal was capable of. The man had a little bit of every kind of supernatural imaginable within him after centuries of harvesting power from others.

Taggert rolled to his knees, bent his head, and put his arms out, showing he was submissive to Cal. "Father, please."

He waited, knowing there was a high chance Cal would deliver a killing blow. When Cal's hands, having returned to human form, found the top of Taggert's head, he looked up to find his leader staring down at him, the red gone from his eyes.

"My son," said Cal, the words warming Taggert. "We have spoken at great length about your darkness, have we not?"

"Yes, Father."

"And what did I tell you?"

Taggert let out a long breath. "That it is to be embraced, not feared."

Cal nodded. "Yes. You are a force to be reckoned with. An asset to me, to the Flock. But, Taggert, the Bringer will kill you if you push him too far, my son. And you should know, if I'm forced to pick between you and the Bringer, I will select him. Brian would be happy to fill in for you, if you were no more."

Taggert fell silent, forcing his wolf to stay

down. If it dared to challenge Cal, he'd end up dead. That being said, he wasn't about to lose Amelia to a Scottish dickhead.

No. He'd see to it the Bringer was no more—and then Taggert would take Amelia himself and run with her.

She would be his one way or another. Even Cal would not be able to stop him.

Chapter Fourteen

GRAM HELD the door to his cabin open for Amelia as she entered. She stopped hastily, and he nearly plowed into her. He caught her upper arms, steadying himself before glancing past her and spotting her little sister on the sofa, out cold.

Amelia twisted partially, her hand coming to Gram's chest. The action made his entire body bustle with need. She gifted him the world's most picturesque smile. "She never sleeps without me holding her," she said softly. "And never this soundly. Clearly, she trusts you. That's rare."

"She's precious," said Gram, kissing the top of Amelia's head before realizing what he'd done. He stiffened.

She leaned into him more, not seeming the

least bit put off by his affection. He was glad one of them was fine with it because it was freaking him the fuck out. He'd never been this attracted to a woman this fast.

Not even Brooke.

"Did you really have visions of me before coming here?" she asked.

"Aye."

She bit at her lower lip. "Um, I had a weird dream. In it, I was with a man who looks a lot like you from behind."

She'd dreamt of him?

"Looked a lot like me or *was* me?" he asked, desperate to hear her response.

"Never mind. It's not important."

He begged to differ but didn't push the issue as he stepped away from her and went for a throw blanket on the back of a chair near the sofa. He covered the little one with the blanket and tucked it around her gently before standing tall once more. When he turned, he found Amelia watching him with a curious expression on her face.

He winked. "I've had some practice with wee ones."

"You have children?" she asked, her voice still

low. There was a coyness about her that he wanted to see go away. He didn't want her to be withdrawn with him.

Gram shook his head. "There is a little one who I see as a daughter, but I'm nae her biological father. She and her mother have been reunited with the wee one's birth father. They are a happy family unit now. She's about yer sister's age."

Amelia came closer and took his hand in hers. She nodded to her sister. "Andie was born when I was almost nineteen. When I found out my mom was expecting, I didn't want a sibling. I didn't want to share her. She was my world. Then I held Andie and couldn't imagine life without her in it."

"Lass, I do nae think we need to whisper. I can hear her heartbeat. She's in a deep sleep," said Gram, glancing around the cabin for the first time. It had its own living room area, a dining room section, and an open, small kitchen. There were two doors that were open, each showing a king bed within. He assumed a bathroom was in at least one, possibly both rooms. Everything was decorated like the lobby in the main building.

Amelia stepped closer, stealing a peek at the bedroom to the right. "Huh, I always wondered what this cabin looked like inside. I wonder if all the guest ones are like this."

"Lass, yer family owns this place and you do nae know what the cabins look like?"

She shrugged. "I know what the one I grew up in looks like, and I know what my father's looks like, but I haven't been in any of the guest ones ever."

Gram stilled. "You do nae live with yer father?"

"My sister and I live on the grounds. Well, a bit from here, but with nearly two thousand acres of land, a lot of things are spread out. But no, we don't live, nor have we ever lived, in our father's cabin. It's the main house on the compound side of things. When my mother was alive, he'd summon her to his home when he needed to, um…well, I guess you could say scratch his manly urges but didn't want to do so with another female from the Flock. Other than that, he didn't really interact a lot with us."

Amelia entered the bedroom to the right and walked to the back window. She opened the blinds and pointed out into the distance. "Our place is that way. It's not super big but it's perfect for just

Andie and myself. Our father's is about a ten-minute walk from there."

"Lass, I do nae understand," said Gram, easing up next to her. "I've never heard of a mated pair living separate. And I've never heard of a male who is mated being able to lie with other women. As you know, children for supernaturals are rare and a gift. I do nae know of many who would be separated in any fashion from their wee ones."

She didn't respond. She touched the window lightly, looking lost in thought. "I didn't want to like you."

"Come again, lass?"

Focusing on something outside, Amelia didn't face him. "The Bringer."

Gram lifted a brow, unsure what in the world she was talking about.

"I thought you'd be like him—like Cal."

"Lass, you call yer father by his name, nae *Da?*" he asked.

She put her forehead to the glass. "He had a hand in our creation, but he's not, nor has he ever been, a father to Andie and me. And no, our mother wasn't his mate."

Gram snorted. "To have children with anyone

who is nae yer mate is nearly impossible. And in those cases, it takes great power to make it so. With great power comes a great price." As the words left his mouth, he thought about their mother being dead. Had that been the price?

Had the fates demanded her mother's life?

Amelia pressed a smile to her face and glanced at him. It was easy to see she didn't want to discuss the topic anymore. "I should take Andie and let you get back to what you'd been doing before you found me. Wait. How *did* you find me?"

He inclined his head in the direction of the other room. "Yer sister told me where you were. She asked me to help you."

Amelia's smile faded. With a huff, she hurried past him, back into the other room, and went for her sister. She lifted the little one, who didn't so much as stir, and held her to her in a caring manner. The feral look in her eyes told him she'd do anything to protect her sister and that she'd make a good mother.

"Lass? Yer upset with me. Why?"

She snorted and shook her head. "Did Cal put you up to this? Did he stage the whole thing? It would be a very him thing to do. Send his right-hand man in to scare me and then send the Bringer in to save the day and make me see you as a white knight. Your plan has a big hole in it—Cal apparently forgot to mention Andie doesn't speak. Ever. She's not said a word in two years since she watched our mother being killed."

Gram flinched. The wee one had seen her mother being slain?

Amelia pivoted and went for the door, carrying her sister, who was no doubt dead weight with as tired as she'd been.

"Lass, wait. Andie *did* tell me where to find you. She introduced herself to me and told me I talk funny. She also asked me to help you. And something about someone being wrong about me," he said, desperate for Amelia to believe him though he wasn't sure why. The very idea of her storming off in anger didn't sit well with him.

Amelia opened the door to leave, paused, cupped the back of Andie's head and glanced quickly at Gram.

He could see the indecision in her eyes. In that moment, he wanted to kill everyone who had ever caused her to get to the point in her young life where she held that much mistrust of others. What had she endured? And where could he find the person responsible? He'd make their death painful.

The next he knew, his wolf was weighing in on matters. It swelled upward, wanting to be free, wanting to hunt the culprit. Evidently, it had taken a shine to Amelia as well. His eyes tingled, and he knew they'd shifted colors.

Amelia backed up fast—and the doorway behind her filled instantly with twin Scotsmen.

Mac was the one who reached out and caught her, keeping her from falling. Still, seeing the unmated male's hands on the arms of his woman was too much.

Mine.

Snarling filled the air, as did the crackle of power.

Mac pulled Amelia and Andie back and out of the cabin as Car rushed in, throwing his arms out wide, fur sprouting on them. As claws emerged from the wolf-shifter's fingertips, Gram found himself and his beast answering the challenge.

Vaguely, he heard a woman arguing with someone—pleading with them. Through the red haze of alpha rage, Gram looked over to see Amelia in the doorway, minus Andie, a worried look on her face as she begged Car to let her past. To let her come to Gram.

"Campbell, pull it together!" shouted Car, his arms still out wide as he tried to keep himself between Gram and Amelia.

It was then Gram realized the twins were attempting to protect Amelia and Andie. That they thought Gram would hurt them.

That cooled his rage almost instantly.

The static in the air dissipated, and while his wolf lingered near the surface, it stopped thrusting up.

"Gram?" asked Amelia, her voice shaky. "What's wrong? They said they're your friends. Are they not with you?"

"What's wrong is he's an alpha. They've all got rocks for brains," said Bill, pushing into the cabin. Thankfully, he was wearing a robe and a pair of boxers with the resort's logo on them. He still had on the flip-flops. "When are you guys gonna learn?"

Confused, Gram stood there taking the verbal lashing from the small, insane man.

Car righted himself, the fur and nails vanishing instantly. "Yer an arse, Campbell."

"Little ears," said Mac loudly from outside the

cabin. He stepped in and was holding a sleeping Andie in his arms.

Gram blinked several times. "What happened?"

"Aye, what happened indeed," repeated Car. "We were nearly to yer cabin to tell you the guid news—we've a cabin of our own now, next to yers —when all of a sudden, the door opened and out popped a family."

Mac shook his head, still holding Andie to him. "Campbell, yer nae here to find fill-ins for what you lost. Yer here to heal your mind, body, and soul. Fighting with yer friends over a woman and her babe willnae help that any."

"Fill-ins?" asked Amelia, staring wide-eyed up at Mac.

Mac cleared his throat. "Nae my place to say."

Car grunted. "I'll say it. This meathead just got out of a serious relationship with a woman who looks a lot like you, from what I've been told. She also just so happens to have a little girl yer daughter's age. It's verra clear to see he has a type of woman he goes for. You know, the unobtainable ones with ready-made families. And trust me, lass, you do nae want to be his rebound chick."

Bill stared at the wall a second. "Gus says the kid is Amelia's sister. Not her daughter."

Amelia gasped. "How do you know my name?"

Bill tapped his temple. "Got told it. You okay?"

"Yes," she said, putting her arms out for Mac to hand her Andie. "I'm sorry I just thrust her at you. I was scared Gram was going to attack your brother."

Car grinned. "Wouldnae be the first time Campbell and I went rounds."

Mac kept hold of Andie. "Lass, tell me where to take her and I'll carry her for you. The wee one sleeps soundly, and she's nae that light for you. She is to me. Let me help."

Amelia glanced at Gram and then pried Andie from Mac's arms. She held her sister to her. "We're fine on our own. And we're no one's fill-ins. No one's rebound anything."

With that, she stormed out of the cabin.

Gram attempted to go after her but found a wall of men in his path.

Bill took the lead, which was amusing to say the least. "Hold your horses there, bucko. Don't you think you've done enough already? That sweet girl needs a friend and someone to trust. Not someone looking to make her a replacement for what he's lost."

Gram began to protest but stopped. Was that what he was doing? Was he trying to fill the void in his life with the first set of people who fit the bill? Did he see Amelia as a substitute for Brooke, and Andie as one for Bethany?

The thought sobered him, and he stepped back, needing to sit down. He went to a dining room chair, took a seat, and then lowered his head into his hands.

Someone touched his shoulder, and he assumed it was one of the twins. When he looked up to find Gus, of all people, his hand on Gram's shoulder, he stiffened.

It was meant to be, said the voice once more in his head.

As Gram stared at Gus, he started to wonder if the voice was his.

The strange man kept his head turned partly, avoiding eye contact.

If it was so meant to be, how is it I managed to fuck it up so royally? he asked down what he hoped was the same mental pathway the voice had originated from.

Simple. If it was easy, anyone could do it. Love is never meant to be easy.

With a snort, Gram bent his head. Of course he'd get a version of fortune cookie wisdom from the voice in his head. As he thought harder on it all, he exhaled a shaky breath. "I do nae see Brooke or Bethany when I look at Amelia and Andie. Yes, I noticed the similarities in ages of the wee ones, but that is all."

"What *do* you see?" asked Bill.

"A future. Happiness." The words slipped from his mouth in something of a hushed whisper. It was as if he were afraid to dare say them too loud. If he did, fate might hear and spite him.

The men all shared glances that said they were concerned. So was Gram. He tried again to go after Amelia, but his friends shook their heads.

"Campbell, you were about to attack us over her. Yer head isnae on straight. James mentioned yer refusing to take the meds he gave you. Let's take some time to gather our thoughts and take a few deep breaths."

"You've a massage on the books," added Car, stepping forward. "Go there now. If anyone needs servicing to loosen up, it's you. Mayhap a hand job will help to clear yer head and get the new lass from yer mind."

The idea of any woman touching him sexually except for Amelia repulsed him.

When he realized the list of women he didn't want touching him now included his ex, he gasped.

They were right. He needed to clear his head. While he hadn't wanted to be at the resort to start with, he couldn't fathom leaving now that he was here. But he wasn't safe to be around in his current state. He did need to relax.

Then he could find Amelia and make her understand he didn't see her as a fill-in for anyone. And she wasn't a rebound chick. Not to him.

She was so very, very much more.

You do nae even know her, he said to himself. *Just leave the lass be.*

Gus began to turn in a circle quickly, appearing agitated.

Bill put his palm to his forehead, looking tired. "Really, Gram-cracker, are all of you alpha males this thick?"

Car laughed. "Gram-cracker. I'm using that."

Gram made a move to go at the small, yet annoying man.

Mac and Car leapt to Bill's defense.

Mac pointed at him. "Yer getting rubbed down whether you like it or nae! 'Tis nae an option, Campbell."

Bill stuck out his tongue.

Gram pointed at him. "I will hunt you down and end you."

With a roll of his eyes, Bill did a fake yawn. "I've had so many of you threaten me it means nothing. I've lost track of the number of you guys who say you're gonna eat me or kill me. All talk, no show. Alphas my ass. I'm more scared of Mona." He pointed to Gus. "We've got to get to our colonics appointment. My pipes need cleaned."

All the men cringed.

Chapter Fifteen

AMELIA CARRIED Andie through their modest
cabin in the direction of the bedroom that had
been Amelia's when she was her sister's age. The
cabin's interior wasn't painted in the same white
and beiges that coated nearly everything in the
compound. No. Their mother had gotten paint
from Jeanie and the two women had painted the
two bedrooms and main living area themselves.
The bedroom that was now Andie's was painted
in yellow, as that had been Amelia's favorite color
when she was younger. Andie seemed to like it, so
she made no attempt to change it.

She squeezed her sister more as she entered
the room, thinking about what Gram had said.

When he'd told her Andie had spoken to him,

she'd felt so betrayed. As if it was the greatest slight she'd suffered in her life. It wasn't, by far, but that didn't take from the feeling any. It was as if she was holding Gram to a higher standard than she did others in her life, and she barely knew the man.

It was grossly unfair, and she recognized as much now.

Still, the idea of him plotting with Cal turned her stomach. She hated her father. She didn't want to hate Gram. The idea actually sickened her, but she couldn't understand why.

Maybe she was wrong. Maybe he wasn't in league with Cal and the others.

But why had he lied to her?

Andie didn't speak.

She hadn't talked since the night she'd screamed in horror at the sight of their mother being eaten by a group of monsters. It was forever etched in Amelia's brain, and she knew it was in her sister's as well. At the time, Amelia hadn't understood what the things were that had been brought in to punish her mother for her transgression—for daring to want to keep her daughters safe from a madman and his followers. It wasn't until Helmuth had come to stay at the resort that

Amelia had finally figured out what the monsters were.

Hybrids.

She'd heard Taggert and Brian talking about it once. They hadn't known she was close, hiding behind a tree, listening as they laughed about Cal's orders to have it done and how fast the hybrids had devoured Amelia's mother. They joked about having Helmuth send more to make disposing of the bodies of the runaways and fodder Flock members much easier.

Bile rose just thinking about it all.

Hate burned deep in her for her father, for Taggert, for Brian, for every one of them who stood side by side with evil. She could only hope they one day got their due, but she doubted it would ever come to pass. Cal was too powerful. Too connected. He'd made bedfellows of powerful people who were as twisted as he was. Maybe more.

No.

Amelia would have to settle for gaining freedom from him. From the Flock.

She'd take Andie and they'd find a new country to settle in, with new names and a new, brighter future. They wouldn't be pawns in a power struggle. And they wouldn't be fed to monsters.

Never.

Amelia glanced at the lonely shelf of a few toys in her sister's room. On it were three dolls their mother had made for Amelia when she was little. They were handsewn and made from left-over material Jeanie had been kind enough to give them. They'd been prized possessions to Amelia when she was little. Much like Andie's red ball was to her. She'd been given the ball by the dragon-shifter who had passed through the resort. He'd made an impression on Andie as well. Unlike Cal, who tried to gift Andie with expensive dolls, custom made for her that had to cost a fortune. The type of things the rest of the Flock didn't have. He'd tried the same thing when Amelia was younger, but her mother had refused to allow her to have them.

That had been fine by Amelia. She hadn't wanted them anyway. Even from a young age she could sense the bad on her father. The truth behind his false smile.

Andie refused to play with the expensive gifts or even accept them from Cal directly. It was Amelia who took them from their father to keep his wrath far from Andie. The bedroom closet was full of them. It was actually kind of creepy. They kept the door to it closed tight.

"Oh no," whispered Amelia, as she realized she'd left her sister's ball at Gram's cabin. She entertained going back for it while carrying her sister, but the twin who had pointed out Andie was heavy was right. She was. Amelia would have to retrieve it later in the day because she'd need it with her when she ran. Andie wouldn't want to be without it for long.

Placing Andie in the bed with great care and ease, Amelia kissed her forehead and went for a blanket at the foot of the bed. Staring down at her sister, she choked up slightly as she thought of how much the little girl meant to her. She was Amelia's world. All she had left, and she'd die to protect her.

Amelia made a move to back away, wanting her to rest.

Andie's eyes shot open and she gasped. While she'd managed to sleep through all the talking and being moved from one location to another, putting her in her own bed did the trick to wake her. It also scared her, which broke Amelia's heart.

Amelia touched her sister's forehead gently and sat on the edge of the bed.

"I'm right here, sweetie," she soothed as Andie looked around her room and appeared confused. "I carried you home."

Andie stared up at her, looking so innocent, so sweet.

"Did you go into Mr. Campbell's cabin willingly? Do you know who I'm talking about? You were resting in his cabin."

Nodding, Andie sat up and put her hand over Amelia's.

Amelia tipped her head. "He didn't make you go in, did he?"

Andie shook her head.

"Was he nice to you?"

Nodding, Andie gave Amelia's hand a tiny squeeze.

Amelia let out a strained laugh that wanted to be a sob. "Sweetie, he said something I didn't believe. He said you told him I needed help. That you talked to him. Did you?"

"Yes."

Air swooshed out of Amelia's lungs as shock hit her full on. It was the first word she'd heard her sister speak in two years.

She'd given up hope that Andie would ever talk again, thinking for sure that trauma would leave her forever silent.

Emotions welled, and the next Amelia knew she had Andie yanked to her, hugging her tight, rocking her as she did. They'd been through so much together and Amelia had sworn to always protect her, to always keep her safe, but had felt as if she was failing.

She cupped Andie's face, still crying. "Sweetie, we're going to do it tomorrow. We're going to run far from here, just like I promised. We'll go and we'll never look back."

Another thought hit Amelia. Gram had been telling the truth.

Amelia had thought the worst of Gram, and he'd been honest with her. She owed him an apology.

"Amelia," whispered Andie, her eyes moist as well. "We can't go without him."

"Sure we can," said Amelia, though the thought of never seeing Gram again made her chest ache and feel as if something heavy was sitting upon it. "We have to, sweetie. Everything will be ready for us to go tomorrow. We have to leave then, or we'll miss our window."

Andie took a deep breath and moved to her knees on the bed. A serious expression came over her. She reached out and wiped Amelia's cheeks dry. "We gotta be with him. He's our family now. We all need to stay together. We're stronger together."

Puzzled, Amelia shook her head. "He's not related to us. It'll be just you and me. And I'll take you far from here and from Cal. Like Mom wanted."

Andie sighed. "*No*. We have to be with Gram."

Amelia fixed her sister's hair. It was slightly tussled from her nap. "He's Gram to you already? And you talked to him after not talking to anyone for a very long time? I take it that means you trust him and like him."

"Yes. I trust him," said Andie in a very grown-up voice. "So do you."

It was on the tip of Amelia's tongue to correct Andie—until she realized her sister was right. On a deeper level, she did trust the man, even having only just met him.

"Gus told me Gram was coming. And he said Gram would be nice and good to us. He's right. Cal is wrong," said Andie.

She shook her tiny head. "Gus talks in my head and I talk in his. We can both do it because we're both special. He said so. He said you can hear Gram too in your head if you listen hard, and Gram can hear you. Gus talked in my head before he came here. He said he was coming and bringing us help. That they would all make sure we were safe."

Amelia fought to keep from crying harder. She'd been so excited to hear Andie talk that she'd thought her sister was cured. That she'd be fine so long as they got far away from their insane father. If Andie was hearing voices, things were far from fine.

"You don't gotta be scared," said Andie, inching forward on the bed. "Gus is our friend. So is Bill. And so are Car and Mac. We gots lots of friends now, Amelia. A big family now. It will be even bigger soon when your babies come."

Amelia stood so fast that she stumbled backward, her eyes wide.

Babies? She wasn't having any babies.

Giggling, Andie slid off the bed and came right for Amelia. She took her sister's hand in hers. "First Gram is gonna make you his wife. Then I'm gonna be a big sister."

Amelia bent and put her hands on Andie's shoulders. "You're not making any sense, sweetie. I'm so excited to hear you talk, but what you're saying is silly. Gram just met me. He's not going to make me his wife. I'm not having any babies. Unless you mean Cal is going to father more children with someone. Do you?"

"Cal will never have any more kids," she said softly. "He's been very bad. Bad men get punished."

"Don't talk like him, Andie."

"But it's true. He will be punished for what he's done. He's been very bad, Amelia," she said in a hushed tone. "He had the monsters hurt Mommy. And he's done other mean and bad things. Gus says he's gonna get his."

Amelia touched her sister's cheek. "Sweetie, I love you so much. And we are going to leave here tomorrow. And we are not taking Gram with us. We can't. We don't really know him."

Andie giggled. "You know him."

"Barely."

Andie touched Amelia's upper chest. "Your soul knows him, and his knows yours. Gus said so. Said it's meant to be."

Andie couldn't possibly mean Gram was

Amelia's mate, could she? For one, she was little and there was no way she could understand mating. For two, mates were very rare. Amelia knew as much. The odds Gram was hers were slim.

"Gram is gonna make you his wife. He's gonna love you and me a lot," said Andie, smiling. "He's gonna be my *new* daddy. A better daddy. A good daddy. Not like the bad one I have now. The bad one I have now is gonna be punished."

Amelia shook her head. "Sweetie, no one is going to marry anyone or be anyone's daddy. We're leaving here tomorrow and we're never looking back."

"There you are," said Susan from the hallway, startling Amelia.

She'd never heard the woman enter the cabin.

Dread filled her as she wondered how much Susan had overheard. Did she know of Amelia's plan now? If so, she'd go straight to Cal. Amelia would be next to be eaten by monsters.

Amelia took Andie's hand and eased her sister behind her, wanting to keep her safe from the woman.

Susan glanced down at Andie and curled her

lip. "You're to stay here for the rest of the day. Your sister is needed at the resort."

Amelia tensed, praying that Andie wouldn't speak in front of Susan. If they'd gotten lucky enough that Susan hadn't overheard their conversation, she didn't want Cal to know Andie was talking again. They didn't need the added attention that would bring. Not with their escape so close at hand. All she wanted to do was go and take her sister far from the Flock.

Andie tugged on her hand.

Amelia glanced down at her sister.

We gotta be with Gram.

Gasping, Amelia blinked. Had she just heard her sister in her mind?

Go with Susan. Do what she wants. I'll be safe here. Gus and Bill are gonna come sit with me. They won't let anything happen to me. Trust me. Trust them.

For a split second, Amelia worried she'd pass out. Somehow, she managed to stay upright.

"Are you coming?" snapped Susan.

Nodding, Amelia released her sister's hand and bent, kissing the top of Andie's head. "I love you."

"Hurry up. You have somewhere special to be," said Susan snidely.

It took everything Amelia had to refrain from calling the woman a bitch. Instead, she left Andie in her room and followed Susan out into the main portion of the cabin. Just then, one of the older women in the Flock entered and offered a warm smile.

The woman was one Amelia trusted.

Relief washed over her.

Susan hurried past the woman and out of the cabin with Amelia following close behind. The last thing Amelia wanted to do was separate from her sister, but she knew if she gave the rest of the Flock any reason to suspect they were set to run, they'd never make it out alive.

Susan centered her attention on Amelia. There was no mistaking the lecherous smile that covered her face. "Your presence is required in the spa area."

Tina appeared on the path and offered a soft smile behind Susan's back. She winked.

Amelia exhaled and followed Susan as she stormed down a path that opened to one of the smaller roads. Brian was there on an all-terrain four-seater vehicle that looked a lot like a miniature Jeep. He laughed when he saw Amelia.

"I figured you'd have to drag the little virgin

by the hair," said Brian with a snort. "Was I wrong? Is she eager to wrap her mouth around the Bringer's cock? Can't wait to tell Taggert she didn't put up a fight."

Cringing, Amelia avoided looking at the man as she climbed into the backseat of the vehicle. Tina sat next to her as Susan went to the front passenger side.

Susan was positively beaming. "Tina was on the books for the Bringer's massage before Cal informed us the VIP coming was actually the Bringer, but obviously that has changed. I just hope the little bitch remembers what we taught her. If she fails to snare the Bringer, she's going to have to deal with Father. When we get there, I'll be sure Amelia changes into something else. Something better suited for the event."

Tina reached out quickly, taking hold of Amelia's hand, giving it a gentle, reassuring squeeze. "You can do this, Amelia. Just like we've shown you before. Okay?"

Unable to keep hold of her emotions, Amelia began to cry softly. She didn't want to be whored out to anyone. It was especially bitter to swallow knowing her own father was the man orchestrating it all. That he'd set the plan in motion years ago, unconcerned with the fact he was forcing his own daughter to trade sexual favors to win over some man.

Not just some man.

Gram.

Before long, they were at the main resort area and parking behind the spa. Brian turned to face her and licked his lower lip. "Wonder if, after you're done fucking the Bringer, we'll all get a piece of you. The rest of the women in the Flock are fair game."

Tina held Amelia's hand tighter.

Once before, Amelia had listened as Tina confessed that Brian had perverse sexual tastes. That he was cruel in the bedroom and got off on pain just as much, if not more than Taggert. Tina had firsthand experience, having been forced to be with the men more than once.

Tina was part succubus and required sex and sexual energy to survive, but there were plenty of men in the Flock for her to pick from. Being forced to be with Taggert and Brian was a form of punishment. One that had been handed down by Susan.

Amelia knew Susan was jealous of Tina. She had a natural allure that appealed greatly to the opposite sex. It had a lot to do with the succubus in her.

Susan also disliked Tina because of how much Cal called upon Tina's services. Cal bedded the succubus often, infuriating Susan. Tina had also gotten stuck dealing with Helmuth during his stay at the resort. The man had a thing for succubi. He also had a strange habit of turning to stone.

That had been something Amelia had never seen before.

Helmuth was as into pain as Taggert and Brian, from what Tina had told her.

Amelia hated that her friend was left in such a situation. She'd tried more than once to convince Tina to go on the run with her and Andie. Tina refused but she never gave a reason why.

Susan exited the vehicle and cast Amelia a hard look. "Come on. We need to get you changed into something more fitting. You better make the Bringer happy. If you fuck this up, there will be hell to pay."

Tina released her hand but gave an encouraging nod as she stepped out of the vehicle. "I can get the room all set up and see to the Bringer to start with. I'll just have him get ready for Amelia. Nothing more."

"Do so now," said Susan.

Brian motioned to Amelia. "Suz, call for me if she starts screaming. I want to listen, too."

"Of course," said Susan.

Amelia wiped her cheeks, knowing if she kept crying, it would only serve to make the two sociopaths happy.

Chapter Sixteen

GRAM DIDN'T WANT anyone looking at his back, let alone touching it. All he wanted to do was seek out Amelia and spend time with her. He wanted to stress that he'd been truthful. Andie had spoken to him. She had told him Amelia needed help. The idea that Amelia thought Gram was scheming with her father ripped at his gut.

Gram stiffened and stared at the floor through the opening in the massage table. A panicked sensation of needing to find Amelia swept over him, and he was about to act on it when the door to the room opened.

Just like that, the feeling died.

The room filled quickly with her scent—the scent of honeysuckle and vanilla—and for a moment hope spread through him that she was in the room. But just like that, the smell was overrun with lavender and something else. It took Gram a moment to place the scents. Comfrey leaves and calendula flowers.

He lay there, face down on the massage table, wearing only a towel over his backside. Gram's eyes widened as his cock lengthened from the scents wrapping around him. Thankfully he was lying face down, or it would be really obvious he was turned on. He'd never had an instant reaction to anyone before, especially from just a scent.

Deep down, he knew the person in the room with him was female. He also knew he didn't want to be there. He just wanted to see Amelia and fix things with her.

As the woman's hands came into contact with his skin, Gram gasped. Heat rushed through him, centering in his groin. He jerked, fearful he'd ejaculate then and there. His wolf came to life within him, wanting to be free. It surged up with a force he'd not felt in weeks. As his mouth tingled with a pending shift, his eyes widened. Losing control of himself and changing shapes in the middle of a spa was not what he wanted to have happen.

It didn't matter if the spa was well-acquainted

with supernaturals or not. With as unstable as his body and his wolf were, Gram didn't want to risk lives should he lose control of his beast. And right about now, it felt as if he'd morph into a wolf and never turn human again.

He felt that disconnected from himself. From his control.

The person massaging him rubbed deeper, her fingers like magik on his skin. Each spot she made contact with instantly felt better. As if her hands were a tonic, bringing with them relief that he'd been seeking for weeks. But now that he had relief, he wanted to get away from it, fearful of his primeval reaction. One too many times he'd seen an alpha male lose control and the end results were devastating.

He couldn't allow that to happen.

Get control of yerself, Campbell.

Scolding himself did little to lessen his response to the female's touch. His balls drew up, tightening, and he groaned, going ramrod stiff, sure he'd lose it and come then and there. The last thing he wanted was word getting around that Striker's idea of a special massage had not only worked to get Gram "back in the game," but it had worked so well he'd come before it really got started.

She worked the knots in his upper shoulders and neck, giving him much-needed relief before working her way down his back slowly, each touch taking him close to the edge of culmination.

As the woman's hands found their way to his lower back, where he'd had so much pain as of late, he tensed more, preparing for pain.

None came.

In fact, there was a total absence of any sort of pain in his back.

She worked the kinks out of the area with an expert touch. Gram would have questioned if the woman was a witch with honest-to-gods healing magik, but at the moment he was pretty sure she was a siren. His cock thought so, anyway.

He wanted to adjust himself but there was no way to handle the matter without being totally and completely obvious. While his buddies might be fine getting special massages, he wasn't. He didn't want to turn the session into a sexual escapade. Sadly, his dick didn't get the memo. It was totally and completely fine with the session going south.

The woman's hands skimmed over one of his

scars, ever so lightly, as if she didn't want to make contact with them. He couldn't blame her.

Need caused his gut to clench. As much as he didn't want his scars on display or touched, he didn't want to lose contact with her.

Fuck his scars.

He wanted to be caressed by her more than he wanted to shy away from the view of others.

If he dared to look at whoever was massaging him, he'd probably do something extra stupid and try to hump her. Anything was possible with as out of whack as his body and wolf were.

He groaned.

Whatever the fuck had happened to him during the attack had left him a hot mess. His feelings were foreign to him and his reactions made no sense. One second he wanted to rush out and claim a woman he'd only just met, and the next he was perfectly content to remain where he was.

He ran hot to cold.

The fucking Corporation had broken him probably beyond repair. How could he heal when he didn't even understand what all was wrong?

Mac and Car thought he needed to clear his

head, but what he needed—what he wanted—was Amelia. She consumed his thoughts.

Protect her.

Your mate.

His mind raced back to the voice he'd heard in his head upon arriving. He thought harder on his reaction to Amelia. Of how seeing her being manhandled by Taggert had left him wanting to kill the bastard. The need to touch her had been overpowering.

His gums began to burn, a sign his wolf incisors were about to push through. The sound of his racing pulse filled his head and he closed his eyes tight, doing his best to control the urge to rush from the room, seek out Amelia, and claim her.

As it all came together in his head, the warning, the visions, the reaction to her, he gasped. Could it be true? Could Amelia really be his mate?

No.

The odds were…

He thought of all the men he knew who had mated over the last year. There had been a rash of matings within PSI and I-Ops. He'd once heard someone say they came in clusters. Did he dare to hope that he not only had a mate, but that he'd somehow ended up placed in the same spot as her when he needed her most?

He needed to find Amelia and see if he was right. If she was who he was fast starting to suspect she was.

Gram nearly leapt off the massage table. As he went to move, someone touched his back, just below one of his many scars. Warmth spread through his body and it centered in his groin. He was sure he was going to come. This time his incisors did break free. His jaw began to re-form, taking on the characteristics of a wolf.

Fearing he'd lose control and hurt whoever was with him, he tried to speak, but couldn't form words with how far gone his mouth was.

Panic assailed him, and he nearly reached out to Mac and Car via their mental links for help. They'd be able to contain him and keep him from doing anything stupid, like hunting down Amelia and claiming her before she was ready for him.

As he thought about how his body was reacting to being touched by another woman, his elation over possibly finding his mate died almost instantly.

If Amelia was truly his mate, Gram wouldn't

be able to get an erection with any other woman. His body would only crave its mate after meeting her. That was simply the way of it with shifters. He didn't know if it worked the same for other supernaturals, but he did understand the ins and outs of shifter matings.

The fact he had a dick currently hard enough to cut glass meant he was wrong. Amelia wasn't his mate.

He grabbed the massage table and gripped it tight as his disappointment coursed through him. He'd been so sure. The idea had felt right, as if he'd been waiting for her all his immortally long life.

It still felt that way.

He made a mental note to reach out to Auberi or James after his massage and confess what happened. They might be able to shed light on why his senses were telling him one thing when that couldn't possibly be the case. That, or they'd confirm everything still wrong with him was psychosomatic and he was basically fucked.

Either way, he'd have more answers than he did now.

All he had to do now was avoid coming while getting his back rubbed. He'd never hear the end of it if he did. The special massage didn't even need to enter bedroom territory for him to lose his load.

He groaned, his thoughts going right back to Amelia. To her eyes, to her flawless skin, her long brown hair, and her scent. He and the wolf wanted Amelia. The intensity with which he longed for her was the only thing that kept him in place. He knew if he dared get up, he'd hunt her down and more than likely attempt to have his way with her. His willpower was that shaky.

The fierce need to lay claim to Amelia was quickly tempered by the knowledge that she already thought herself a replacement for Brooke. A fill-in. Thanks to Car, he'd have that mess to clean up before he could even attempt to see if anything more could develop. Mate or not, he wanted to be near her.

Hell. Who was he kidding? He wanted to be in her.

"Gram," whispered a soft voice.

One that made need slam through him. One he knew.

When he realized it was Amelia's hands on his back, that she was the one massaging him, he gasped and sat up faster than he should have,

MANDY M. ROTH

considering that all he had was one towel draped over his ass. Other than that, he was naked.

It had been her hands on him all along? He really had caught her scent to start with?

His body hadn't reacted to some other woman. It had reacted to *her*. Hope surged through him.

Looking up, he found Amelia there, her hazel gaze snapping to his exposed erection. Her eyes widened, and she leapt back as if his cock were a snake about to bite her. In many ways, it was.

Gram was torn between laughing and being mortified. It was an equal split.

"Good goddess, did *it* just get bigger?" asked Amelia, her upper chest flushing with pink.

Gram was positive he was about to shoot a load all over his leg at the rate he was going. He grabbed his cock, attempting to shield it from view. Even with two hands, he couldn't cover it all. He'd never been ashamed of his body before he'd been hurt and scarred. As a shifter, nudity came with the territory. But the woman he was positive was his mate looked like she might pass out at the sight of him naked.

Never a good sign.

Of course she'd find the sight of his scarred

body repulsive. "Lass."

She just stared at him, her eyes still wide.

He grabbed for the towel and brought it over his groin quickly. There was so much he wanted to say. The problem was, Gram couldn't focus. Not with her there, looking stunning in a nearly sheer white gown that was different from the other one she'd been in. This one gifted him a view of her nipples—and the fact she had nothing on beneath the dress. All he had to do was lift the dress and he'd find paradise.

Sitting up fully, he draped his long legs over the edge of the table. He noted the look of shock on Amelia's face, and his cock picked then to wilt. "Lass, I'll put clothes on. You do nae have to be alone in here with me. I know yer scared of me, and you do nae care much for me. And I know I'm no prize to look upon. Nae now. Nae after what happened."

"W-what?" she asked, as if coming out of a daze. She met his gaze. "Scared of you? I'm not. It's just, well, I wasn't expecting you to be so… much. Not that I'm complaining or anything. I just don't know how to respond or act. I really want to play it cool, like it's no big deal to have you naked in a room with me, but the rest of me is thinking I should run away, that you're way more man than I can handle. And what do you mean by no prize? Wait. Do you think you're unattractive? You can't be serious. You're the most attractive man I've ever seen, like, ever, and in case you missed it, I live in a compound with hundreds of males."

Relief that she didn't think he was hideous came over him. "You find me attractive?"

"Yes. Very." Nodding, her gaze slinked down him, and she bit at her lower lip. It was then he caught scent of her desire. The smell was pure perfection, bringing his cock back to life at once.

At the rate he was going, he'd never be able to walk right. Not from his injuries but from an endless hard-on.

There were worse things to suffer from.

"Amelia."

She jumped in place slightly as he said her name. Her gaze snapped to his. "Yes?"

"I find you verra, verra, verra attractive, too."

"Oh. Okay," she said in a shy manner that suited her—a second before she lurched backward. "Oh! Um, yes. Thank you?"

Gram did his best to avoid laughing. It didn't quite work. He had a pretty good idea that she wasn't well versed on the inner workings between men and women. That only served to make him happier. If happy thoughts really could make someone fly, he'd be able to go around the world twice over.

She thought he was attractive and more than likely didn't have an ex who would swoop in and try to take her from Gram. The very idea of a man attempting such a thing set him on edge. He growled.

She jerked more.

"Lass, no," he said quickly. "My wolf and my imagination got the better of me. By chance, you do nae have a long-lost love that you've had a child with, do you?"

She glanced around the room.

"What are you looking for?"

"Medicinal marijuana. It would explain your senseless line of questioning." She righted herself, easing away from the door, keeping a safe distance from him. "No to all of that. I've never even had what someone would label a boyfriend. That isn't really done here with the Flock. Mostly, when you're of age, Cal hands you off to whoever he sees fit. Some men get more than one woman given to them."

"Cal is an arsehole," said Gram and then sighed. "Sorry, lass. I dinnae mean to call yer father such a thing."

Shrugging, a smile spread over her face. "It would be offensive if you were wrong. You're not."

Gram realized how dry his throat was and understood it had something to do with his state of longing for Amelia. "Lass, can I have some water? I'd get it myself but I'm nae in naught more than I was born in, and I'm worried you will pass out if I flash you again."

Her eyes tracked to his groin once more. "Yes. Let's get you me. Wait. I mean, let's get me some you. No. I mean *I'll* get you water. Don't move."

Gram snickered. "Aye. I'll be right here, waiting to be given you."

He winked.

She squeaked like a mouse, making him laugh as she fumbled to unlock the door. She didn't bother closing it, not that he cared. He strongly suspected she hadn't meant to leave it open but was in a hurry to put distance between them.

It had to be overwhelming for her. It was for him, and he had her by centuries. He could sense her age and she was barely into her twenties.

Chapter Seventeen

AMELIA HURRIED to the area where glass pitchers and fresh-cut fruit to infuse water was kept. The smell of lavender increased the closer she got to it. The scent was overpowering on purpose. At least that was what Tina had told her once. She said it kept supernaturals from being able to easily smell anything else.

As she turned the corner, she ran right into Brian. He caught hold of her and raked his gaze over her.

"Fuck, Amelia, you've been hiding a body like that all these years?" he asked, his very voice making her uneasy. He skimmed the backs of his fingers over her arm before gripping her once more.

She tried to squirm free of his grasp, but it didn't work.

Brian sniffed her, putting his face close to her neck. "You haven't done what was expected of you. You haven't fucked the Bringer. Cal is going to be disappointed, and we all know what happens when Father is upset."

"Let go of me, Brian," she said firmly, pushing on him, careful to only use a small portion of her strength. No sense tipping him off.

"Is there an issue?" asked Susan as she entered the area with papers in her hands. "Amelia, why are you out of the room? Do not tell me that you already managed to screw up making the VIP happy. Really, Amelia, it was a simple task. How hard could it be? Massage him everywhere, make him find release either with your hand or mouth. We were very clear in the training sessions."

Amelia's face reddened. The last thing she wanted to discuss was what she did and didn't do behind closed doors with Gram. Mostly, she just wanted away from Brian and his grabby hands. She tried again to break Brian's hold, but he didn't let go.

He glanced at Susan. "I could show her how it's done. But this time, we won't need one of you to demonstrate. She can learn on her own with me."

Susan arched a brow. "Taggert won't be pleased with you. He's already looking for excuses to attack the Bringer. You don't want to end up in his crosshairs too."

"He won't find out," said Brian. "You owe me, so you won't say a word. After all, I've not said a word about your little pets, have I?"

Pets?

Amelia wasn't sure what Brian wasn't talking about. Susan didn't have a pet that she was aware of. Or did she?

Susan grunted. "And you won't."

"Hey, what you do with a dozen Flock-fucks is your business. For now. But push me and Cal will find out you've been enthralling them and getting them to do your dirty work."

Amelia stiffened.

Brian grinned as he focused on Amelia once more. "I think we both know you hate Taggert."

She nodded. No point in denying as much. She hated Susan and Brian too, but she held that part back. Amelia knew better than to rock the boat this close to launching her escape plan.

Brian put a hand on her hip, and the idea of

letting him go onward twisted her gut and physically caused her pain. She didn't know why it hurt so much when all he was doing was making contact with her hip, but it did.

As much as she wanted to hide what she could do, there was no way her body would permit Brian to go forward with what he wanted.

Drawing upon her resolve, she yanked her arms free from his hold and stood tall, shaking her head. "Not happening. You even try it and I'll rip off anything that comes near me."

Susan's eyes widened, and the color drained from her face. For a female Flock member to speak to a ranking male in such a way wasn't just forbidden and not done, it was punishable in the worst way. Amelia wasn't sure if her position as Cal's daughter would protect her from Brian's wrath, and she didn't care. She wasn't going to back down.

"Back up. Last warning, Brian."

She expected to be struck.

When she found Brian looking at her as if he was proud of her, she couldn't help but be confused.

"Lass, there you are," said Gram, appearing in the doorway, wearing nothing more than a

towel around his waist. His entire body was chiseled and the scars only served to make him look
more rugged.

More manly.

More delicious.

When she'd first entered the massage room
and saw him there, on his stomach, his back on
display, her dream of running with the man who
had scars on his back came to her. It was then
she'd fully understood that she'd been dreaming
about fleeing with Gram.

Susan put on a fake smile but not before she'd
looked her fill of Gram's nearly nude form. The
scars did nothing to take from how spectacular he
was, and Susan clearly noticed. "Mr. Campbell,
my apologies that Amelia is lacking in the skills
department. I'll call for Tina. She'll be able to see
to your needs. Or, if you'd prefer, I could handle
them."

"Like hell," snapped Amelia, surprising
herself at her tenacity. She clenched a fist, ready
to sock Susan a good one if she even so much as
exhaled any closer to Gram. No way was the
woman going to handle anything for him. Gram
was hers.

Mine?

Gram's jaw set as he glared at the woman. "The lass is seeing to me just fine, thank you. I've no need or want of yer services. She's what I want."

Anger flashed quickly through Susan's gaze, but she hid it well. "Of course. I was told you had a certain fondness for her. I just assumed when I found her here that she'd somehow managed to displease you. Here at Caladrius, we want only the best for our guests. Especially ones of your caliber."

Gram's eyes slid to Amelia. He licked his lower lip, appearing pained for a moment. "Aye, I've the best already. And the lass is only here to get water for me because the verra sight of her in that gown had my throat dry and my dick hard."

Amelia stiffened.

Brian crowded Amelia's space ever so slightly, in a way that left him inching closer and closer. It was a threat and she knew it. With as crazy as her body was reacting to him touching her, she was likely to sock him a good one too.

Gram bristled with anger as he glared at Brian. "I'll thank you kindly to back away from the lass afore yer head is removed from yer neck, boy."

Boy?

Brian was at least a hundred years old, maybe more. If Gram thought he was a boy, just how old was he?

She wasn't sure she wanted to know.

Gram's eyes flashed from blue to brown as the air in the room thickened. It took Amelia a second to recognize there was magik around them—and it wasn't hers. Susan didn't possess any, as she was born from a shifter union but couldn't even shift forms, and Brian wasn't a magik.

That meant it was Gram's power.

Brian must have sensed it as well because he stepped back fast, giving Amelia a wide berth. She may be the daughter of a nutty cult leader, but she was no fool. Seizing the opening to get away from Brian, she hurried to the refrigerator and retrieved a pitcher of infused cucumber and lemon water. She held it to her and moved quickly toward Gram, who held his towel with one hand and put his other out to her.

Every muscle on his body rippled with the action and suddenly it was her mouth that was dry. Goodness, the man was downright sinful and wearing nothing more than a towel was hardly helping her control her lustful thoughts.

The front of his towel lifted on its own somewhat. When Amelia realized what was causing it, she instantly thought of what it had been like to stare at him completely naked. She hadn't been kidding when she pointed out exactly how well-endowed the man was. As intimidating as that may be, she found herself curious and craving everything on him.

It was easy to imagine herself doing to Gram all the things she'd watched the women doing to Taggert and Brian in the training sessions. Before meeting Gram, the very idea of having her mouth on any part of a man did nothing for her. The thought of taking a man's shaft into her mouth had seemed downright ludicrous. That had been when the man was Taggert. Gram was an entirely different story.

She very much wanted to taste every single inch of the man.

Gram's eyes flashed colors again as he sniffed the air. A low grumble started deep in his chest that quickly became a full-blown growl. The sound wasn't threatening as she'd heard him do around Taggert. No. This growl held the promise of maybe getting to taste him after all.

At the thought of losing her virginity to

Gram, she accidentally splashed water down the front of herself, and Gram's gaze moved to her chest. He gulped loudly, looking pained.

"Are you okay? Did I hurt you when I was giving you a massage?" she asked. "Did I rub you wrong?"

"Dear gods above, lass, yer trying to kill me," he said, his voice tight.

She shook her head. "No. I would never try to hurt you."

He snorted. "I do nae mean in the literal sense. Come. You rubbed me just right. We've a massage to finish—and no one is to interrupt." He glared at Susan and Brian.

Neither dared say a word.

"Gus, don't you yell at me again. Just because you don't like people touching you doesn't mean I can't get stuff done to me," said a man with a rather loud voice.

Bill came storming out from the hall that led to the colonic hydrotherapy rooms. He had a magazine and was fanning it behind his bottom. "I can't help I have gas now. I told you my pipes needed cleaned but no. You won't let anyone touch you, let alone your bum so you ruined it for everyone."

"Bill, what are you doing now?" asked Gram.

He looked Gram up and down and then set his gaze on Amelia. His bushy eyebrows raised and met in the middle, forming one giant brow that looked a lot like a moving caterpillar. He inclined his head. "Hi, Amelia. Glad Gram-cracker found you. I'm not sure if you know but your dress is wet and see-through."

"What?" she asked, looking down at herself. He was right. She yelped. She'd known the material was thin but now it might as well have not been there at all for all the good it was doing.

Bill made a move to remove his robe. "Here. You can cover yourself with this."

Susan shot past Amelia. "Bill, we had a talk about you getting naked where guests could see all of you."

He shrugged. "What's the big deal? You know, for a hippie commune, you're really uptight about nudity. I once joined a commune. We blew glass, smoked a ton of weed, and dropped acid." He worried his jaw. "Wait. That wasn't a hippie commune. It was the military. And a lot of LSD. There was glassblowing though. Had to make our own bongs and shit. You'd think Uncle Sam would be kind enough to supply those. Uncle Sam gave me the LSD so there is that. Then again, they didn't give it to me to be nice. They tested on me. Serves them right I blew glass then. Assholes."

Amelia stared blankly at the small man. Was he mentally ill?

Chester, who worked in the colonics room, came running out into the hall. He glanced at Susan. "Sorry. He's faster than he looks like he'd be."

"And Gus?" asked Susan.

"I had no luck with him." Chester shook his head. "He spun in a circle, clutched a helmet with a doll head in it to his chest, and proceeded to repeat 'no bum cleaning' over and over again. Then he ran off in the other direction. The last I saw of him, he was racing down one of the paths headed toward the staff cabins. I can send someone to look for him."

"That won't be necessary. I'm sure he'll be fine," said Susan.

Bill groaned. "He's with our friend, making sure she's okay. He forced Mac and Car to help. They weren't happy. They were trying to get laid. Gus was macking on their game. I told him as much. He never listens to me. He's already got himself a woman. He doesn't remember what it was like to be single before Mona."

"Mona?" asked Susan.

Chester groaned. "Doll head in the helmet. Don't ask."

Gram lifted her hand to his lips and kissed the back of it. "Come, lass. Let's go back to the room. You do nae need to be on display for all to see. Susan, see to it she's brought a dress that is dry and nae see-through. Place it outside the room and do nae bother us when you do. And you," he said, looking back at Brian, "if I ever see you near her again, you will become a missing person."

Bill grunted and then picked his nose. "That happens a lot around this place. Want me to deal with him, Gram-cracker? I ain't scared of a punk-ass shifter boy."

Brian growled.

Bill narrowed his gaze on him. "I've been bound-up for decades. I was so close to relief. Do not push me, shifter boy. I'll kill you and then shit on your dead body."

Amelia cringed at the vivid picture the small crazy man painted.

Gram shook his head. "Bill, go back to the room and finish what was being done."

"Gus keeps yelling at me," said Bill, before looking at the wall and falling silent. There was several seconds' worth of pregnant pause before he spoke again. He looked right at Amelia. "He says your sister is fine and wants you to spend time with Gram. He says it's meant to be. It's time. And that you're the one. Says Gram-cracker will know what he means. And the twins can reach him if anything changes."

Gram held her closer to him. "Aye. I figured it out."

"Took you long enough," said Bill as he rolled his eyes and flicked his booger at Brian, as if daring the shifter to attack him. "Alphas are thick-headed."

Amelia couldn't stop a laugh that bubbled up. The man was insane but in the best possible way.

Bill faced Chester. "All righty, let's get this shit moving. Pun intended. I'm pretty sure a burrito I ate back in '92 is still lodged in there. There is an extra twenty in it for you if you can get it out in one piece. If you do, we can get a picture and send it to my friend Striker. He once got a ten-inch...never mind. There is a lady present and then that mean chick who keeps making me put a robe on. I'll tell you about it when we're alone. It was epic from what I heard."

Amelia wrinkled her nose. She did not want to think about anything coming out of Bill's backside.

Chester looked tired but led Bill back in the direction of the colonics rooms.

Susan and Brian shot her dual warning looks but she didn't cower or cry like she normally would. Next to Gram she felt emboldened, like she could take on the world and live to tell the tale.

It was foolish but how she felt.

"Come on, love," said Gram, as he walked her down the hall, holding her hand. He led her into their room once more. When they were inside, he shut the door, and then took the pitcher from her with his free hand, still clutching his towel with the other.

His blue gaze roamed over her chest and then lower. His breathing increased and sweat beaded on his brow.

She reached for him, worried he'd overexerted himself. "Gram, are you okay?"

Lifting the pitcher, he began drinking straight from it, spilling some down the front of himself, still looking at her chest and body the entire time.

It was then she remembered what Bill had said.

Her dress was now totally see-through, not that there had been a lot to it to start with.

Amelia blushed again and was about to put her back to Gram when rivulets of water running down his steely chest caught her attention. Her gaze fixated on the action, tracing the path the water took before it vanished under the towel.

Moisture formed at the apex of her thighs and she felt the need to shift her legs slightly, back and forth, trying to alleviate the pressure. Need made her body ache.

Gram inhaled deeply, his eyes flashing to brown once more. He gulped even more of the water before lowering the pitcher and staring right at her. "Lass, I can smell your arousal. You should go now. Run from me. Yer nae ready for everything I want—everything I need from you, and I'll nae take yer choices."

She didn't make any move to run. In fact, running was the last thing on her mind. Licking the lines of water from his chest consumed her thoughts. Amelia found herself stepping toward him and pushing his hand and arm with the pitcher away from his chest. Once he moved it, she touched just above one of the scars on his torso, positive it was smaller than it had been only minutes before.

Absentmindedly, she traced a finger over another line of water, and then did something that stunned her—she stepped even closer to the man and licked the water from his chest.

Heat flared through her as her tongue swiped over his salty skin. She moaned and slid lower, with her tongue on him the entire time.

Gram fell back against the door, still holding the pitcher outward. "For fuck's sake, woman. Did you nae hear me? I cannae control myself around you! I want to ravish you. I want to put you on that table, climb on top of you, and sink into you."

She glanced at the massage table and then back at him. While she hated knowing she was doing exactly what Cal wanted, giving her body to the Bringer, she wanted the man more than she'd wanted anything before.

With her escape plan in motion and the knowledge she'd be gone from the compound in a little over twenty-four hours, she threw caution to the wind. She wanted to get lost in reckless abandonment just once in her life. She wanted to know pleasure. Gram could give her that.

"Okay."

"Come again?" The man looked scared of her, which was amusing.

"You can put me on the table, climb on me, and sink into me," she said, staring at another rivulet of water on his chest.

Gram dropped the pitcher and caught it again quickly before it would have hit the floor. He stared at her with wide eyes before he went to the side table and set the pitcher there. Facing her, he started to speak, only to stop and start several more times. He blew out a frustrated breath.

"Lass."

"Yes?"

"You do nae understand what yer giving me permission to do," he said softly, though he looked to be straining as he gripped the towel around his waist for dear life. "We need to have a long, *long* talk. I need to prepare you for what will happen when we join."

"I may be a virgin, but I understand fornication," she said.

He closed his eyes tight and said something in

a language she didn't know. When he looked back at her, he sighed. "Lass, do nae make me beg. Go."

"But you said you wanted to sink into me. I want you too. Why should I go?" she asked.

He closed the distance between them in one big step. He then cupped her face and dipped his head, his lips capturing hers. His kiss was hot and branding, making additional moisture flood between her legs.

Chapter Eighteen

GRAM ATE at Amelia's mouth, wanting to explore every inch of her with his tongue. The smell of her arousal sent his wolf into high gear. It wanted to lay claim to her. So did he. But he couldn't. Not yet. She needed to understand fully that he believed they were mates—destined for one another. She didn't need him pawing all over her in the process.

If he dared to give in to his carnal urges for her, there was a high likelihood he'd claim her. He wouldn't be able to stop himself. That wasn't fair to her. No. He needed to gather control of himself and his hormones and explain everything.

Then he'd claim her.

He broke the kiss but didn't stop touching her face.

She stared up at him with passion-glazed eyes.

He gave her a chaste kiss on the lips, despite wanting far more than that.

"I wanted to find you before I came to get a massage," he said, unsure where to start, but he felt like blurting out the fact he thought they were mates might be a bit too much. "To explain that I was nae lying to you before, lass. Yer sister spoke to me."

She nodded. "I know that now, and I'm sorry. You were right."

It warmed his heart to hear her say as much. "Lass, I should get dressed so we can talk. I think, well, I'm sure, erm, we need to have a long talk."

Her cool palm made its way to his hot chest. She ran her hand over one of his scars and teared up. "What happened to you?"

Already he'd have so much to explain away when it came to his past. A piece of him feared Amelia would reject him if she knew he'd cared for another woman—that he'd loved someone as much as he could, considering they weren't true mates. He actually considered lying to her but thought better of it. "The woman and child Car spoke of before…"

She nodded.

He cleared his throat. "Brooke and I had nae been an item for a couple months as it was when her true mate came into her life again. She'd thought him dead, and I'd thought I dinnae have a mate of my own. I was wrong."

Amelia remained close to him and he had to stare at the ceiling to avoid looking at her nipples through the sheer wet gown.

"Yes?"

"She and her wee one were tested on by horrible people. And these people were hunting them nonstop," confessed Gram. "Once, they found them, and I was shot in the process. Brooke ended things with me then. She dinnae want me hurt in her battle. But, lass, I dinnae want to let go. I thought we could still work it out. It was nae until her true mate appeared in her life that I knew it was well and truly over. But that dinnae mean I'd leave them to defend themselves. When another attack came, I was there. I was attempting to get the wee one to safety when I was overrun by the enemy, injected with something that had an adverse effect on me, and then blown up."

She gasped. "W-what? Blown up?"

"Aye. Was nae one of my finer days. But I dinnae let the little one be harmed." He kept looking upward, more out of the fact he couldn't face the woman he knew in his heart was made for him when he told her of another. "I wasnae expected to live, the wounds were that serious."

He was greeted with dead silence.

She pulled her hand away from his torso, and her rejection hurt him worse than any explosion ever could.

"Lass, I've no right to ask for yer understanding, but…" He looked at her—and found her in tears.

"That is the sweetest, kindest thing ever, and I'm sorry you were hurt." Amelia launched herself at him, tossing her arms around his neck and hugging him tight. She then sucked in a large breath and released him. "Ohmygoddess, did I hurt you more? I didn't mean to."

Gram caught her wrist. "Lass, you dinnae hurt me. I'm battered, scared of your reaction to what I just told you, and nae quite at full strength, but I'm nae glass. I'll nae shatter. Unless you tell me to stay away from you, then I might verra well break into a million pieces."

A questioning expression fell over her lovely face. "Why am I so drawn to you, and why do you care what I think?"

"Lass, I know we've only just met, but would you believe me if I told you I think we're mates?"

Amelia took a small step back from him, but she didn't run. He'd take that as a slight win. Any victory, even a tiny one, was welcome. "What makes you think that?"

A shaky laugh fell free from him as he adjusted the towel on his lap. "For starters, like I already told you, I had visions of you before I came here. You were in a gown much like the one yer in now, yer hair down the way it is now. And I could smell yer scent—honeysuckle and vanilla. It did to me then as it does to me now."

She stared blankly at him before speaking. "I had a dream with you in it before you came."

Gram did his best to hide his elation. "Aye, you mentioned as much, but you dinnae tell me what happened in the dream."

"We were running. You were leading, holding my hand, trying to get me somewhere safe. But I didn't know it was you right away when I saw you by the river."

"How do you mean?"

She let out a long breath. "In the dream, I only saw you from behind. You were shirtless. I could see the scars on your back. When I came in here to give you a massage, I realized who you were—the man I dreamed about."

Gram averted his gaze. "Lass, I'm sorry about all the scars. I understand they are nae appealing."

"Gram, everything about you is appealing. I want to lick you all over."

He groaned, trying to will his cock down. "Lass, the verra sight of you makes my cock so hard I think I could hammer nails with it."

"Oh." Her gaze went to his groin. "I think it probably could hammer nails. It's really big."

That was it, she was trying to kill him. He was sure of it.

Chapter Nineteen

STIFLING ANOTHER GROAN, Gram did his best to hide the fact he had another hard-on. It seemed to be a constant when it came to her. The towel didn't do much to mask it though. "Aye, it's *verra* big when yer near."

"And because your, um, thing reacts when I'm close, that makes you think I'm your mate?" she asked.

My thing?

Her innocence was a blessing and a curse.

"There is more to it than that, lass," he stated evenly. "Do you nae feel anything for me? You mentioned you feel drawn to me; is that all?"

Lowering her gaze, she shook her head. "No."

"Tell me what else you feel."

"I feel like I'd tear off anyone's face who tried to hurt you. That I'd do anything and risk everything to protect you," she whispered before looking up at him with tears in her eyes once more. "And not because I think you're weak. I don't. I can't explain why. I just know that the idea of you being hurt by anyone sets my teeth on edge. It makes me want to let the darkness in me out fully."

"Amelia," he said, wanting to drag her to him, but he knew better. He sat on the table quickly, knowing if he dared to get off the table, he'd end up taking her then and there. She wasn't ready for that. "What yer describing is common for mated pairs to feel for one another. And, lass, I do nae for one second think you've any darkness. You are like sunshine. Sweet. Warm. Pure. Glorious. And beautiful. Nae just in looks. I can sense yer soul. It's caring and guid."

She bit her lower lip, and then gasped, her eyes widening. "Andie was right!"

"About?"

"She said that you and I were going to be a couple—a married couple. And she mentioned babies and getting to be a big sister, but that didn't make sense since she wasn't talking about Cal having children."

Gram did his best to keep from jumping for joy. "She said all that?"

Amelia nodded.

"Lass, yer the most important person in her life, and I'm guessing that to her, yer a mother figure."

Amelia seemed to think on it before nodding. "Yes. I guess. She was two when our mother died. I'm who watches over her, who is with her every night, who sees to her bath, her education, everything."

"You love her."

"Yes. So much," she said.

"As a sister or as a mother would for a child?" he questioned, already guessing the answer.

Amelia swallowed hard. "As a mother would. I'd kill anyone who tried to hurt her."

"If we're mates, as I believe we are, and we joined, mating fully, that would make *me* yer husband. Our babes would technically be Andie's cousins, but my instincts tell me all of us, her included, would see them more as siblings. Nae cousins. And she'd see us as her parents. I could be wrong though."

Her lips trembled. "You're not wrong. She told me you were going to be her new daddy. A better one. A good one."

He held tight to his emotions. All he'd ever wanted was a family. He didn't need to be a child's biological father to love it. Bethany had taught him that.

After taking several deep breaths, she began to pace, wringing her hands in front of her as she did. "This is a lot. I wasn't planning on this, on you. I thought the Bringer would be a jerk. Not my mate."

He let her rant as he stood slowly, keeping the towel in front of his groin.

"Sure, my mate is in love with another woman. Why not? Who would want me?" she asked, clearly speaking to herself, not him as she continued to pace. "I know what I look like to the rest of the world. I must look simple to him. Being raised here made me sheltered. I'm not very worldly. I'm not like other women. I can't compete with what he's used to. He's seen and done so much and all I've done is try to stay alive and keep my sister safe."

"Lass, I do nae see you as simple. Far from it. And I do nae see you as a substitute for anyone. Please know that," he said, wanting to touch her but holding back. "And I did fully believe myself to be in love with Brooke. I understand now that wasn't really the case. That she and I loved one another as much as possible for supernaturals who are nae mates. That love pales compared to what one feels for their mate."

She whipped around to stare at him. "How would you know?"

"Because I've nae even known you a full day and already I want to wrap my arms around you and never let you go. I want to whisk you far from here and start a life with you—with Andie. I want to show you the world, give you anything you could ever want, and I want you to know love." He took a deep breath, but he didn't stop. "Lass, I want to see yer stomach swollen with my babes. I want to wake up every morning with you there next to me in the bed. I want to see our wee ones come to be, and grow to have children of their own—and yes, I am including Andie in that. The second I saw her, I wanted to protect her. So, that's how I know."

She paled. "Sorry I asked."

He chuckled. "I come on strong. Sorry. I'm old enough to know what I want and smart enough to nae let it slip away. I know who you are to me. I think fate brought me here, to you. Nae yer father. Destiny. Well, destiny and my dipshit friends."

"Gram, you can't trust my father," she said, stepping closer to him. "Promise me you won't be alone with him or his men. You can't trust any of them. And don't trust Susan. She's as bad, if not worse than Taggert."

"Lass, I surmised as much for myself. But I am nae worried about being alone with any of them. I am only worried about you," he said.

She met his gaze. "What do you mean when you say your friends are responsible for you being here? Be honest with me. I'll know if you're lying."

His lips twitched with the urge to smile as he sensed the same power he'd felt near the river float over the room. It was her. She was magik. "I'm here because my friends kidnapped me—staging an intervention, if you will. I was nae healing as I should be. They think it's in my head. They may be right. My friends had the bright idea that I could heal here."

With a pensive look, she took a step closer to him. "Your friends forced you to come here?"

The edge of his mouth curved upward. "Aye."

Her eyes widened. "Do they hate you?"

He laughed. "There are days I wonder. What of you, lass? What are you nae telling me?"

Amelia radiated fear as she glanced at the doors to the room. She went to the main one and engaged the lock before doing the same to the back one. Much to his surprise, she bent her head...and the feel of magik pulsed around him more.

When she looked up, her eyes were icy blue.

"Yer Fae?" he asked, even though it was obvious she had at least some Fae in her.

His own Fae side instantly recognized it and knew she was of a similar line. A powerful one at that.

"Yes, but I don't know all of what I am. I know my mom was part Fae. And part shifter. I can't shift and I know I don't have a lot of shifter traits. My father is a lot of things. I think I am, too," she said, and he could feel the truth of her words. "No one else here can know about me or my magik, Gram. Please."

He nodded. "Yer secret is safe with me. But will they nae sense it radiating from this room?"

"I'm sure they will but they'll assume it's you," she said nonchalantly. "And I'm only drawing on my power to prevent anyone from hearing our conversation. Gram, you and your friends need to leave here at once. This is not a safe place."

"Yer here. Did you miss the part of me telling you we're mates? I go where you are. Period."

She closed her eyes a second, appearing pained. "Please, Gram. I can't tell you anything more, but I can say that you're in danger. Whatever my father wants with you can't be good. He's spent my life grooming me for you, for your arrival. He calls you the Bringer of Change. And in his mind, you're going to help him lead the Flock into enlightenment, into its next stage of evolution even. I don't know what that next stage is, but it can't be good. Deep down, I think he wants to rule over supernaturals and enslave humans. Something tells me I'm not wrong."

Gram had to fight to keep from laughing. "No offense, lass, but yer da sounds as if he might be hitting the hash a bit too hard. I know it's now legal out here but still. Too much of a good thing is just that—too much."

She continued to coat the room with magik, and he worried that it might drain her. "Gram, Cal and his men, they've killed so many alpha males that I've lost count. And that is a drop in the bucket compared to the number of women and humans they've murdered. I don't know if you heard about the dead women showing up in the area, but I know the Flock is behind it all. I'm pretty sure Taggert might be the main one responsible for the deaths of the women at least. But in truth, they're all more than capable of doing it."

He stiffened. "W-what?"

She teared up. "Please. You have to believe me. You can't tell them I told you this. I just need you to go far from here. I need you to be safe. If Cal thinks I can't bring you into the Flock, my value to him will be gone. My gut says he'd give me to Taggert then. That is the best-case scenario. If they find out I warned you away, Cal and the men who serve him will do to me what they did to my mother when Andie was two years old—kill me in front of the Flock. They won't be quick about it, and they'll make everyone watch it happen, so they know better than to go against them. They'll bring in

Helmuth's monsters and feed me to them like they did my mother."

His wolf roared. "No one will fucking touch you! Helmuth? Walter Helmuth?"

She nodded.

"Lass, yer father let hybrids attack yer mother?" he asked, horrified at the idea.

"Y-yes," she said, her voice shaky. "He didn't just let them. He ordered them to do it—and he made us all watch it happen. Even Andie. They tore our mother to bits and ate her, Gram. It was horrific. I'll never, ever forget that night."

Gram snarled. "I will kill him with my bare hands. I'll kill them all!"

"No! Please." Tears slid down her cheeks. "I'm going to take my sister and run. I've been planning it for two years. I didn't think you were real. I thought the Bringer was another one of my father's weird prophecies that wouldn't come to pass. And honestly, a piece of me assumed if you were real that you'd be like him—evil. Deep down, I know that isn't true. You're a good man. I can't let you be hurt or brainwashed like the rest of the Flock. Promise me that you and your friends will leave here tonight, before the gathering."

Gram stepped closer to her. "A team of a hundred men couldnae drag me from you, Amelia."

"Why?" she asked, swaying slightly, an indication she'd pulled upon too much juice. "You don't owe me anything."

"Lass, are you always this stubborn?"

"What do you mean?"

He gave her a pointed stare. "You. Me. Mates. Destiny. Fate."

She tensed. "Gram, I'm the daughter of a man who thinks he's a god and who others worship. You'll have to forgive me if I'm a tad cynical when someone stands before me talking about divine intervention."

Reaching out with one hand while holding the towel with the other, he touched her face and strained with the need to hold her.

She pushed at his chest. "Please go. Just leave. Run and don't look back."

He grabbed her to him with both hands and inhaled her scent, letting it wash over him. He had no intention of leaving without her. "I promise I'll go."

Some of the tension leaked from her frame. "Good."

"But, lass, I'll be taking you and yer sister with me. No arguments, or I'll walk out there right now and have it out with yer father. If it's change he wants, it's change he'll get. Though it may nae be the change he was hoping for."

She gasped and stared up at him, her eyes flickering back and forth from hazel to icy blue. "He's been feeding off the power he drains from the alphas he's killed for thousands of years. It's changed him somehow. He's a blending of many things, but not any one thing, if that makes sense. And while he seems harmless and peace-loving, he's not. He's evil and he wants to rule the world. He will kill you if you try to stand against him. You said it yourself, you're not at full strength."

He didn't like the fact she had no faith in him, but he knew arguing with her was pointless. Plus, he had to admit that her worry for him warmed his heart, melting the ice that had started to form around it. "Lass, tell me everything. Start at the beginning."

"I can't," she said, sniffling, nearly pulling out of his embrace. She stopped and licked her lower lip. "Erm, Gram?"

"Aye?"

"If both of your hands are on me, what is holding up your towel?"

It was then he realized the towel was pooled on the floor near his feet. "Do nae panic. I'll cover myself. I know yer nae ready just yet. Nae really."

Chapter Twenty

AMELIA STARED down the length of Gram and her breathing increased. Desire raced through her and she skimmed her fingers down his torso. She hadn't been joking when she'd said he very well could hammer nails with his erection. The thing was massive and currently very, very hard.

She gulped.

The desire to touch it won out and she gave in, doing just that. As her fingers wrapped as far as they could around his velvety-smooth girth, he jerked, and she thought he'd pull away.

He didn't.

His hand closed over hers on his hot erection and he dipped his head, his other hand finding the side of her head. He ran his hand into her hair and put his forehead to hers. "Lass, do nae start this if you do nae intend to finish."

Closing her eyes, she thought on what he was saying. Could she do it? Could she surrender to him fully? Everything in her screamed yes, but a niggle in the back of her head held her back. She held his shaft as she kept her forehead to his. "This is what Cal wants. He wants me to lure you to the Flock. I'm supposed to use sex to do it. This would be giving him what he wants."

She let go of him and took a big step back, her emotions running the gamut. Her entire body buzzed with excitement and need for the man before her, but she couldn't do it. She couldn't be a pawn in her father's demented game.

Gram shuddered, making no move to cover himself. "Lass, do you nae want to act on what is clearly between us because you do nae want me, or is it because yer worried I'll think you did it because yer father told you to?"

Her eyes widened. Was she worried Gram would see it as her using him? "I hadn't even thought of that. Now I will. Great. One more thing to worry about."

Gram reached down and began to stroke himself slowly at first, his eyes never leaving her. "Lass, then I'm to take it you do nae want me the same as I want you? That you do not burn for me as I do for you? That must be so since you were nae worried if I'd suspect you had ulterior motives."

Her hand went to her throat. She swallowed hard. "Oh, I want you. A lot. A whole lot, but I can't. You weren't part of my plan. And I want you far away from this place, not joining it."

"Life is what happens when you're busy making plans," he said with a wink, still stroking his cock boldly.

When she'd watched Taggert and Brian being serviced, she'd felt disgusted. The entire ordeal had sickened her, and she'd wanted to run and hide. A part of her feared that would always be her reaction to sexual situations. That the Flock's training and their sexual rituals had left her damaged in some respect.

Seeing Gram touching his cock didn't turn her off. It did the opposite. It ignited her sex drive. She wanted to be the one doing it for him. She wanted to touch him. Please him. Be one with him. And she didn't want to let fear or worry about plots and schemes take that from her. It was her moment to be with a man she wanted and who appeared to want her in return.

Amelia edged forward, her hand going out as if it had a mind of its own. She made contact with Gram's rock-hard lower torso and the heat she'd felt before flared through her once more. The air around them seemed electrified. Raw need took root in her and she nearly whimpered.

"Lass, I want you, and I can smell yer want of me." Gram increased the speed in which he touched himself, only serving to excite her more.

Her pulse thumped erratically, and she found herself pressing against him. While her mind screamed that acting on her impulses would be playing into her father's hands, the rest of her stopped caring. She sank against him and the next she knew, her mouth was on his, wanting to feed the insatiable hunger inside her.

Gram took over almost instantly, showing who was the master and who was the student. His tongue circled hers and he wrapped an arm around her waist, keeping her held to him. It was a good thing too because the more his tongue explored her mouth, the less she felt she could stand on her own two feet.

His tongue stroked her mouth to the point her toes started to tingle. She wasn't even aware that was a possibility. The kiss moved quickly to the point of no return. Not that she was complaining any.

With a seductive growl, he jerked her against him harder, his erection digging at her stomach. She ached for it to be between her legs. To be diving into her recesses, unifying them.

She bit at his lower lip. "Gram."

"Lass, if you bite my lip again, you had better be prepared to be claimed," he warned. "Because I'll nae be able to stop myself or my wolf. It wants you too, lass. It wants to possess all of you. If yer nae ready for that, speak now."

Passion clouded her judgment and she froze.

Gram sighed and made a move to pull away from her.

Amelia did the only thing she could think to do to prevent the pleasure from ending. She bit his lower lip again, this time harder.

Hunger flashed through his eyes.

In an instant his hands roamed over her body, tugging at her dress, lifting it as she squirmed against him, wanting more. Cool air eased over her now exposed legs and Amelia whimpered into Gram's mouth.

With a growl, he grabbed the sides of her waist and lifted her with ease, depositing her on the massage table. He then jerked her butt toward the end of it and pushed her enough to force her to lie back. She followed his lead and nearly bolted when he shoved her dress up more, lifting her legs as he did. He stared down at her nakedness and a wolfish grin spread over his face. "Och, lass, I've found heaven."

Embarrassed and exposed, she made a move to push down the bottom portion of her dress to cover herself. No one had ever seen the area before, outside of herself, and she'd only looked long enough to follow Tina's directions on womanly "spring cleaning."

He shook his head and stopped her from covering herself. "No."

She squirmed.

He hooked his arms around her thighs and kissed her knee before kissing his way down her inner thigh. When he reached her mound, he inhaled deeply. "Lass, you smell guid enough to eat and that's exactly what I intend to do."

"W-what? I didn't train for that," she blurted, feeling foolish as the words left her mouth. But it was true. She'd trained on various ways to pleasure him. Not the other way around. She felt every bit the bumbling virgin she knew herself to be.

He chuckled. "I'm all the teacher you'll need."

As he planted a kiss on top of her mound, Amelia stiffened.

Gram caressed her legs. "Lass, I promise you'll enjoy this. I know I will. Hell, I am already and I've nae even started yet. This is the best kidnapping I've ever been subjected to and you should know that's saying something as it's nae the first one I've fallen victim to. When we're done, remind me to thank Striker."

"What?" she asked, totally lost on what he was talking about. "Who is Striker?"

He winked. "Never you mind that. Just focus on how guid this is going to feel for you."

"I'm supposed to be pleasing you, not the other way around," she protested. "I'm supposed to be rubbing, erm, massaging you. It's me who should have my mouth on your *thing*."

"All in due time, lass. But for now, I get to taste you first." He put his hand over her mound and stared up at her. "I like that yer nae shaved bare. I like that you've hair here."

She tensed. Her girl part maintenance help had come from Tina. It had been her friend's suggestion that Amelia kept a neatly trimmed triangle of hair there. Apparently, she owed Tina a big thank you. It looked as if more than one thank you card would be sent when the act was complete.

Gram parted her folds and cool air moved over her exposed nether regions. Sweet goddess. The man was going to do her in before he even got started.

When he swiped his tongue over the area, Amelia nearly came up and off the table. She'd never felt anything that good before. He laughed against her pussy and used one hand to keep her pinned in place. He licked more, his blue eyes swirling to brown almost instantly.

A low grumble started in the back of his throat and she knew then his shifter side was showing itself.

Was he going to lose control and shift forms with his head between her legs?

Her eyes widened.

She sure in the heck hoped not. It was

enough that she was about to hand over her virginity to a man she'd only just met. Giving it to a wolf was simply out of the question. "G-Gram?"

"Shh, lass," he said, looking up at her from under thick lashes. "I'll nae harm you."

"But your eyes."

He nodded. "My wolf is here, sampling you too. It's the way of things with mates. I cannae help it, but I can tell you that I'll nae let it harm you. Do you trust me?"

Nodding, she tried to relax but it was nearly impossible. She was lying on her back, on a massage table, in a room with people she hated down the hall, with her sex totally exposed to a man who was a shifter and had already licked her intimate regions once.

As he licked his lower lip, she knew he was about to do so again.

He caressed her stomach with his thumb as the rest of his hand kept her held in place. With his other hand, he spread her lower lips more, flicking his tongue back and forth. Each swipe, each lick sent jolts of pleasure pulsing through her body. Within minutes, her thighs were quivering, and she was fairly positive she was about to burst into flames, that or run for the hills. She honestly wasn't sure which might occur.

He pressed a finger to her soaked core and she held her breath. She expected a lot of pain. When she'd seen virgins being taken for the first time in Flock rituals, it always looked painful—then again, the men doing the taking during the rituals were sick bastards.

Gram sucked gently on her swollen bud as he pushed a long finger into her. There was slight pain, but it was fleeting and followed quickly by nothing short of pure bliss.

Closing her eyes, Amelia arched her back, her hips moving of their own accord. They wanted more of what Gram was doing as much as she did.

He began easing his finger in and out of her as he continued his oral sensual assault. Never had she felt like this. Her hips undulated of their own accord, encouraging Gram to increase his actions. He did, and Amelia gasped, clamping her thighs shut as far as she could get them with his head there. She was left effectively squeezing his head and holding it in place.

As he chuckled into her pussy, he looked up the length of her. The man then had the nerve to wink of all things as if her body's response to the pleasure he was giving her was humorous.

Maybe it was.

All she knew for sure was she wanted more.

Much more.

He moved his finger just right at the second his tongue struck her sweet spot. Her body constricted around his finger, grasping at it as immense pleasure slammed into her, causing her to become dizzy. Thankfully, she was already lying down. She clamped her legs tighter to the side of his head and jerked involuntarily on the massage table. The pleasure didn't end there. Whatever Gram was doing kept it going, kept making her body jerk like she was a fish out of water.

Tiny gasps of shock came from her as her body shattered around his finger.

"That a girl," he said, staring up at her, his chin even wetter than it had been. "Keep coming for me, lass."

Her body obeyed and for a split second, Amelia was positive her magik was going to break free from her and level the entire compound. It clawed at her from the inside out, wanting free, wanting to go to Gram. Fearing she'd harm him,

Amelia held tight to it, focusing on it instead of Gram's tongue on her clit.

When he added a second finger, she stiffened. It wasn't comfortable.

Gram lifted his head and his lips glistened. He licked them, his eyes still brown. "Lass, I'll stop if you want me to."

She shook her head and put her hand over the one he had on her stomach. "That hurts a little."

"Aye, because you've nae had anything or anyone there before," he said as he withdrew his fingers from her core, put them in his mouth, and licked them clean. His eyes rolled back in his head a moment.

Gram stood fully and stepped back fast. He put his back to her and his shoulders heaved.

She sat up. "Gram?"

He looked strained. "Do nae descend upon her like a rutting beast. Be gentle with her. She's trusting you, do nae betray that trust."

It took her a moment to realize he was talking to himself. The restraint he was showing as an alpha-male shifter in the throes of passion was impressive. It made her chest tighten. He didn't want to hurt her. He wanted the entire experience to be pleasurable for her.

Unlike the men of the Flock.

Gram was nothing like Taggert or Brian. He didn't get off on the pain of others.

She may have only just met him, but she felt something for the man. More than she was willing to admit. For a second it felt as if her heart would leap right out of her chest and soar.

Chapter Twenty-One

GRAM CLENCHED HIS FISTS, willing his beast to calm itself and give him this moment with Amelia. He'd spent his entire life thinking he'd never know love with a true mate. Then, the little niche of happiness he'd carved out for himself with Brooke and Bethany had been ripped away. He understood now that everything happened for a reason, that everything had led him to this town, this resort, this woman. And he wasn't about to let his wolf fuck it all up for him.

Not when his future was so close at hand.

Let me do this, he said to his wolf. *Give me this time with her.*

His wolf snarled at him, warning him that it wasn't going to back down and take a backseat to their destiny. The wolf wanted him to claim her, to sink its teeth into her, forever marking her. He was all for the idea of claiming her, but she wasn't ready for that.

Not yet anyway.

With time she would be. Such was the ways of things between mates and he knew she was meant for him. No one would be able to tell him different. He felt it in his bones.

He could still smell the small amount of blood that had come from her losing her maidenhood to him. It excited his wolf even more. Not that the asshole beast needed any help to be motivated when it came to Amelia.

His jaw began to change shapes and his teeth lengthened. Such a thing had never happened to him before during sex and he knew why—he'd never been with his mate before. If he kept going, he'd end up claiming her when she wasn't ready for that step yet and all it would entail.

Forever with him.

Gram wasn't an easy man to live with. No alpha male really was. They were never exactly easygoing when it came to their mates. Often, their need to protect their women outweighed their better judgment.

Gram had always found it amusing when his friends suffered from the issue. Now that he was in their shoes, the humor had faded. All he wanted to do was turn around, drive himself into Amelia, and sink his teeth into her tender flesh. He wanted to make her his wife. To forge an unbreakable bond between them.

"No, do nae harm her," he said, as best as he could to his wolf considering his mouth was no longer quite human. The words were there but low, deep, partially garbled.

The dick of a beast in him ignored his command. It kept pushing at him, wanting free. If it was able to separate itself from him, he knew it would just as soon tear his throat out than let him captain the ship any further.

To be fair, Gram had done a great job of fucking things up in his life to date. Maybe the wolf had a point. Maybe it should be left in charge. Running on instinct might be better than overthinking every single tiny detail—like he'd been doing since the attack.

But letting the wolf loose right now would put Amelia at risk. That wasn't acceptable. She was to be protected at all costs. Even from himself.

Swaying, he grabbed for anything he could to

hold himself up. His hand connected with the side table and he drew in long, deep breaths, trying to gain some semblance of control again. His body spasmed and he knocked a candle off the table and onto the floor. By the grace of the gods, the flame went out before anything caught on fire. He jerked more and inadvertently bumped a small jar of something that smelled a lot like whatever Amelia had been rubbing on his scars. It too hit the floor.

"Gram," said Amelia, her soft voice easing over him like silk. He heard her sliding off the table and hoped beyond hopes that she was going to flee, to run far and fast from him. If she was smart, she'd go and not look back.

He couldn't blame her.

Who would want him?

He was damaged goods. His spirit was as broken as his body.

She could be my salvation.

"Gram, look at me. Please," she pleaded. The smell of her cream still coated his mouth and chin, making it impossible for him to concentrate. All he wanted to do was bury his head back between her legs and watch her reach culmination again. The sight had almost done him in. He licked his lips and all that did was make him hornier and set his wolf even more on edge.

"Trust yourself with me, Gram," she said in a barely there voice. "I do. Everything in me is screaming at the top of its lungs for me to put all my trust in you."

Her words helped him gain control of his mouth once more. It returned to human form but the threat of it changing once more was there, just below the surface. "I'm sorry. I thought I could do this. That I could control my beast."

"You're doing just fine."

Clearly, they had *very* different definitions of fine.

There was no way he could face her. Not unless he was fine with descending upon her and ravishing her. Which he was not. "Lass, I'll nae break my promise to you. I told you that I'd nae hurt you."

As her cool hand touched his back, he jerked away, terrified he'd harm her without meaning to. Gram expected her to misread his attempts at keeping her safe as rejection. He was prepared for her to storm off, angry with him. That would be for the best. At least she'd be safe from him then.

Instead, she traced her way over his back and

eased up next to him, doing the exact opposite of running in the other direction. "I can feel you struggling with what's inside you. It's breaking my heart. I don't want you to fight with your inner nature."

"Lass, my inner nature is close to fucking you senseless."

"I know," she said, and those two little words sent additional need spiraling through him. "Let go. Trust yourself. You won't hurt me."

It was painfully clear her father's lift didn't stop on all floors, but he hadn't thought she took after him in any way. Hearing her ask him to stop fighting his wolf and what it wanted to do to her made Gram second-guess her level of sanity.

His mate was batshit crazy.

And hot as hell.

Fuck.

He growled.

Her fingers moved sensually over his bare, feverish skin. Pinning his gaze on her, he shot her a look that more than questioned if she'd lost her mind.

The temptress had the nerve to return his stare, her expression one of reverence.

He was well and thoroughly screwed.

And so would she be very soon if she didn't wise up and run from him.

She slinked her body closer to his. He shut his eyes, trying to get the image of her spread open before him out of his mind. The more he tried to stop thinking about her pussy—how tight, warm, and sweet it was—the more it consumed his every thought.

He slammed his palms down on the side table and claws sprang forth from the tips of his fingers.

Not an ounce of fear radiated from his mate. The woman, who he was fast beginning to think might be certifiably insane, had the audacity to slide her hand down his arm and over his hand. She then bent and planted a tender kiss to the back of his hand like him partially shifting in front of her was no big deal.

Yep.

Batshit crazy.

One flew over the cuckoo's…

The sight of her pert nipples under the sheer fabric of her dress killed his train of thought. Instantly, he was hit with thoughts of holding the glorious globes in his hands before placing his cock between them and doing very, very naughty things. For half a second, he was fairly sure he'd been wrong about the candle falling and the flame going out. How else could he explain the spike in the room's temperature?

"Gram, what's wrong? You have a strange look on your face. Are you okay?"

Hyper-focusing on her breasts, he nodded. "Aye, I'm thinking of how guid it would feel to rub my cock between yer tits right before I come all over yer…erm…now would be a guid time to get as far from me as you can."

She ran her fingers up his arm, her expression innocent, yet tempting all in one. "I didn't train for you doing that to my breasts, but I'm game."

Groaning, he shook his head. She was destroying his self-control. "Lass, being blown up hurt less than trying to restrain my wolf right now. If you understood that, you'd nae joke."

Tipping her head, Amelia licked her lower lip and ran her hand higher up his arm. "Who said I was joking?"

"Oh for fuck's sake, lass! Help a wolf out here."

"I may not have been shown how to do that, but I did learn some other things." She leaned and kissed his upper arm before grabbing him and trying to turn him. He faced her slowly, still unsure of himself. Amelia kissed his right pec and then moved to his left. She then shocked the hell out of him by slinking down quickly and going to her knees before him.

His jaw dropped.

She couldn't possibly be thinking of sucking him off when he was on the verge of a shift and claiming her. Could she?

She took hold of his hot, turgid shaft and licked the end of it.

He shuddered and looked down more to be sure his legs hadn't actually begun to sprout fur on their way to turning into a wolf. "Amelia!"

A sly, sultry smile touched her lips a moment before she licked a line from the base of his cock to the tip, making him quake. She pinched the loose skin at his base, exposing his cock head even more. The next he knew, she had her mouth wrapped around the head of his cock. Pure ecstasy engulfed him.

Gram whispered a prayer to the gods he'd believed heavily in back when he was just a young man. The prayer was in Gaelic and it was one that asked for strength in the trials ahead.

His entire body trembled, and he fought to stay vertical as Amelia artfully worked his dick.

He knew he was on his own—forsaken by the gods—and about to be done in by a virgin.

Not just any virgin.

My mate.

With a hesitant movement, he touched her cheek as she took him deeper into her mouth. She added her hands to the mix, using one to cup his balls and the other to stroke his exposed shaft.

Gram's hands went back, and he grabbed the side table again, using it to hold himself up as the wanton vixen on her knees before him continued to work her magik. The air began to thicken, and it took him a second to realize it was buzzing with power. Her power.

His magik flared to the surface, having a mind of its own as it merged with hers. It had been unpredictable since he'd been injured and for a fleeting second, he worried it would harm her.

When the room seemed to burst with nothing but sexual energy, he realized she'd be just fine.

Well and thoroughly fucked soon, but fine.

She sucked on him, increasing her hand actions. He wasn't sure he wanted to know more about the training she'd mentioned, but he strongly suspected he was deeply in debt to whomever had shown her what to do because it felt fucking amazing.

Gram was delirious as pleasure assailed him and magik moved all around them. When Amelia moved her mouth off his cock, the action made a popping sound and he instantly mourned the loss. She lifted his long shaft, moving it sideways slightly as she buried her face against the base of his cock. The blasted woman had the audacity to take one of his balls into her mouth with great care. She sucked on it and he nearly came then and there.

She was going to do what The Corporation and the explosion failed to do.

She was going to kill him.

He was sure of it.

"Sweet mother of…lass…I cannae…*fuck*." His eyes widened as she jerked on his cock, using her mouth to toy with his ball sac more. Looking upward, he did his best to gather his wits.

Too bad he didn't have any common sense left to speak of.

The best he could do was cling to the table to stay upright as he tried hard to think about anything other than how good her mouth felt around his dick. Gram began to recite poems from his younger years in his head before moving to thinking of every mission he'd gone on over the past decade. Anything he could do to shift his focus from her gifted mouth. For a fleeting moment, he even thought of Bill down the hall getting his pipes cleaned.

Nothing worked.

Her mouth and her touch felt too good. Too right.

His hips took over his thought process since it was clear he couldn't handle the task himself. They moved all on their own, as if they were no longer controlled by him, thrusting slightly at first, causing his cock to go deeper into Amelia's mouth.

She adjusted, accommodating him as best she could.

Gram increased his pace.

Their magik thickened around him and his incisors exploded in his mouth. Straining to keep from shifting fully, Gram tossed his head back, the muscles in his neck drawing tight. He pumped faster into her mouth and his balls drew up, tightening in anticipation of his orgasm.

Amelia splayed her hands on his thighs and held her head to his body just as his cock exploded, jetting seed into her mouth. Small jerks rushed through his hips as he emptied himself fully. She swallowed and then eased off his shaft, licking her lips as she did.

"Hmm, it's saltier than I thought it would be. But not bad," she said as if it were no big deal that she'd nearly unmanned him, and he was extremely close to walking on all fours with the ability to lick his own fucking balls.

She tugged at her lower lip, a pensive expression covering her face. "Gram? I did it wrong, didn't I? I hurt you. I didn't mean to. I tried to be gentle."

"L-lass," he managed, his teeth still that of the wolf.

Her eyes widened as she lifted a hand, feeling the air around them. "What is that? Is that our power?"

All he could do was nod as his legs felt as if they'd turned to rubber. On a good note, there was no longer any pain in his injured leg. On a not-so-great note, he was fairly sure he'd never walk straight again regardless because of how good his body still felt after climaxing.

Amelia stared harder at him and lowered her gaze. She sighed. "I knew I shouldn't have given in to the pull to you. It's what Cal wanted and that alone made it wrong. Seeing how you're acting right now, it's clear this was a mistake. I'm sorry. I thought, well, I thought it would make you happy. That it would make you feel good. Like how you made me feel. I'll go."

Go?

"No," he ground out, reaching for her only to find his hands had started to shift once again as well. He stiffened and hated how weak he was being.

Amelia backed up more, heading in the direction of the door.

Gram wanted to charge after her and explain that she'd done nothing wrong. In fact, she'd done every single thing right. Beyond right even. But he wasn't in control of himself.

Don't go thinking this was a mistake, lass. Please. It was anything but a mistake.

Stiffening, she looked over her shoulder at him, her brows meeting. "Your hands and teeth… is that something you can't control right now?"

He nodded.

"Are you staying away from me because of that?" she asked, her eyes growing moist. "Because you're still worried that you'll hurt me?"

Again, he nodded.

A partial laugh broke free from her. "So, you don't think this was a mistake and I didn't hurt you?"

"Not. A. Mistake." The words were hard to get out, but he managed, just barely.

"Can I do anything to help?" she asked, the sincerity in her voice moving him.

Unless she was willing to be mounted and claimed, there wasn't much she could do beyond keeping her distance from him. Their joint power continued to fill the room and he wondered how long it would remain.

Amelia drew in a large breath and he watched as she straightened her shoulders. "Gram, when you're like this, do you have intercourse a special way? I've seen the shifter males when they're partially shifted, bending their women over and taking them from behind. Is that something you need right now?"

Was she serious?

He blinked, his eyes wide, his body burning with the need to shift fully and do just as she'd suggested.

Chapter Twenty-Two

AMELIA ENTERTAINED LEAVING the room and not looking back, leaving Gram to his own devices. She'd done what had been expected of her—she'd pleasured him. But her reasons for doing it hadn't been because she wanted to follow commands. No. She'd done it because it felt right and she'd wanted it for herself.

She still wanted him.

Still felt the pull to him.

Torn between turning and throwing her arms around the man, and fleeing in order to salvage her escape plan, Amelia froze, her hand on the door handle. Leaving was the smarter option. If she did, she could keep getting everything in order for leaving tomorrow. Gram was an unnecessary complication. A wrench in her plan. But she couldn't deny she was drawn to him in a way that suggested she might never actually get enough of him.

He was like a drug.

And she craved him.

It was painfully obvious that Gram feared hurting her and that meant something to her. It meant that he was a good man. Unlike the men she'd spent her life around. He was different and while they may have only just met, he cared about her in some way, even if only small.

She knew she cared for him already.

More than cared, not that she could explain the reasoning behind it all.

Was he right? Were they fated mates? It would certainly explain the attraction she felt for him, the desire she had to please him, and the hollow pit in her stomach at the thought of carrying out her plan to flee with Andie but leaving Gram behind.

Whatever the reasoning behind it all was, she knew she couldn't do it. She couldn't go without him. She couldn't walk away from him now when it was clear he was struggling with his shifter side and she understood that inner battle was because of her. Because he didn't want to hurt her. Deep down she also knew she could help him. It was within her power to give his wolf side what it was craving, ease Gram's longing, and in return, handle her own desires as well.

With mustered courage, she took hold of her dress and pulled it up and over her head. Casting it aside, she stood with her back to Gram, totally naked and exposed to him. She'd never felt so vulnerable in all her life.

Would he reject her?

Would his fear of hurting her win out?

She waited with bated breath, unsure if he'd still refuse to touch her or not.

When his hot, hard body crowded hers, pressing her against the door, she knew otherwise.

He put his mouth to her ear. "*Mine.*"

Heat rushed over her and she nodded, tipping her head, giving him access to her neck if he wanted it, knowing that was what he and his wolf needed. "Yes. *Yours.*"

He pushed against her more. He put his hands up to the door and leaned, causing her to press to the hard wood totally and completely. His cock nudged at her backside and she gasped.

Gram dragged his chin over her shoulder and

the stubble on it tickled, making her laugh and bend slightly. That only served to push her butt against his erection more.

The magik around her began to swirl. It was suddenly caressing her everywhere all at once. Tiny gasps of pleasure came from her as she arched her back more, wanting Gram fully.

He moved an arm down and slinked it around her waist. When he lifted her feet off the floor, she yelped. He held her there suspended and she felt compelled to lean forward more for him, understanding what he was doing—ensuring they'd fit together while they were both standing since there was such a height difference. It was on the tip of her tongue to suggest they use the table when she felt the head of his cock nudging her wet core.

The power around them increased, caressing her intimate areas to the point she felt as if she'd burst. When Gram pressed his shaft into her, it was painfully tight at first, but quickly eased. He went deeper, slowly, inch by inch, and she understood the restraint he was showing in order to make that happen.

Another sign he was nothing like the males of the Flock.

Amelia gasped as pleasure continued to rack her body.

He buried himself farther into her wetness and growled against her ear in male triumph. Liquid heat flooded her sex and he began moving in and out of her with more ease, filling her past the brink of full. She pressed her hands to the door, easing one up and over Gram's hand. The claws on his fingers receded and suddenly he was kissing her neck, her ear, anywhere he could seem to get his mouth. She knew then he was gaining more control over his wolf side.

Oddly, she wanted him to keep being wild.

He didn't disappoint as he continued to pound into her, holding her off the floor, their bodies locked tight together. He controlled the entire situation and that only served to turn her on more. She liked knowing how powerful yet gentle he was with her. He was a true alpha. The kind that didn't need to fling power or strength around endlessly or rule with fear. He was the kind that understood violence wasn't the answer to every situation.

She gasped and panted as he thrust in and out of her, again and again, the pleasure bordering on mind-numbing.

Pumping, he made low, animalistic noises before grunting.

She moaned and gasped at the feel of his big, thick, long shaft pounding like a piston in and out of her. The magik continued to pulse around them and it, combined with Gram being buried deep in her, was too much for her system to handle.

Pleasure tore through her and she cried out in ecstasy, digging her nails into the back of Gram's hand. She hadn't meant to draw blood, but it happened all the same.

The man didn't stop or even seem to notice.

No.

He kept going.

Kept drilling in and out of her.

Blinded by passion, she cried out again as her body constricted around his cock.

Gram went faster, bucking against her, making her hit her zenith over and over. She couldn't take it anymore. For a second, she thought she might go up in flames if he kept going.

Growling, he jerked her hips tighter to him, locking deep in her body with a shuddering roar. She felt him erupting deep in her as his cock twitched. "*Mine!*"

The slightest of pinches happened in her neck at the same moment her entire body lit with bliss.

The pinching stopped, and Gram licked the area, only seconds before Amelia gave in to the urge to lean forward. She licked the bloody scratches on the back of his hand and paused, whispering as she did, "Mine."

The power swirling in the room slammed into them.

It felt as if someone was there, stitching their hearts and souls together, forming an unbreakable bond. For one moment, she felt as if she was experiencing it all from Gram's point of view. What confused her was how much the man cared for her already. If she didn't know better, she'd have thought she was sensing love.

As quickly as the glimpse into his world had come, it vanished.

"It's done," he said, his voice deep. "But we're far from done, lass."

Gram lifted her higher and began to fuck her so hard and fast, she feared they'd fall through the door and into the hallway. That or he'd break her in two. If it happened, she'd die happy.

Really, really happy.

She cried out again in pure bliss as he rooted

deep, his cock twitching once more. When he made small, jerky thrusts, she found herself swiveling her hips as best she could considering the fact he was holding her around her waist, locking her body to his.

With a quivering breath, he eased from her body and she felt their combined juices instantly start to leak from her.

Gram kissed her ear and then lowered her with the utmost care to her feet. He didn't move, choosing instead to keep her facing the door. He wrapped his arms around her and held her to him.

She sank against his embrace as their power evaporated, leaving her slightly dizzy, but thoroughly satisfied.

Her mind wandered to what little she knew about supernatural matings. As she thought about the fact that he'd bitten her, and she'd licked his blood, while they were climaxing and verbally claiming one another, she tensed.

He let out a long, shaky breath. "Aye, lass. I was nae wrong. Yer my mate. And no one will be telling us otherwise from this point onward."

Amelia gulped. "We're mated now?"

"Aye." He planted a row of kisses on her

shoulder before turning her to face him. He raked his gaze over her and a lopsided grin spread over his face.

"Gram?"

"I have the hottest wife ever," he said with a wink. "Lass, all I want to do right now is play with your boobs. Can I?"

Unable to help herself, she laughed. It was the result of his odd humor, nerves, and fear.

Cal would kill them all if he didn't get what he wanted from the Bringer. Then again, maybe he'd wanted Gram to claim Amelia all along. The thought sobered her, and she nearly started to panic once more.

There was no way to take it back. No undoing a claiming. The act was done. They were officially mated. Man and wife in the eyes of the supernatural community.

It was a lot to absorb and take in. Her mind was having a hard time wrapping around the knowledge, despite her knowing it was true. She was his and he was hers.

"Lass?" he asked. "You look pale. What's wrong? Do you regret what happened between us? I thought when you lifted your dress that you understood what was going to happen. That you knew I was going to claim you fully. I'm sorry. I dinnae mean to take yer choices. Did I hurt you? Amelia, I'd never hurt you intentionally."

Amelia grabbed him, keeping him close. "No. I'm not sure how to explain this right. I mean, I do regret it."

He lowered his gaze. "Amelia, I'm sorry."

"Let me finish please," she said, as she touched his chin. "But it's not for the reasons you're thinking. I regret it because now you're in my father's crosshairs even more. Gram, I'm scared he'll hurt you. That this isn't what he wanted, or worse yet, it is. Maybe we just played right into his twisted plot. But I don't regret getting *you*. And I don't regret the fact I'm now yours forever, and you're mine.

"You're the bright spot in all of this. I didn't start out today thinking I'd meet a man who captivated me and that I'd end up his wife before the day was out. I'm not going to ask your age. I probably don't want to know right now. Save that revelation for another day. I'm only twenty-three. I've been raising my little sister for two years already, all the while trying to get her away from a madman. When I had a small taste of the outside world, it became very clear to me how sheltered I was in the Flock. I may have seen unspeakable atrocities, but I'd not ever seen a movie in a theater. And the movies I did get to see were carefully screened. No sense letting the Flock get ideas to start thinking on their own or anything."

She took a deep breath, keeping hold of his chin. "I've barely had a chance to live my life. I've never really been able to live it just for me, and now, I'm tied to a man who oozes alpha and is, I'm guessing, a lot older than he looks. Are you going to take my freedoms like Cal has, but in other ways? Did I just trade one domineering male for another?"

"Never," said Gram, taking hold of her hand and kissing her fingertips. "I'd never take yer freedoms, Amelia. If you do nae want me, I'll do my best to stay on the fringe of yer life, but I'd be lying if I told you I could be far from you. A shifter male is hardwired to nae let that occur. But maybe I could turn my magik on myself. Maybe I could find a way to help you be as far from me as you want to be."

His words eased her worries.

She'd been right about him.

He was nothing like the men of the Flock.

She skimmed her fingertips over his lips more,

hating the sadness that filled his blue gaze. The man was more than she could have ever hoped for in a mate. More than she'd ever expected anyone to be. He was willing to forgo his own chance at happiness to please her. "I don't want that. I just needed to hear you say that if I did want it, you'd not fight me on it."

A shaky breath fell free from him. "So you do nae want me to stay far from you?"

"No. I don't want that at all," she said with a smile.

"Guid thing, lass. I think I'd have had to resort to asking the twins to hogtie me to make sure I kept my distance from you. Trust me when I say they'd have loved to do it. In fact, it would nae be their first time doing such a thing to me."

She grinned. "Bet Bill would have helped."

"Aye. For sure." He chuckled. "You do realize we're standing here naked and I can still smell yer cream?"

"We just did a lot. How can you still be thinking about sex?" she asked.

He bit his inner cheek. "The fact yer nae makes me think I'm nae as guid a lover as I've thought I was. You've managed to make me the happiest man on earth and offer a serious blow to my ego all in one afternoon, lass."

Her eyes widened. "Oh, no! That isn't it at all. It all felt amazing. More than amazing even. But, well, my friend Tina talks about men and sex and she told me that while supernatural males have more stamina than a human male, they still require downtime between sexual acts. You don't. That's what I meant. I'd tell you that you're the best lover I've ever had but I'm not sure that would hold much weight considering you're the only lover I've ever had. What I can tell you is that it was amazing, and I hope we can do that a lot more."

He nodded, wrapping his arms around her. "Aye, and I'll be the *only* one you ever have, too. Yer mine, lass."

This time, the idea of being mated to him didn't send her into an instant panic. A piece of her wanted to believe that together, she and Gram could accomplish anything—even beat Cal at his own game.

Whatever game that may be.

His prediction of Amelia being the one to attract the Bringer had been right. She just hoped the rest of what he was thinking might happen wouldn't come to pass. "Figures this would be one of the predictions my insane father got right."

Gram laughed softly as well, rubbing himself against her as he waggled his dark brows. "Wait until he figures out that he's nae gaining another follower but rather losing two daughters."

"Gram?"

He caressed her side, making her laugh as it tickled. "Amelia, I told you already, I plan to take you and yer sister from here. I'll nae have either of you here if it's nae safe for you. Understood?"

She nodded. "He won't let us just walk away. I have a plan set up to run. We'll need to be secretive about it. You're too important to his grand designs. Andie and I are disposable. Like our mother was to him when she'd served her purpose and gave him children."

Gram growled, and she worried he'd revert and end up in shifted wolf form. "If he attempts to take you or yer sister—my family—from me, or harm either of you in any way, he'll see just how fucking much I really do *bring* to the cult."

Pressing herself to him, Amelia stared up into his handsome face. "Shh. They'll hear."

"Guid."

She went to her tiptoes and kissed his lips tenderly before drawing back.

Gram came for her mouth again, but she touched his lips, blocking his path. "Lass, my dick does nae seem to care that he should want downtime."

Glancing down, she saw he was right. She stared harder at his shaft.

"Amelia?"

"I'm trying to figure out how that fit in me and how it is I'm upright and not split in two," she said flatly, meaning every word of it.

His deep chuckle tugged at her gut. "Truth be told, I was nae so sure it would fit. It was touch and go for a moment there."

She laughed and traced her hands over the planes of his upper chest. "Gram, are you over three thousand years old?"

His eyes widened. "Och. No! Lass, do I need to invest in moisturizer? The last time I checked I dinnae look much beyond thirty. I could be wrong though. When I see some teens driving now, I think they look ten, so I may nae be a guid judge of age."

She grinned and found herself running her thumb over his lower lip. "I was pointing out the fact Cal *is* nearly three thousand. He's had a long time to build his powerbase. A long time to learn all the tricks in the book. I didn't mean you looked that old. You are so handsome. I really don't think I'm ever going to get tired of looking at you. Or tasting you. You taste really yummy."

He flashed a sexy smile. "So do you, wife. And if you do nae wish to be taken again, right this moment, we should get dressed, find Andie, the two Scottish dipshites who brought me here, the hairy nutty old man, and his silent buddy with the doll head, and then discuss an exit strategy."

"Yes. Before Cal enacts whatever plan for you that he has."

"Actually, I'm more worried someone will try to give me a mud bath and put cucumbers on my eyes than I am of yer father."

She couldn't help but smile more at his humor. "Thank you for coming here."

He touched her cheek with the back of his hand. "Thank you for nae giving up on me. For trusting me even when I dinnae trust myself. For knowing I would nae hurt you when I claimed you. And for letting me claim you when you've only just met me. The faith you have in me means everything, Amelia."

She smiled and then gasped as she looked down the front of him and did a double take.

His brow furrowed. "Lass?"

"Gram, your scars."

He glanced down too and stepped back fast, running his hand over his smooth torso. Gone were any signs he'd been burned or hurt.

Amelia went to him and spun him around. The smallest of burn marks remained on his upper right back area. Everything else was gone. Totally healed over as if it had never happened. "Your back is pretty much healed, too. There is just a small bit that isn't. It's the size of my hand. How?"

He turned slowly, took her hands in his, and brought them to his lips. He kissed them. "That is nae important. All that matters right now is that yer with me. Let's go collect our family and get the hell out of here before someone offers us grape-flavored drinks or a ride on any comets."

"But, Gram, your scars. They're gone. Don't you want to know how and why?"

He kissed her knuckles, one by one. "It's pretty plain to me already. You've healed me, Amelia. The man and the wolf."

She teared up, realizing that the constant fear

she'd been living with for years was lessened. For the first time in a long time, she had real hope about her future—about getting Andie far from their father's clutches and schemes. It was then she realized Gram had, in a way, healed her too.

He eased around her and moved her over out of the way of the door. He opened it boldly, seemingly unconcerned he was totally naked. She noticed the spot he'd put her in kept her from view of anyone who might be in the hallway.

Gram stiffened, his back to her. "Susan, guid. You brought the dress. Is there anything else you need, seeing as how yer lurking outside the door?"

Susan was out there?

Amelia tensed.

How much had the woman overheard?

Did she know Gram was planning to take her and Andie and leave? If she did, she'd go to Cal. Susan prided herself on being Cal's eyes and ears.

Gram stayed where he was at the door. "I'm going to spend the rest of the day with Amelia, unless there is some problem with that?"

"No, no problem," said Susan, something off in her voice. "I'll let her father know she'll be with you."

"Guid."

Amelia held her breath, fear of what Susan may have heard too much to take. At some point, her power had fallen, letting others hear what was happening in the room, but Amelia didn't know exactly when that had happened. Her mind had been elsewhere.

Shutting the door, Gram glanced at her. "Lass, yer pale. What's wrong?"

She didn't say anything, afraid Susan would hear her.

Gram came to her with the dress in hand. He dragged his knuckles over her exposed neck before cupping the back of her head and kissing her thoroughly. He drew back, grinning. "Wife, let's go."

Chapter Twenty-Three

GRAM WALKED hand in hand with his wife, still unable to fully grasp the fact he was indeed someone's husband. It hadn't been on his mind when his day had started, and he'd not been kidding when he'd told Amelia this was the best kidnapping he'd ever had.

He didn't exactly relish the idea of having to admit as much to his buddies, but since it meant he had Amelia, he'd consider sending out an interoffice memo, so no one missed the news.

His wife was perfect.

More than he deserved. And while they'd met under odd circumstances, they'd at least met.

He'd been in such a dark place mentally. And

hadn't seen any way out of it. She'd been his guiding light. His port in the storm.

The pain and heartache he'd endured to get to this moment, this point, all seemed worth it to him now. Though part of him feared that it would go as quickly as it had come. That something or someone would come along and rip away his bliss. He couldn't help but think of Cal and the entire bizarreness that was the Flock.

Within four seconds of meeting Taggert, Gram had thought the man was a dick. No surprise there. Brian was much the same way for him. But Cal had been an altogether different beast. He'd sensed something about the man; he just wasn't sure what that was. From what Amelia had told him, the man was a Grade-A whack job, but so far, Gram hadn't seen anything to support the statement.

Not that he didn't believe his mate.

He did.

He just had a hard time wrapping his mind around a hippie bent on world domination being any kind of a real threat. The man was named after a bird for crying out loud. How deadly could a bird be? How much damage could ruffling his feathers really cause?

Then again, hippies didn't tend to surround themselves with men like Taggert and Brian. And then there was Susan, who he could sense didn't like Amelia one bit. To the point that hate seemed to drip from her very core when Amelia was either brought up or near.

Gram had overheard Susan and Brian when they'd cornered his mate in the kitchen area of the spa. He'd felt Amelia's fear, her unease, and it had prompted him to go in search of her, to hell with the fact he'd been in nothing more than a towel.

For her, he'd walk naked down the interstate.

The twins would do it too, just for fun.

Cringing, he got a visual of Bill wanting to join in.

Now *that* man would for sure walk down a busy road wearing nothing more than the permanent fur he seemed to be covered with. The twins were right: Gram had never seen a fuzzier human in his life, and he'd been around a hell of a long time.

"You're quiet," said Amelia as she tugged lightly on his hand.

"Sorry, lass," he returned, bringing her hand to his lips, kissing it as he continued to steal glances at her. The gown Susan had brought for Amelia was also white, which seemed to be all anyone in the Flock wore, and it fit snugly over her breasts. His cock hardened at the thought of what was and wasn't under her dress. She wasn't wearing any undergarments. Under it all, she was naked.

The sweet taste of her cunt had spurred him onward and he wanted to sample her again. Lick her for hours. Hell, years.

His mate would be well and thoroughly pleasured every chance he could get. And if Fate was on their side, they might even be blessed with little ones of their own one day, not that he didn't already feel a strangely deep connection to Andie.

He wanted to take the little one away from everything and make sure she was raised right, knowing love, knowing what it was like to have a father who cared. He smiled as he thought about Andie and Bethany playing together. He suspected they'd end up being good friends since they were so close in age.

His mind raced with all the things he needed to see to the second they got back home. His home was already well-equipped for a little girl, but he'd change everything to suit Andie's likes, whatever they may be.

He'd buy her six hundred red balls if that was her toy of choice.

He needed to reach out to the preschool at PSI to see about getting her enrolled. There was so much to do. Everything had to be perfect for the little one since he'd be uprooting all she knew and asking her to take a chance on him.

To possibly find it in her heart to love him as he already knew he'd love her.

When Gram realized he was spiraling down a panic-induced path, worrying over things that didn't need to be addressed right this second, he cleared his throat and his mind. As he did, his gaze slid over his mate's form once again.

Dammit if his cock didn't instantly rise to the occasion.

His dick was Pavlovian in its response to her. Evidently, old wolves could learn new tricks.

His mouth watered at the thought of taking one of Amelia's pert nipples into his mouth. The next he knew, he began to shake as raw need rippled through him.

She took another step and her breasts bounced slightly.

He nearly moaned at the sight and suggested they jog so they'd bounce more.

"You keep looking at me funny," she said. "Is something wrong? Do you regret what happened between us? It was really sudden and unexpected. I'll understand if you changed your mind."

"If by regret you mean I want to lift you, drive into you, and never leave yer body again, then aye. *Huge* regret," he said with a smile. "Fucking ginormous regret. I'm running over with it. Can I touch your boobs?"

The grin she gave him only made him harder.

"What?"

He bit his lower lip. "Lass, you have to know what you look like in that dress. Hell, every dress I've seen you in today. And what you look like out of them. Woman, you've a body to die for."

She turned several shades of red and tugged at her dress, only serving to show off her nipples more.

He wished he'd have just remained naked instead of bothering to get dressed when they left.

Fuck who saw him.

Walking around in jeans with a hard-on was easier said than done. With his free hand, he tried adjusting himself with limited success. Short of getting naked again, he wasn't going to find a comfortable spot for his cock.

Well, *in* his mate would be pretty fucking comfortable.

He growled as he thought of her wet sheath wrapped around his cock. "Lass, the likelihood of you wanting to be barefoot and pregnant the rest of our immortal lives is…?"

"Gram?" she asked with a laugh. "What kind of question is that?"

"The kind a man asks when he knows he's going to want to spend every waking second in his mate. Seemed wise to get yer input on it. So, think about it and get back to me." He waited a moment and then locked gazes with her. "What did you decide?"

"Honestly, my only thoughts have been getting Andie far from here. Beyond that, I've never really given my future much consideration."

"Tell me what you had planned. *All* of it," he said, wanting to know what, exactly, she'd had planned for her exit from the Flock. Somehow, he doubted she'd planned to use the front door.

He did.

He'd walk his mate and Andie right out of the front gate and if anyone tried to stop him, he'd

MANDY M. ROTH

tear their fucking heads off and put them on a
pike in front of the resort as a warning to other
would-be cults.

Mess with his mate or his family, and he'd
unleash a fury the likes of which they'd never seen
before.

Her gaze moved around as she took in their
surroundings. "Not here. I need to check on
Andie and then I can take you somewhere private
to talk."

"Lass, the wee one is fine. Car and Mac would
use our mental link to alert me if she was
nae okay."

"Mental link?" she asked.

He nodded. "We can communicate with our
minds. It's something the men I work with all
practice. It's harder to do with different species.
But we've done it so much over the centuries that
sometimes it's as easy as exhaling."

The worried look on her face pained him.

He focused on Mac and reached out with his
mind. *Are you with Andie?*

Och, aye. And I do nae want to discuss it more.

Gram tensed. *If she's hurt in any way…*

*The wee one is nae hurt. She's…erm…well, she's
putting bows in my hair. It's making her happy and keeping*

362

her occupied. In a little bit, we're going to take her out to play. She mentioned something about pretending to be airplanes since she's never been on one. We'll figure some-thing out, said Mac, sounding less than pleased to be having his hair done by a four-year-old.

If anything changes… pushed Gram.

Aye, you'll be the first to know. And, Campbell, you owe me big for this shit. I was going to spend the night in my own cabin, surrounded by hot chicks in white dresses, getting a full-service treatment. Now I'm getting a makeover from a three-year-old.

Gram snorted. *She's four.*

Big difference.

Mac.

There was silence a second. *Sorry, the wee one is now drinking a grilled cheese smoothie with Bill and Gus. Correction, they're pulling out spoons. Apparently, it's too thick for the straws. I'm going to vomit but she seems to like it.*

Gram smiled, pleased to know his friends were coming through and helping with Andie. *Mac, I did it.*

Did what?

Claimed Amelia.

A long pause greeted him. *You couldnae have waited and let us throw you a bachelor's party first? For*

MANDY M. ROTH

fuck's sake, Campbell, we've been here like five hours and you've already found yer mate, claimed her, and have us babysitting. What's next? World domination?

Gram smiled wide. *Possibly a cult overthrow, but we'll talk about that later tonight.*

Aye. I'm always up for a good takeover. Mac's laugh reached him, and Gram closed the connection to find his mate's eyes wide as she gripped his hand.

He hissed and pried his hand loose from hers. Amelia had one hell of a grip. "Lass?"

"You went all quiet and got a weird look on your face. She's hurt, isn't she? Oh gods, she's dead."

He drew her to him. "Shh, no. She's fine. Though I do nae think you'll be pleased to hear what the twins are letting her eat, but she's in guid hands. It would seem she's been verra busy putting bows in Mac's hair."

Amelia laughed loudly. "I'm almost sorry I missed that."

"Do nae worry. I know Car well. There will be photos, video footage, and maybe a social media channel devoted to it by the time we get there. For sure Mac will be up for an Asshole of the Week award."

She tipped her head. "A what?"

"Never mind. But, as I said, the wee one is fine and in guid hands."

She exhaled and some of the tension seemed to melt away from her. He hated that she carried the weight of the world on her shoulders. She was so young and had already been through so much. He'd fix it all for her. He'd take her and her sister far from Cal and the Flock and they'd be a family.

"Take me to this private place where you wanted to talk to me," he said, kissing her forehead lightly. "You can tell me everything I need to know now while Andie is tended to."

Nodding, she pointed at a fork in the path. "My greenhouse is that way."

Chapter Twenty-Four

AMELIA CLUTCHED Gram's hand for dear life as they headed in the direction of her greenhouse— her sanctuary. Normally, she disliked anyone, other than Tina and Andie, being in it or near it. But she found herself wanting to share it with Gram. Wanting him to see what she loved and what held meaning for her.

He'd probably think it was silly that she enjoyed herbalism so much. She couldn't imagine what she and the Flock looked like to him, or why he kept acting like he'd won some prize by getting tethered to her for the rest of his life.

He was signing himself up for a life on the run. A life of looking over his shoulder, forever wondering when Cal would make his move and find them. She hadn't thought hard enough before she'd surrendered herself to him, wanting what he offered. Had she, she'd have realized she was quite possibly signing his death warrant.

Staying and letting Cal have his way would be safest for Gram, but Andie would pay the price in the long run. She'd end up forced into a mating with Brian one day. And Taggert wouldn't let the slight go of losing out to Gram. He would prove to be nothing but trouble for them for as long as they remained in the compound or part of the Flock.

Gram drew her closer, kissing the top of her head as they walked. It soothed away some of the gnawing worry in her gut, but she knew it was merely a mask. The troubles were still there and no amount of kisses would solve or end them.

"Lass, the worry in yer eyes tells me yer overthinking this again."

"Yes, but how did you know?" she asked, staring up at him.

"Because you tensed and looked faraway in thought. I assumed you were thinking of what we'd just done—of the fact yer mine now," he said. "Was I wrong about that?"

She shook her head and then shrugged.

"Maybe. Kind of. I was actually worried for you, since you got stuck with me."

"Stuck with you?" he echoed.

She nodded. "You got a poorly trained virgin, whose father is a false prophet and head of a fanatical cult, not to mention saddled with a four-year-old when all you'd done today was show up at a spa. Seems like it's not really your day, is it?"

He drew her to a stop and took hold of her shoulders, making her face him fully. "This is the single best day of my life, Amelia Campbell."

She squeaked at the sound of his last name in place of hers. Heat rushed over her, as did a feeling of nausea as it all really sank in.

He grinned. "Looks like it's you who is nae so sure they're having a guid day."

She gasped. "Oh Gram. You're amazing."

"Lass." He took hold of her hands and lifted them high above her head, pulling her closer, dipping his head as he did. "If you were any more experienced in the bedroom, I'd come on my fucking leg before I even got in you. Hell, I nearly did that already. You were perfect. You are perfect. Continue to doubt that and I'll fuck you here and now, on the path, where any zealot could be out for a late-day count-the-crazy-apocalyptic-signs stroll."

His words and unique outlook on life made her laugh softly.

The heat continued in her but this time it didn't make her want to puke. It centered in her chest. As she realized just how much the man before her meant to her, she closed her eyes, breathing in his scent.

He growled lightly, still holding her hands up high. He ground his body against hers, causing a torrent of cream to flood her thighs. Gram inhaled deeply and growled more. "I'm about to give in and take you here and now."

"As much as I want you in me again, can we not? I saw a snake out here last week. If one of them slithers over me while we're on the ground having sex, I will be too traumatized to ever let you touch me again."

His eyes widened, and he lifted her up and off her feet.

"What are you doing?"

"I'll nae risk a snake getting near you and no sex for guid."

If she smiled anymore around the man, her face would crack. "Put me down."

He did, but she noticed him glancing around at the foliage around them. When she realized he was indeed scouting for snakes, she managed to smile even more. Life with him would never be boring or dull for her. It was easy to see her mate had a unique sense of humor. One that greatly appealed to her. Everything about the man did.

"Tell me about yerself, Amelia. Nae yer father. Nae the Flock. You. What do you like?" he asked, taking her hand in his once more as they began to walk again.

She was about to say nothing when she thought of her greenhouses. "I like to grow things. And I love herbalism and holistic medicines. I'm always trying to come up with something new and natural to help others. It's my favorite place and it's where we're headed now. That is something that means a lot to me. Silly. I know."

"Lass, that is nae silly in the least," he said. "If it's plants you like, I'll see to it you have a special area to work with them until yer heart is content. I've more than one home, but I think the main house will be perfect. There is an old greenhouse on the property, as well as an old, overgrown herb garden on one of the back acres. It was on my list to one day tear down…"

She gasped.

He winked. "But now that I know you have a love of it all, I'll bring in someone to restore it to its former glory. And if you need more space, I'll have it built as well."

"You don't have to do that. I'm capable of getting the garden and the greenhouse back into working order. The one I love here, the one that is just mine, it's old, but I keep it in good working order. I don't let Cal send anyone to help me. I let Tina help me change out glass panels when they break, but that's only because I trust her, and she is always encouraging me to pursue a future in holistic healing. She thinks that when I go, I can do that anywhere."

Gram slowed his pace. "This Tina knows of yer plan to leave?"

"Yes."

"Does anyone else?"

She nodded. "Jeanie, she's not part of the Flock. In fact, she thinks the Flock are a bunch of fruitcakes and she can't stand my father. She's helped me so much with everything. She even drove me to Denver to meet with a contact I found. She wasn't happy about me making her stay in a parking area that was several blocks from the back alley I was meeting the man in at night, but she didn't argue too much."

Gram stared blankly at her and stopped walking altogether. "Lass, you went to the city, walked alone around it at night, and went to an alley to meet some man you knew, all by yerself?"

Her lips pursed a second. "Yes, and no. I didn't actually know the man before I got there. When I first saw him, I couldn't stop thinking about how big he was."

"You met a stranger, in an alley, at night, alone?" he asked, his eyes widening. For a second, she thought steam might actually come out of the man's ears.

She nodded.

Looking up, he said something in a language she didn't know and then looked down at her. "I know I swore to nae be an alpha douchebag to you, Amelia, but can you maybe *never* do something like that again? Ever?"

"Yes. I can never do something like that again. Ace was big but very nice. He was gruff and rough around the edges, but he has a big heart. He didn't let me pay him for the new identities and he wanted to help me. He also said if I didn't reach out to him in forty-eight hours—which would be tomorrow night—he was going to come here. I got the sense he was really worried about me and that he really would storm the gates."

"Lass, yer lucky he was nae a serial killer or something," he stressed.

"I know, but, Gram, the man I'm trying to get away from is far worse," she reminded.

He sighed.

She offered a slight smile as she led him in the direction of the greenhouse. When they reached it, she instantly felt more at ease. The place always had that effect on her since she was little. It had been a place her mother enjoyed working as well. She still felt connected to her mother there.

Amelia went to the door and opened it. "It's not much. Cal tried to make me work in the fancy one he had built on the other side of the compound, but I like this one. I like how it catches the morning light just right. I like the view of the mountains from it. And mostly, I like that I feel safe in here. It's kind of my own personal refuge."

Gram entered and went to one of the various glass jars of liquid. He reached out to touch it, but she stopped him. "No. That's *Hippomane mancinella.*"

He gave her a questioning look.

She sighed. "Most people would know it by the name the *little apple of death*. It's very deadly."

"Why would you have it here?" he asked, moving her back from it as if he was worried that she'd somehow die from proximity.

She averted her gaze.

"Lass?"

"I work with a lot of things that, in their pure, base form, would be toxic or at the very least dangerous. But it's okay. Sometimes, Cal makes me increase the potency of something so that he can use it to suit his needs. I know he's taken some of what I've created over the years and used it in nefarious deeds and acts. I hate that he takes my passion for healing and twists it into something perverse. Mostly, I hate him."

"What is it he wants you to do with the death-apple juice?" asked Gram.

"Actually, this is one of the few times my father didn't have a direct hand in the wrongdoing. His friend did. Helmuth had it shipped in to the compound and insisted I work with it. Almost everything toxic in here right this moment was brought in at his request. Cal tasked me with trying to find a remedy for the man's condition. When conventional means didn't work, the suggestion to try other means came into play. And by suggestion, I mean Helmuth didn't give me a choice."

"Yer father forces you to handle dangerous herbs and chemicals and do his friend's bidding?"

She nodded.

His jaw set. "Lass, how much would you dislike me if I killed yer father before this dinner I'm supposed to attend with him tonight? I mean, I know you wish to be away from him, but that could just be some form of rebellion. I wouldnae want to strip you of him if you truly wish him no ill, but right now, I want to rip out his spleen."

She'd forgotten all about the dinner. "Gram, pretend to be sick or tired from a day of travel. Don't attend the dinner. I'll go, and pretend everything is normal and fine. Then I have to go to the weekly mandatory Flock gathering. If I'm not there, everyone will notice."

"Lass, I'll nae cower and hide from him or anyone for that matter. And you'll nae be going anywhere without me by yer side. Nae here. Nae until I know better what is really happening. Besides, I'm curious to see what he's about," Gram admitted. "I'll have Mac and Car watch the wee one while we attend, and I'll be crashing this gathering of theirs tonight, too. If yer required to be there, then they get me as well. Push me on this and I'll have the twins watch you too while I go alone."

She grabbed his arm so hard her nails dug into his skin. "No! I'm not letting you go to dinner with my father—alone. Not happening. No way. Nope. Try it and I'll have the twins stage a secondary kidnapping of you today and take you far from here and me. Understood?"

A strange look came over his face.

"Gram? What is it?"

"Yer scolding of me is hot. Can I touch yer boobs now?"

She snorted. "Only if you're a good boy and don't try to go to dinner alone with my father."

He winked. "Aye, yer learning. I suspect I'll be eating out of the palm of yer hand by nightfall, if nae before."

Her lips twitched at his joke. "I'd think it was the best wedding present a girl could get."

Gram glanced at the vial of the toxin and turned to leave.

She caught his arm. "Where are you going?"

He glanced back at her. "To kill yer father."

She gasped. "Gram! I already told you he's dangerous."

"Lass, no disrespect, but he's a delusional hippie who runs a health resort," he returned. "He's nae really that big a threat."

She took his hand in hers and then led him through the greenhouse to the back exit. Amelia said nothing as she walked him through thick brush. There wasn't an actual path there, but she'd traveled that way more than once in the last few weeks. When they emerged, there was a steel warehouse tucked in amongst the trees. She glanced around.

"Do you smell anyone?" she asked, already knowing his senses would be far better than hers.

"No. And I do nae hear anyone either. There is no one in the area." He stilled. "I smell gun oil. A lot of it, all of a sudden. Why?"

Nodding, she tugged on his hand and led him around to the side of the building. There was a loose piece of metal there and she pulled it back, motioning for him to go in. The second they were inside, Gram drew up short.

"Fucking hell," he said in a hushed whisper as he took in the sight of rows and rows of various weapons. There were automatic rifles, explosives, and so much more. "He's arming a militia."

She exhaled slowly. "Gram, this is only one of the weapon caches he has on the grounds. There are three more of these. This is the *smallest* of them all. The one they don't bother guarding. Do you understand me now? He's not a good man. He's not just some hippie. He's deadly. He's dangerous. An ideological zealot who will do anything to get what he wants."

He wrapped his arms around her. "Lass, we're leaving tonight. Fuck dinner. Fuck gatherings."

She gasped. "No. Not tonight. It *has* to be tomorrow. Everything is in place for tomorrow night. Not now. Trust me, if I don't show for dinner, he'll send people for me and there are a lot of Flock members here. Nearly every single one of them is willing to kill and die for him."

He looked around the warehouse as he held her. "If we do this yer way, yer to listen to me. If I give you an order, it's nae to be an alpha douchebag. It's to keep you safe. Are we in agreeance?"

She nodded. "Yes. But, Gram, even if we go tomorrow and not tonight, he won't stop hunting for *you*—you're really important to him, but I don't know why. He's always only wanted me to get to you. I'm not sure how hard he'll hunt for me when I'm gone now that he has you. But he does have a temper. He could have me hunted and killed just to prove a point."

"Lass, I only want to get you and yer sister to safety. Then, he and I can go rounds." He kissed her forehead. "I won't let either of you be hurt. We can head back to yer cabin and discuss all of this with the twins. We've friends in the area and co-workers. We can call them to assist in our exit. If it's a war Cal wants, my friends and I are more than willing to give it to him, but nae until you and yer sister are far from here and safe."

He took her hand and led her to the loose metal once more. He then stopped and put a hand up. "Do nae move from here."

She stood perfectly still as he rushed off deeper into the warehouse. When he returned, she tried to figure out what was different. "Gram?"

He winked and then held the metal piece as she exited. When they emerged on the other side, he took her hand in his and began walking quickly in the direction they'd come from.

When they emerged at the back of her greenhouse, she expected him to veer off and head toward the cabins. He didn't. He took her right back into her greenhouse. "Lass, gather anything that can confuse a shifter's senses. Anything that would mask you and Andie specifically."

"What? Why?"

"You agreed to do what I asked of you in all of this," he reminded.

Hesitantly, she set about doing what he'd asked of her. When she was done, she had two small jars of salve. "I have something better in the works. The percolation extraction method that I'm using for one of the ingredients is time consuming. It won't be finished until tomorrow morning."

"Lass, I've no clue what you just said to me."

She grinned. "The stronger one I'm trying to make needs something that I don't have finished just yet. These will have to work for now."

He stared at her for the longest time before his eyes swirled to icy blue. Sniffing, he bent and lowered himself in front of her, his hand splaying over her stomach as he did.

"Gram? What are you doing?"

He pressed his face into her lower stomach and clutched her hips, looking up at her then standing fast. "Lass, can you hurry whatever it is yer working on?"

"Hurry it?"

His eyes continued to swirl. "Aye. The stronger masking agent. Can you accelerate its time frame?"

"Maybe, but I'd need to spend the evening in here working. How can I do that if I have to be at dinner and the gathering?" she asked. "And why are you doing the freaky eye thing over it?"

He skimmed his hand over her abdomen again. "Lass, whatever you make, it needs to mask you, Andie, and the baby."

Nodding, she turned to start working on it— and then stilled, his words racing over her. Slowly, she glanced over her shoulder at him. "The what?"

"The wee one takin' root in you as we speak," he said. "I can smell the changes in yer body. I can sense it there. Hints of my magik combined with yers. And my verra bones tell me yer carryin' my babe already."

"But we just…"

He wrapped his body around hers and hugged her back against him. "Do what I asked. And do nae even glance at anything in here that is remotely harmful. I'll nae risk you or the little one."

He held her but glanced to the side, staring at a row of shelves. She knew then he wasn't really looking at the shelves but rather was doing the mental connection thing he could do with his friends.

He grunted but kept staring off at nothing in particular. He then snapped out of it. "The twins are getting Andie ready to leave now. They'll reach out to our friends in the area now. This cannae wait. One will go with Andie, Bill, and Gus and get them all away from the resort. The other twin will come here to help me get you out of here. Hurry and do what you can in the next few minutes, after that, we leave. Now."

"But, Gram," she protested.

He turned her to face him and kissed her greedily. When he was done, she was whimpering in his arms. "Amelia."

She sighed. "I know. I'll do what you asked. Are you sure that I'm…"

He nodded. "Aye."

A deep resolve settled over her and she focused, looking around at what she had at her disposal. She went to work on the task at hand, working quickly. She smeared various things on her wrist and held it out to Gram for him to smell.

"That will do for now."

"Campbell?" Car came in and looked around. "Yer mate is a witch?"

She laughed softly.

He gave her a strained look. "Do nae be hexing me. I had a witch do that to me once. My dick dinnae work for a whole week. Was torture. A week of no sex. I still have nightmares of it."

Gram motioned to him. "Car, come. We need to talk."

They stepped out through the backdoor and Amelia looked around, gathering anything else she could think of that they may need. She was about to turn to join Gram and Car out back but looked up to find Susan standing in the doorway of the greenhouse.

The evil bitch stepped in and grinned. "Amelia, it looks as if you're packing up shop. That can't possibly be. I mean, where is it you'd be going? Surely, not away from the Flock. So where are you headed to, Amelia?"

"Nowhere," whispered Amelia, weighing her options.

At least twelve male Flock members made

their way into the small greenhouse work area. Amelia knew they were all loyal to Susan, used to handle her wants and desires, regardless of how twisted they were. They were more than likely the pets Brian had mentioned. Susan had clearly overheard everything that had transpired in the massage room with Gram.

Susan glanced around the room and grinned more. "Odd, I would have thought your mate would be here, with you. What happened? Did he claim you, get what he wanted, promise to help you get away, and then bolt? Did the Bringer abandon you? Was all the buildup about his arrival for naught? Hmm? What will your father say about it all? He had so much hope and faith in you. Too much. You're nothing. No power. No worth. And he'll know that soon enough. Brian has gone to get him. When he finds out you're trying to run, there will be hell to pay."

Amelia's mind raced and then she took a deep breath, wanting to protect Gram and the others. "Yes. That's what happened. The Bringer is gone. He's probably already back at his cabin, packing to leave. He regretted what he did almost instantly. When he learned Father made me trick him, entrap him, he lost trust in me."

Susan tossed her head back and laughed. "Little miss perfect finally did something that will earn her an ending like the one her mother suffered. I can't wait to see my pets rip you to shreds. Just like the hybrids did to your mother. Then, I'll feed them Andie."

Amelia stiffened. "You won't touch her."

Susan snorted. "And who will stop me? You? Please. You're powerless. The only reason you're even alive is because you're Cal's offspring. But even he knows you only had one use—to fuck the Bringer. It's evident you didn't even do that well."

She looked to the man nearest her. "Find Andie. Take her to the grove. Wait there."

Amelia took a step forward. "No."

One of the men tried to grab her and she twisted and grabbed the very same jar she'd warned Gram not to touch. She hurled it at the man and it splashed in his face and eyes. The next Amelia knew, all the men were coming at her.

A shot rang out and the one closest to her lurched back, a crimson dot appearing in the center of his forehead. Another shot went off and yet another male dropped.

Everything seemed to slow as Amelia turned to find Gram and Car there, just inside of the backdoor. Each had a handgun and they were systematically picking off the male Flock members.

Susan's eyes swirled, and she leapt up and over one of the long tables full of various mixtures. She landed in front of Amelia, grabbed her, and whipped her around, using her as a shield. The bitch had the nerve to grab a piece of the broken glass from the little apple of death extract. She held it to Amelia's throat.

Gram put his hands up fast. "No! Do nae harm the lass."

Car lifted a brow. "I do nae want Amelia harmed either, but I'm thinking we can kill the crazy lady before she does much in the way of damage with that wee bit of glass."

Gram looked at him but no words were spoken—at least not out loud.

Car's eyes widened and he put his hands up as well.

Susan jerked harder on Amelia. "Looks like I was wrong. He didn't leave you after all. Shame. That isn't the story I'll be telling Cal later. I'll tell him you didn't want to do what he asked and in the chaos the Bringer and his friend were killed. That I happened upon your plot and tried to stop you but was too late. But you left me no choice but to kill you."

The air charged with magik and it wasn't Amelia's.

Susan pulled harder on Amelia and pressed the glass into her skin, cutting it, drawing blood.

Gram's face went ashen. "No!"

Amelia had suffered under the woman for too long. Endured too much. She was done. She pulled upon her gifts and looked at the remaining Flock members. She knew the second she held their minds, something her father could do to some extent. She held them enthralled with her magik. "Kill her."

They charged at Susan.

Amelia managed to jerk free from the woman and Gram was suddenly there, having cleared two tables without issues to get to her. He lifted her and rushed her to the side of the room to the sink and started trying to dump water on her neck, but only really succeeded in soaking the front of her dress.

Car stared wide-eyed as the Flock males partially shifted and clamped their jaws down on a screaming Susan wherever they could. "We should go, now!"

The pets went wild, tearing into the woman's flesh, ripping her apart, just as she'd threatened to have them do to Amelia. Just as had been done to Abigail. While the sight of her mother suffering the same fate had haunted Amelia, seeing Susan meet the same end oddly made Amelia almost want to smile.

As sick as that was.

Gram's attempts to dunk her under the running water killed the moment.

"Gram, stop!" she shouted.

He didn't. "Lass, the grape of wrath is in yer blood."

She took a calming breath. "The grape of wrath?"

"The poison shite!" he shouted, past hysterics.

She understood then what he was talking about. "Oh, the little apple of death? Yes. It's in my bloodstream now, more than likely."

He gasped, lifted her, and she got the sense he was going to shove her entire upper half into the sink to rinse her.

She jerked free and shook her head. "Gram, are you nuts? Stop trying to drown me with a faucet."

"Lass, it will kill you and the babe and…"

She cupped his face. "No. It won't."

"But you dinnae let me touch it. You said…"

"Gram, I'm not like others. I'm different. Remember that I told you my father is a blend of many things, but not one of anything?"

"Aye," he said, his hands shaking.

"I'm his daughter. That means, I'm like him. That all he's done to himself was passed down to me and to my sister. That makeup gives me an immunity to the things in here. I can't be poisoned. I figured it out by accident last year. My father doesn't know. No one does."

He didn't stop shaking. "Amelia, the babe. The wee one may nae have the same immunity."

Car swept in, grabbed her, and ran. "Figure it out later, Campbell."

Gram rushed out of the greenhouse behind them just as Flock members swarmed it. They were all heavily armed. Gram threw magik out and at them, knocking them back as he did.

Car spun around, set Amelia on her feet, and then froze, his gaze going to her chest. His eyes widened. "Lass, yer dress is wet."

Groaning, she glanced down to see that yet again she was in something that was see-through.

"Stop staring at my mate's breasts!" shouted Gram.

Car snapped out of his stupor and turned just in time to knock an automatic weapon from the hands of a Flock member who wandered into the area. He used the butt of it to bash in the man's head and then twisted, putting himself in front of her. "And now the fun begins!"

Gram continued to fight back the enemy with magik and Amelia was about to help when the strongest urge to grab Car and yank him back came over her. She trusted her gut and did just that. She ripped the Scotsman back and they stumbled into the exterior of the greenhouse.

He twisted and caught her, righting her. "Lass?"

In the next breath, an all-terrain vehicle came bursting through the brush. Mac was driving, and he had white ribbons tied at random through his long hair. He also had a crapload of weapons with him. He tossed one to his brother and then another to Gram.

He leapt off the vehicle and joined the fight.

"Took you long enough, arsehole!" shouted Car.

"Bite me," returned Mac.

"Nice hair," added Car.

Mac flipped him off.

Gram growled. "Fight each other later. Kill the enemy now!"

The twins shared a look, shrugged, and then began doing just that.

Amelia barely had time to register what was going on when another all-terrain vehicle burst through into the area. This one had Bill at the wheel. He was wearing a vest that was covered in bullets. He had a rocket launcher with him and stood fast.

He aimed right at all the men. The good guys included.

Amelia gasped. "Get down!"

Car, Mac, and Gram dropped just as Bill fired the launcher.

It hit its mark, cutting a large hole in the Flock.

Gram spun around. "What the bloody hell?"

Bill grinned. "I love the smell of burnt hippie in the evening!"

The twins didn't seem too worked up about nearly being shot with a rocket. They came up and charged the bad guys.

Another thought occurred to Amelia. If they were all here…where was Andie?

"My sister!"

Bill tipped his head. "What?"

"Where is Andie?" She shouted it as loud as she could.

He shook his head. "No. I don't have any candy! Is this really a time for that? Wait. Are you getting your monthly visitor? I once dated a chick who was so bad around her period that I had to throw chocolate at her and run in the other direction. Only safe thing to do. Hey, your dress is still see-through. Want my vest? It's got grenades attached to it too. Sweet, huh?"

"Where is—?"

He grabbed an automatic rifle and began firing at Flock members from his position on the vehicle.

Frantic and worried for Andie, Amelia turned to run toward her cabin only to step out and directly into the path of an oncoming golf cart. It came to a sudden stop and bumped ever so slightly into Amelia. This one had Gus driving, with his eyes closed, his hands gripping the wheel so tight his knuckles were white, and Andie sitting next to him, strapped to the seat with an honest-to-gods belt for a man's waist. She had on the football helmet, which had gotten turned around on her head, so she couldn't see out of it and the front was in the back. In her arms was Mona's head. There was a red strip of cloth tied around the head and someone had put black paint under her eyes, like a soldier would wear.

Bill smiled wide and nodded to her. "My lady, your chariot awaits! Hop in and I'd suggest driving. Gus is using the force. Not sure we're gonna be able to pry his hands loose though. Oh well, just climb on his lap and steer. He won't mind. Mona won't be jealous. She knows you're mated to Gram-cracker and expectin' his baby."

Amelia's jaw dropped.

She'd thought growing up in a cult had been weird. Meeting these men really made having a crazy cult leader for a father seem mundane.

"Amelia, come on!" yelled Andie from under the helmet, which was still backward. "We're going for a ride! Gus is driving!"

Amelia looked around. She didn't want to leave Gram, but her gut said to go. That Gram would want that.

He turned as he threw his hand out, claws

emerging and slicing through the neck of a Flock member. He locked gazes with her. "Go! Now!"

Nodding, she hurried to the golf cart.

She climbed in and was about to ease her way between her sister and Gus, to take over trying to drive it, when Gus slammed on the gas pedal. Amelia tumbled into the backseat and grabbed the bar, holding on to keep from falling out. She'd never seen one of the golf carts go so fast before.

They went right through the battle. Gus never opened his eyes, never took his hands from the wheel, and somehow, never hit anything or anyone. They burst through the other line of brush and achieved a fair amount of air.

Andie threw her hands in the air and Mona's head went flying. "Whee!"

Amelia reacted on instinct and snatched hold of the head, pulling it into the cart. She leaned forward, grabbed her sister to be sure she was still secured, and thrust the head back into Andie's hands. She also kept the helmet turned backward. It was best Andie not see what was happening. As it stood, the only one actually looking was Amelia.

She lost her balance and nearly fell out of the cart, which was still going far faster than any golf cart should. They hit another bump and this time, Amelia *did* go airborne.

She was just about to wrap her fingers around the bar again when something ripped her off the cart with a force that knocked the wind out of her.

Gus slowed the golf cart.

Amelia looked up. "No! Go! Get her to safety!"

The man never glanced back as he accelerated away with Andie.

Someone snarled and spun Amelia around.

She found herself face-to-face with Brian who was in partial shifted form. He backhanded her so hard that she went down.

Chapter Twenty-Five

GRAM BLOCKED a strike from a cat-shifter and then spun, slicing out as he did, cutting the man's chest open. The shifter dropped, and Gram stepped over him, grabbed a discarded sidearm and came up, firing at more of them.

They were like locusts, descending upon the location. There seemed to be no shortage of them.

"Fire in the hippie!" shouted Bill a second before there was an explosion to Gram's right.

The force of it slammed into Gram, knocking him into the air.

When he landed, it was near the vehicle Bill was standing in. He looked up at the hairy man. "Really?"

Bill shrugged. "Stop bitching. You guys are hardy stock. Hey, Little Bow-Mac could use a hand."

Gram pushed off the ground to find Mac getting swarmed by a mass of men in white clothing. He wanted to get the assholes beat back enough to go after Amelia and Andie. He needed to be sure his family was safe. He ripped off his shirt and did a partial shift, his wolf more than up for the task of killing cult members and getting to their mate.

"Well, now you've gone and done it," said Car, holding one shifter in a headlock. "You've pissed off Campbell."

A fully shifted wolf lunged at Gram and he bent slightly, coming up fast and ramming his clawed hand through the wolf's side. It fell away with a whimpering thud.

Energy filled the area and it wasn't Gram's, nor was it Amelia's. But it was powerful. More powerful than anything he'd ever felt before. One second, he was upright and the next he was on his knees, struggling to stand.

The same happened to Car and Mac.

"What the fuck is this shite?" demanded Mac.

The Flock fanned out, making room as Cal strolled casually in from the side, as if it was no big deal that grenades, automatic weapons, rockets, and general pandemonium surrounded him.

He nodded slightly to his followers and they willingly bowed to him. When his gaze found Gram's, his expression was a mix between amusement and curiosity. "Mr. Campbell, I'm told you greatly enjoyed the afternoon services provided, but that you've decided to check out early."

Amelia was right.

He was nuts.

"Who is the guy with the man-bun?" demanded Mac, still straining to stand.

Car snorted. "Asked Little Bow-Mac."

"Fuck you, you, ugly arsehole," snapped Mac.

Cal stopped in front of the twins and stared down at them, sizing them up. "It seems I have found what will be my main course this evening. You see, I find alpha males very tasty." With that, his face morphed quickly into something that looked to be part wolf, part bird, part vampire, part dragon, and fully horrifying.

Car grunted. "Campbell, yer father-in-law is a dick."

"Aye," added Mac.

Gram glared at Cal.

Cal's face returned to normal. His lips drew up in a thin smile and he lifted his hand, motioning for someone to come to him.

As Brian stepped into the area with Amelia's limp body over his shoulder, Gram lost it, fighting against the power holding him, snarling, growling, spittle flying—anything he could do in an attempt to get to his mate and unborn child.

"Here will do," said Cal, pointing to the ground right in front of Gram.

Brian tossed Amelia down with no concern for her safety.

She fell to the ground but didn't move or make a sound.

Gram strained to touch her but whatever Cal was doing to him left him just shy of making contact with his mate. He roared, his own power beating against the magik around him. He was no slouch when it came to magik, yet his power didn't make a dent in what was holding him in place.

It was then he remembered Amelia's warning about her father, his age, and what he'd done to alpha males for centuries.

He stopped fighting and his upper half re-formed to human. Gram stared at his mate. She was face down, her head turned toward him, her long hair spread out in every direction. "Amelia, lass."

Brian laughed.

Gram drew his gaze upward slowly. When he found Brian, he pinned him with a murderous glare. "You had better pray the man holding yer leash kills me. I will hunt you, I will find you, and it will be me feasting on yer innards when this is over."

"Yeah, sure," said Brian with a huff. He bent and lifted long strands of Amelia's hair and inhaled. "Damn, she smells so good. She always does."

"Get. The. Fuck. Away. From. Her." Gram's entire body tensed.

Cal snorted. "Brian, step back so that Mr. Campbell and I can speak. His attention will only be on you if you remain near his mate."

Gram flinched at the word because it meant Cal knew the truth. If Amelia was right, her father would have no use for her anymore now that she'd done what he wanted—ensnared the Bringer.

Cal grinned. "Yes, Mr. Campbell, I'm aware you claimed my daughter. Just as I'm aware that she already carries your child."

"What?" asked Taggert, appearing on the edge of the circle. His gaze flickered to Amelia and worry flashed through his gaze. "Father?"

"Ah, Taggert, join us. We were just about to discuss Mr. Campbell's role here with the Flock. The position he is going to agree to fill."

"I'm not filling shite!" spat Gram. "I am going to cram a vat of grape-flavored drink down yer damn throat, you sick son of a bitch!"

Cal folded his hands before him, appearing amused. "Well, now that you have gotten that outburst out of your system, shall we discuss the terms of our arrangement?"

"Fuck you," returned Gram, his voice low.

Cal shrugged. "Very well. If that is your final answer. Brian, kill his mate."

Brian licked his lips and tossed his hands out, letting claws emerge from his fingertips.

Mac and Car shouted.

Gram was unable to form anything close to a full threat. He was blinded by a blending of rage, fear, and desperation. It was guttural as he reached but could not make contact with his mate —his wife.

Brian lifted an arm and Gram shook his head.

"No! I'll do it. I'll join!" shouted Gram.

Cal lifted a finger, stopping Brian, who didn't look please but obeyed. "Ah, good choice, Mr. Campbell. Tonight we will indoctrinate you into our happy family. It's simple really. You will kill your friends, offering them as a sacrifice to me in exchange for my generosity in allowing your mate to live."

"That plan blows!" shouted Car.

"Aye!" added Mac.

Gram stared at the cult leader. "She's yer child. She's carrying yer grandchild. Have you no heart? No love of yer own babe?"

Grinning, Cal bent and touched the back of Amelia's head. "The man of years ago cared greatly for her. He had wished for a family for so long that he did anything he could to see that goal achieved. She was such a beautiful baby, Mr. Campbell. And when I held her, she looked up at me with love and trust. And then over the years, her mother poisoned her mind against me. Her mother made her hate me. And if I permit her to go on, she will do the same with Andie."

Gram stiffened. "You said you'd let her live if I did as you ask."

"Campbell, you do remember the part about killing us, right?" asked Mac. "I like the lass as much as the next guy, but not enough to get fed to her father. I'm still debating."

"I'm with ugly," said Car.

"I will permit her to live until your child is born. Then, you, Mr. Campbell, will be the one who kills her," said Cal, grinning more. "If you refuse, your child will be killed in her place."

Taggert eased closer. "Father, no. Give her to me. Like you once promised."

"Taggert, we have already had this conversation. It grows tiresome," said Cal.

Someone whistled and Gram turned his head to find Bill standing in front of his all-terrain vehicle, holding an M16. "Listen here, Caladrius Manson, I happen to like Amelia a lot. She's a good girl. Has shit taste in men, but hey, can't be perfect at everything, I guess. I don't take kindly to hearing you threatening her."

Cal laughed, long and loud. "Little human, you think you can do what to stop me? I can kill you without touching you."

Bill winked. "Yet, I'm standing and not on my knees. Think harder on *that*, jerkoff."

Cal seemed surprised by his words.

Bill puffed out his chest. "Oh goodie, backup is here and we're gonna hand you and your hippies their asses, birdman!"

The entire area seemed to explode all at once.

He caught sight of Armand, Cody, their friend Ace, and countless other men Gram knew from PSI and from years of serving as both a team member and a Shadow Agent.

Bill had been right. Backup had arrived and in huge numbers. Enough to take on the Flock.

Cal's power dropped, and Gram threw himself over Amelia's body protectively.

Brian snarled and lunged at Gram.

The man was tackled by someone Gram never thought would lend an assist.

Taggert.

The wolf-shifter began to beat the other male to a bloody pulp. Taggert drew upon his magik and moved his fingers around in the air. A bolt of power struck Brian as Taggert roared.

"What the fuck?" Brian pushed at Taggert but there was no moving the man. He was on a mission.

Taggert's face shifted partially and he clamped his jaws down on Brian's neck, tearing through the flesh. A gurgling sound came from Brian as his eyes glassed over. When Taggert looked up, his face returned to human and was covered in blood. He looked every bit the sociopath Gram suspected him to be.

"Save Amelia!" the man shouted.

Gram didn't wait around to see what other inmate was going to take over the asylum. He scrambled to his feet and grabbed his mate, his intention to get her to safety. As he turned, he ran right into Cal.

Cal flicked his wrist and Amelia's body was ripped from Gram's hold.

"No!" shouted Gram.

Taggert growled and went at Cal, shifting fully in the process, as Amelia was propelled high into the air.

Gram threw power at his mate, his intention to catch her and slow her descent. Before his power even reached her, her body stopped in mid-air instantly and somewhat violently.

Taggert yelped and it was followed quickly by the sound of a neck snapping.

Gram highly doubted that neck belonged to Cal.

No.

Cal had killed the wolf-shifter, of that Gram was sure, especially since he no longer felt Taggert's magik in the air. Gram had no remorse for the man and wasn't sorry to know he was dead. He'd planned to kill Taggert himself once Amelia was safe. Cal simply beat him to the punch.

Gram ran in the direction of Amelia. He didn't care how or why she'd stopped. He just wanted her safe.

"Oh, I do not think she will be joining us for dinner this evening, Mr. Campbell," said Cal as his power went ripping upward toward his daughter.

Gram threw himself in its path, taking the hit meant for his wife.

Pain consumed him, causing his body to contort, but he didn't go down. He remained upright, using his own gifts to draw down Cal's power, taking in the madman's death-magik. He would not allow Cal to hurt his wife or child. He'd gladly die for her.

For them.

He'd absorb every ounce of the madman's dark magik if it meant his family was safe.

Gunfire filled the area more as did additional explosions. Countless PSI operatives and Outcasts fought with Flock members.

Armand was suddenly there, trying to get to Gram to no avail. The vampire hissed and made a move to go at Cal.

Cal knocked Armand clear with a flick of his power.

Gram strained to look behind him.

Armand struck a tree and came up, looking pissed and worried. "Gram!"

"G-get the girl," managed Gram. "Save her."

With a pained expression, Armand nodded and defied gravity—something Gram had seen the vampire do only once before.

"I saw a *doco* once with a priest and a chick with the devil in her!" shouted Bill. "Looked just like that. Back up! The vomit radius on that devil-chick was wicked wide. Oh and avoid steps."

"Doc*u*!" shouted Armand on his way to Amelia.

Amelia's head snapped up a second before Armand would have gotten to her.

Cal threw more power at them and it hit Armand, knocking him back again.

Confusion coated his mate's face. "Gram?"

"Lass," he said, feeling Cal's power beginning to rip him apart from the inside out. "You will always have my heart."

With a gasp, she looked directly ahead at her father as she continued to be suspended in mid-air, high off the ground. In an instant, she was no longer horizontal, but upright, facing Cal as she continued to float. She put her arms out and her hair lifted on its own.

White light began to form around her as she glared at Cal.

In that second, images of paintings that depicted gods and goddesses flashed through Gram's head. His mate reminded him of those deities. Of a thing of great beauty and power.

And from the looks of it, a whole heap of wrath.

She jutted out her chin and Cal's power was instantly stripped from Gram.

Ignoring the intense pain, Gram stayed upright—barely.

Cal looked stunned. "Amelia?"

"Father, your reign of terror ends here and

now. You will never hurt an innocent again. You will never hurt anyone again," she said in an oddly calm voice.

Cal's eyes began to glow. He thrust his hands out, and Gram didn't need to be told he was throwing everything he had at his own flesh and blood.

Drawing upon his own magik, Gram added it to his mate's power. The combination left Cal stumbling backward some.

Gram dug deep and pulled upon his rage. He then charged Cal.

White light engulfed the area and Gram let his other senses guide him since he was temporarily blinded by the brightness.

He reached out, grabbed hold of Cal's head, and twisted fast, snapping the man's neck.

The cult leader fell away from Gram as the white light faded away.

"Holy hippies!" shouted Bill. "Did you see that? I thought it was the end of days there for a minute. But look. It was just the end of the hippies."

Confused, Gram glanced around to find every single Flock member lying dead. PSI-operatives,

Shadow Agents, Crimson Ops, and Immortal Outcasts were all standing, looking totally and completely unharmed.

Not a scratch on them.

It was then Gram realized he was no longer in pain.

Gasping, he spun around to find Armand putting his arms out, helping Amelia as she lowered to the ground. Her magik faded away fully and she nodded her thanks to Armand before running at Gram.

He grabbed her and lifted her, hugging her tight.

She clung to him. "I thought he was going to kill you. I was so scared for you."

Gram covered her face in kisses and set her down gently. "How hurt are you? Where are you hurt? The babe?"

She cupped his face. "I'm fine. The baby is perfectly fine."

"Lass?" He glanced around to find all his friends, watching them with stunned expressions on their faces. "Amelia, what did you do? There are hundreds of dead Flock members."

She nodded and eased out of his hold. She

walked to where her father's body was and put a hand out, holding it above him. White light emanated from her palm, engulfing Cal's body. His body exploded into light and Amelia tipped her head back as the light seemed to rain down on her gently.

She touched her cheek. "Good-bye, Daddy."

Squaring her shoulders, she looked at Gram. "He's free of the darkness now. Of the evil he drew upon for so long."

"Campbell, yer wife is fucking hot and she can death ray people!" shouted Mac. "Does she have a sister?"

"Yes, and she's three!" shouted Car.

Mac winced. "She's four! I dinnae mean that sister. I was talking about another secret one—who is, you know, an adult. Och, never mind."

Armand approached. "Gram, you have no more scars."

He nodded and went to his wife, drawing her into his arms. "Armand, this is Amelia. My mate."

Lifting a brow, Armand stared at him a second before smiling and bypassing Gram, pushing him out of the way and embracing Amelia. He lifted her gently and kissed her forehead. "Welcome to our family, Amelia."

She smiled and hugged him back.

As Armand set her down, he stiffened, his gaze going to her stomach. "Gram? You said baby. She is pregnant with your child!"

"Aye, I'm aware of as much," said Gram with a laugh. "I need you to stay with her while I check on my daughter."

"Daughter?" asked Armand.

"Clear the way!" shouted Bill as the golf cart driven by Gus came bounding into the area.

Gus's eyes were still closed tight as he gripped the wheel.

Andie was still on the seat next to him, with Mona's helmet on. It was still facing the other direction. She held the head under one arm and waved with the other. "Hi, Daddy! You did it. You punished Cal for being a bad boy. He's on a very long time-out now, Daddy."

Gram rushed to her and went to lift her out only to find she was belted to the seat. What was more troubling was that she was strapped in with one of Gram's belts. He looked at Gus. Who had yet to open his eyes or say a word.

Bill strolled up leisurely. "Hey, Little Bow-Mac, what do you say we take the kid for ice cream while the rest of your pals clean up what's left of the hippies?"

Mac began yanking bows from his hair, stepping over dead Flock members on his way to the cart.

No one dared to comment.

Car walked into the center of the circle, put out his hands, and smiled. "I have video footage of him getting his hair done. Who wants it?"

Every hand shot up.

Mac grunted but didn't snap at his brother. Instead, he put his hand on Gus's shoulder. "I've got it from here. Thank you for keeping the wee one safe. Lass, do not turn that helmet around."

Andie touched it and giggled. "I know. Gus said I had to wear it this way. He said I wasn't allowed to watch Cal and the Flock get punished. Was it cool?"

"Aye," said Mac with a grin.

Gus released the wheel and got out of the front seat. He batted at his ears on his way to the backseat, avoiding being touched again.

Bill climbed in next to him. "Gram-cracker, we'll take Andie for a bit. She'll be safe with us. The worst that will happen is Little Bow-Mac may end up with very pretty highlights in his hair."

Mac growled.

Andie giggled. She then turned her head in Gram's direction. "Daddy?"

He choked up and bent, wrapping his arms around her as best he could, considering she was strapped to the seat back very snugly. "Aye, wee one."

"I'm gonna be a big sister," she said, hugging him back. "When my sisters get here, we're gonna have so much fun. Uncle Mac will say you've got girls coming out of your ears. That's silly, huh?"

As Gram registered what Andie was saying, he tensed. "Lass, you said sisters. Not sister."

Andie nodded, and the helmet bounced on her head.

Gram put a hand on it, holding it in place as he handed Mona to Gus in the backseat.

Gus snatched the head and began to stroke it lovingly.

Bill simply picked his nose.

Andie touched Gram's arms. "Uh-huh. They match. Like Uncle Mac and Uncle Car. And then another sister comes and she looks like you do,

Daddy. Same eyes. And then another sister comes."

Mac eyed him. "Campbell, way to go. Yer a stud. Though you've managed more in one day than Car and me have in a lifetime. I'm a wee bit jealous and oddly scared it might happen to me. Do nae be getting that mating vibe on me. I'm a free agent."

Andie giggled again. "For now."

Mac gulped.

Gram touched Andie's side, a wash of emotions moving over him for the child. He bent more. "Lass, if anyone ever tries to harm you, they'll have me to deal with."

"I know," she said, laughing. "Because you love me, Daddy."

"Aye, little one. I do," he whispered, glancing up to find Mac misty-eyed.

The Scot cleared his throat. "So, what's this I hear about ice cream?"

Andie squealed. "Gus said I can have a banana split. I don't know what that is."

Mac feigned surprise. "Well, then yer in for a treat, lass. Hold your helmet, we're going to eat so much ice cream we pass out from sugar comas."

"Yay!" yelled Andie as Mac started the golf cart and pulled away.

Andie lifted her hand and waved. "Hi, everyone! I'm Andie. I'm Daddy's daughter! Bye, everyone! Nice to meet you! I'm gonna get a banana split, then I get to go play with my new best friend Bethany, and then I get sisters, and then…"

Her voice trailed off.

Gram smiled at Andie's words. The little one could tap into something he'd never understand. But whatever it was, she knew she'd be close to Bethany, a child she'd not even met yet, and that she was going to be a big sister. Gram turned and locked gazes with Amelia.

She touched her stomach. "Twins?"

Car laughed. "Guid on you, Campbell. Though I'm told twins are hellions. I do nae personally see that though."

Gram walked quickly to his mate, swept her up against him, and kissed her passionately. "I love you."

She smiled against his lips. "Why, Mr. Campbell, I think I might love you too."

"Might?" he asked with a grin.

She shrugged. "I'll let you touch my boobs."

"Might it is!" he shouted.

THE END

BE sure to be on the lookout for the next Immortal Ops Series World book—*Wrecked Intel*. To be notified of its release, sign up for Mandy's newsletter today.

Sources

Anthony, Ben, director. *The End of the World Cult*. FilmRise, 2007.

Bon, Gustave Le. *The Crowd: A Study of the Popular Mind*. Origami Books Pte. Ltd., 2018.

Britannica, The Editors of Encyclopaedia. "Ruby Ridge Incident." *Encyclopædia Britannica*, Encyclopædia Britannica, Inc., 15 Aug. 2018, www.britannica.com/event/Ruby-Ridge-incident.

"Children of God/The Family." *Cult Formation*, goo.gl/n53mYw.

Cunningham, Scott. *Encyclopedia of Magical Herbs*. Llewellyn, 1985.

Dempopoulos, Maria and Jodi Wille, directors. *The Source Family*. Gravitas Ventures, 2012.

Gisiger, Sabine and Beat Haner, directors.

Guru: Bhagwan, His Secretary & His Bodyguard. Jason Media, 2010.

Gladstar, Rosemary. *Herbs for Common Ailments*. Storey Publishing, 2014.

Gladstar, Rosemary. *Rosemary Gladstar's Herbs for the Home Medicine Chest*. Storey Books, 1999.

Guinn, Jeff. *The Road to Jonestown: Jim Jones and Peoples Temple*. Simon & Schuster Paperbacks, an Imprint of Simon & Schuster, Inc., 2018.

Layton, Deborah. *Seductive Poison: A Jonestown Survivor's Story of the Life and Death in the Peoples Temple*. Aurum Press, 1999.

Mundo, Nadine and Rena Mundo Croshere, directors. *American Commune*. Gravitas Ventures, 2014.

Myers, Sergio, director. *Heavens Gate: The Untold Story*. UFOTV, 2017.

Noesner, Gary. *Stalling for Time: My Life as an FBI Hostage Negotiator*. Random House, an Imprint and Division of Penguin Random House LLC, 2018.

Olsson, M D Peter. *Malignant Pied Piper: A Psychological Study of Destructive Cult Leaders from Rev. Jim Jones to… Osama Bin Laden*. Strategic Book Publishing, 2017.

Ridley, Jane. "I Grew up in an Apocalyptic

Sex Cult, Just like Rose McGowan." *New York Post*, New York Post, 11 Mar. 2018, goo.gl/wwPNnd.

Sargant, William. *Battle for the Mind: A Physiology of Conversion and Brain-Washing*. Malor Books, 1997.

Smithson, John, director. *Children of God*. FilmRise, 1994.

Taylor, Kathleen E. *Brainwashing: The Science of Thought Control*. Oxford University Press, 2017.

Thibodeau, David, and Leon Whiteson. *Waco: A Survivor's Story*. Hachette Books, 2018.

Walter, Jess, and Alan M. Dershowitz. *Every Knee Shall Bow: The Truth and Tragedy of Ruby Ridge and the Randy Weaver Family*. The Notable Trials Library, 2015.

Wilson, Jason. "Ruby Ridge, 1992: The Day the American Militia Movement Was Born." *The Guardian*, Guardian News and Media, 26 Aug. 2017, goo.gl/X9dQFN.

About the Author

Dear Reader

Did you enjoy this title and want to know more about Mandy M. Roth, her pen names and all the titles she has available for purchase (over 100)?

About Mandy:

New York Times & *USA TODAY* Bestselling Author Mandy M. Roth loves 80s music and movies and wishes leg warmers would come back into fashion. She also thinks the movie The Breakfast Club should be mandatory viewing for...okay, everyone. When she's not dancing around her office to the sounds of the 80s or writing books, she can be found designing book covers for New York publishers, small presses, and indie authors.

Learn More:

To learn more about Mandy and her pen names, please visit www.MandyRoth.com

For latest news about Mandy's newest releases and sales subscribe to her newsletter: Sign Up For Mandy's Newsletter

Want to see all Mandy's books? Click here.

Printable PDF list of all Mandy's titles: Click here.

To join Mandy's Facebook Reader Group: The Roth Heads.

Review this title:

Please let others know if you enjoyed this title. Consider leaving an honest review on the vendor site in which you purchased this title. Reviews help to spread the word and boost overall sales. This means more books in the series you love.

Thank you!

facebook.com/AuthorMandyRoth

twitter.com/mandymroth

instagram.com/mandymroth

goodreads.com/mandymroth

pinterest.com/mandymroth

bookbub.com/authors/mandy-m-roth

youtube.com/mandyroth

amazon.com/author/mandyroth

30345951R00265